The Long Harbor Testament

Tom Minder

BLACK ROSE writing™

Second printing

ISBN: 978-1-61296-800-1
PUBLISHED BY BLACK ROSE WRITING
www.blackrosewriting.com

Printed in the United States of America
Suggested retail price $19.95

The Long Harbor Testament is printed in Book Antiqua

I would like to thank my beta readers: Mark Doenges, Gregg Feistman, Ellin Jones, Pete Desmarais, Gina Desmarais, and Paula Minder. Your input and frank feedback helped to shape the novel.

Special thanks both to my developmental editor, Patti O'Brien, whose encouragement and attention to detail helped to make the work flow consistently, and to Dawn Byrne, my critique leader, who patiently provided guidance on craft.

Finally, thanks to my wife Paula for her feedback and support, sometimes through a closed door.

The Long Harbor Testament

Part 1: Advent

Chapter 1

Genesis and the Garden

Father Jim had writer's block.

He glanced out the frosted-over window of his small office in St. Augustine's rectory on the cold November Saturday afternoon. He'd been a priest for five years and actually liked creating sermons while in seminary. Now he would gladly just wing it from the pulpit. Most people don't listen anyway.

So here he was preparing another sermon for folks who would rather skip it and get on with the mass. Those extra ten minutes could be used at home to open a beer, grab some Doritos, and position oneself on the Lazyboy to watch your team under-perform and destroy your football picks. He reached for his own sheet. Another $150 down the drain.

So what's the sermon for this week? Genesis and man's fall from grace.

My friends in Christ, God in his abounding love created the first man, Adam, in his image and likeness and built for him an earthly paradise free of pain and suffering... and free of surprisingly accurate football point spreads and over/unders.

God understood Adam's need for companionship and so constructed a helpmate, Eve, to share paradise with him and make him happy. Bad move, God. Things will go downhill from here. Why is the over/under for the Bears and Eagles set at 46? That's too high.

But Adam and Eve were flawed, as we all are, and were convinced by the serpent that they would become as powerful as God if they merely ate of the Tree of Good and Evil. When confronted by God, Adam replied with the first recorded cop out in human history..."The woman made me do it." And here we are now. SSDD: Same shit, different day.

Jim mulled over his options: keep it brief, or delve into Cain and Abel. Now, there were prototypical siblings. Who's to say Cain didn't have a good reason to club Abel? There's always a good brother and a bad brother, isn't there? Abel and Cain, the Prodigal son and his nose-to-the-grindstone brother, the sainted Gabe and Father Jim Cooper.

My friends in Christ, like Adam and Eve, we face difficult decisions every day. We don't always make the right choice. Maybe we can't even be certain what the right choice is. God Knows. But he isn't telling.

All we can do is follow our God-given instincts and keep to the faith. Let's live every day knowing that God expects an accounting for our actions and the decisions that we make. Not bad. Now for the big question. How can the Lions be giving six points?

– – –

Chapter 2

David and Bathsheba

Silvio returned to his office after a lunch of a double cheeseburger, large fries, and enough soda to ensure he would never be thirsty again. To make sure he burned no unnecessary calories, he piled his 5 foot 10 inch, 270-pound frame into his Explorer and drove the two blocks to Smitty's and back.

When he entered, he was surprised to see Mario Gallante waiting. Although a silent partner in Fortunato Brothers, Mario rarely showed interest in the day-to-day business of stopping leaks, unclogging toilets, and installing water heaters. What did interest him was Silvio's real profit center: sports betting and associated gambling interests. Silvio knew this was not going to be a social visit, but started with pleasantries anyway.

"Mario, it's good to see you. This is a surprise." He pulled his chair and dropped a Snickers bar onto his desk. "What brings you to Long Harbor?"

Mario closed the Ladies of Construction calendar he had removed from Silvio's wall and tossed it on the desk. Silvio picked it up, turned to November, admired the faucets of the young tradeswoman and returned the calendar to its position of honor. He knew it was a good idea to sponsor the calendars. They made nice Christmas handouts.

"Silvio, we need to talk about your bookkeeping. Let's go into your back office."

The back office was little more than a desk with a lamp, phone, internet connection, and a few plumbing manuals for show. This room was for betting.

Mario closed the door and settled himself. "Silvio, there seems to be less revenue coming from your office. I know that there's no shortage of gamblers in Long Harbor, and those folks increase their bets over time. What the hell's going on?"

Although Mario had always been a father figure, Silvio knew that he was about to see the bad side of that relationship.

"Mario, I've been building a nice trade here and have always brought in good money for Gallante Supplies. In this tough economy, some clients are having trouble covering the full amount of their bets."

Silvio studied Mario's expressionless face and decided to revise the approach. "The vote to rezone key land for residential use is coming up soon. I want to be sure that we're in the middle of this. We need to bring in a more affluent set of residents who, I assure you, will want to wager large chunks of their paychecks on football and whatever else we can make available to them."

He grew more confident. "I don't need to put the screws to people right now. Don't worry, those bettors who came up short are paying interest on their debts and in cases where someone has leverage locally, I'm pressuring them to talk up Fortunato Brothers and the zoning change."

"Silvio, I get what you're doing, but we need to bring in more money. Gallante Supplies has a bottom line too. I answer to people even less patient than me."

He leaned forward, picked up Silvio's Snickers bar, broke the chocolate masterpiece in half, and took a bite. After an open-mouthed chewing process that disturbed Silvio, Mario swallowed and let out an "ahhhh." He looked at Silvio. "Neither of us wants to end up on a road side ditch or feeding the Long Harbor aquatic life."

"Like my brother Enrico?"

"I didn't mean to bring that up, Silvio. We still don't know who killed him, but we haven't given up on it. It wasn't from the organization, I know that for sure. It was someone who was either lucky or knew how to cover his tracks."

Silvio leaned forward. "I think it was someone Enrico was pressuring. That's my point, Mario. These folks can come unhinged easily."

Mario growled through a peanut lodged in his front teeth. "I expect the next month's set of payments to be twenty percent higher than you sent in last month. And I want to see your books. There has to be a few marks that jump out."

Pushing back in his rolling chair, Silvio removed the manuals and empty fast-food containers covering the safe. This was not going well, but he had few options. Mario could replace Silvio in a minute with someone more willing to drag money out of the locals. Silvio was facing the loss of his position in the community, and maybe a few appendages. Severance in this line of business was a lot different from most occupations.

He handed the ledger to Mario, who started with the latest set of entries and worked backwards. Specially coded line items indicated the betting transactions.

"Silvio, I see several clients who need to catch up with their payments. Father Jim himself seems to be down quite a bit. Go to confession and unburden yourself that if the good father doesn't make good on his debt, he'll be facing pain and suffering not mentioned in the bible. Tell him to dip into the collection basket if he has to."

He thought for a minute and smiled. "Father Jim seems to be well liked in this community and his word carries. Tighten the screws on him. Tell him that if he talks up the zoning and does what he can to show Fortunato Brothers in a good light, his trespasses will be forgiven and his penance not so heavy as he deserves."

He continued to look at other entries in the ledger. "Now let's find some more deadbeats who need to cash up before they meet an unexpected misfortune. Same rules as Father Jim. Pay up or convince us you can make up your debt in other ways."

- - -

Gabe's cell spat out his answer message: "This is Cooper Renovations. I cannot answer your call at the moment but please leave a message and I'll get back to you as soon as I can."

Jessie Fortunato took a breath and responded to the beep. "Gabe, this is Jessie. Silvio and I are thinking of adding a room onto the back of the house. We would like you to come over and give us an estimate on how much time and work would be involved. I'm home anytime and look forward to seeing you."

Gabe returned the call, arranging to stop by in the afternoon. He never felt comfortable alone with Jessie. Still attracted to her, he regretted not continuing their relationship past high school.

His foreman Lou would come along on the estimate to help measure and assure propriety. However, a late morning emergency call about a retaining wall meant Lou was needed elsewhere. Gabe drove to Jessie's alone.

Gabe tapped lightly on Jessie's door, hoping for no answer. She answered quickly, wearing a short, tight blue skirt that would get her arrested in some states. Waving Gabe inside, she explained that Silvio was off working, and Rico was in class at the community college.

The requested addition was straightforward in scope and seemed unnecessary since the house was large and nicely laid out. Jessie seemed more interested in talking to Gabe than in understanding the work involved. Gabe sensed this and tried to keep the conversation focused on the effort, price, and time estimates.

"So Jessie, I'll write up a full estimate so you and Silvio can look it over. Frankly, I like your house as it is and don't see how adding the room would improve things very much."

Jessie tapped the counter. "Gabe, I want to talk about Rico. He seems to be distracted and unclear about what he wants to do with his life."

As she stepped closer, Gabe took a half step back, pinning himself against the counter. "He loves Silvio and wants to win his respect," she continued. "But Silvio has always seemed disappointed in Rico and makes no attempt to hide it. Rico respects you, Gabe. Can't you speak to him?"

She closed the distance between them making slight lower extremity contact with Gabe. He was moved by Jessie's emotion, some parts of him more than others.

After a pause to choose the best words and allow sufficient blood to return to his brain, he asked, "Has Rico spoken to counselors at the community college? Maybe he can focus his studies on an area that attracts his interest."

He put his hand on Jessie's shoulder to comfort her. Probably a bad move, but it felt right.

"Maybe after a time, he'll decide what is best for himself and realize that Silvio's approval is Silvio's issue and not his. He has to realize that he won't please everyone and shouldn't live his life trying to do that."

Jessie reached around Gabe's shoulders and hugged him, pinning him to the counter. "This is why I rely on you, Gabe. You know just what to say."

It felt good to embrace her. The front door opened and Silvio lumbered in. Seeing Jessie and Gabe in mid-embrace, he skidded to an unplanned stop.

"What's going on? Cooper, what the hell are you doing?"

Jessie spoke up while drying a tear. "I called Gabe to give an estimate on adding a room to the back. I wanted some more exposure to the afternoon sun."

"I don't remember discussing any addition. And if I was a few minutes later there might've been lots of exposure."

Gabe slid from between Jessie and the counter. "Silvio, this was, uh, just two friends supporting each other. I gave Jessie the estimate and if you're interested in having the work done, we can discuss it later."

"Why don't you leave now, Cooper? I have friends of my own who would be happy to talk to you. You aren't needed or welcome here."

Rico walked in and sensed the tension. Silvio turned. "Ah, here's my son. Nice of you to join us at this time. Your hero, Mr. Cooper, was helping your mother to work out some issues with her posture. He's leaving now."

Rico looked at his mother, then at a red-faced Gabe. Rico considered the posture remark, decided to let it pass, and turned to his father. "Dad, Mr. Cooper is a friend. I'm sure this was just friends talking."

Silvio faced Gabe and snorted. "Rico, if you don't think there's anything going on, you're nuts. Your lack of common sense comes from hanging around that community college, and not having the stones to make something out of yourself.

"Cooper, maybe we can have a short supportive talk sometime ourselves. Maybe we'll even hug. But for now, it's late and you should be on your way. I'm sure you have other appointments."

Gabe picked up his supplies and walked towards the door. "I look forward to our talk, Silvio. Maybe we can understand each other better."

When he was outside, Gabe's cell vibrated. Lou. "We're done with the wall, Gabe. How'd things go at Silvio's?"

"I don't think we're getting the business. Silvio has something else in mind for me." He sighed. "Lou, it's been a long day. I'm going to grab some dinner and a beer at The Wharf. Care to join me?"

"Thanks anyway Boss, but I'm heading home. Stay away from Silvio. He's bad news and he's not someone we want to associate with. Have a good night and don't drink too much."

– – –

Gabe made his way to The Wharf at Quincy Pier at the south end of the harbor. The popular after-work watering hole was perfect for him, as it also served a limited menu of easy-to-dump-on-a-plate meals.

The Wharf had replaced a gentleman's lounge called The Long Haul. Gabe's waitress tonight was Carla Ciccone. She was an ex-mermaid, the name given to the dancers at the club. Famous for pleasing the male guests both with her interpretive dancing and individual attentions, Carla was arrested in the last raid of The Long Haul and might have been charged with solicitation if Silvio hadn't intervened.

Being a regular, Gabe had no need to order. Carla brought a draft, smiled, and asked about his day. Gabe mumbled a quiet "okay" and started into the beer.

After he'd eaten and downed a few more brews, Carla came over to check on him and drop off the check. "Here's how my day was. I went to Jessie and Silvio's to give an estimate on building an addition."

He drained the remainder of his draft. "I hate going to Jessie's because she's the one who got away and now she's married to that Neanderthal, Silvio." He held up the mug to make sure no liquid remained. He sighed, belched, and continued. "That bastard treats Jessie and Rico like shit. Anyway, Silvio caught Jessie and me in a friendly embrace and freaked out."

He looked up at Carla, who was paying close attention, as good confessors do. "Here I am dumping this on you when I have my brother the priest I can bother with my personal life."

Carla smiled. "Gabe, I've heard things no priest will ever hear. Just tread lightly around Silvio. He's possessive and overreacts. Better not to stir up a fight. He has friends."

Gabe continued to explore for one last drop. "I wish it was that simple. I'm thinking I wasted a big opportunity with Jessie and now she and Rico are paying for it. Silvio's not worthy of Jessie, damn it."

"Gabe, you've had too much. Take it from a friend. You don't want to mess with Silvio. He's not rational."

"Thanks, Carla. But there must be something I can do to protect them."

"Nothing can be done while Silvio is around, believe me. He and Jessie just don't work. Maybe they should split up. It would solve a lot of problems."

Gabe wondered what that meant but knew Carla was right. He should sleep this off, and maybe things would be clearer in the morning. He paid the bill, tipped extra for the counseling, and headed out into the night.

Realizing that driving back to his apartment in his current state would be unwise, he decided to walk the two miles or so and get some fresh air.

- - -

Silvio had gone home to change clothes and prepare for a late night when he'd discovered Jessie and Gabe. He'd lost all romantic feeling for Jessie during the last year as things with Carla heated up. He was angrier about Gabe's presumption that he can fool around with Jessie and insult him, than with feelings of hurt for Jessie's affections being given to someone else.

He showered, changed into casual clothes, and headed to The Wharf.

Jessie was no fool. As he drove away, she picked up the phone and dialed a local number. "He just left and is heading to The Wharf.

See who he talks to and where he goes when he leaves. Yeah. Love you, too."

Silvio parked his Explorer in his usual spot and entered the popular but dingy Wharf. What a dive, he thought, as he wiped a greasy substance from the doorknob onto his pants. I'm gonna buy out the other owners, knock it down and build a sports bar that the yuppies will go for. How about Silvio's Extra Point or maybe Silvio's Over/Under?

He had missed Gabe by 10 minutes. Carla brought him a large draft. "So, how was your day?"

"It sucked. I'm getting pressure from Mario to expand the betting and bring in more money. He's even threatening to bring in someone to run the territory and add muscle to the collections. I need to start leaning on some of the deadbeats to pay up completely."

He took a quick gulp of the brew then slammed the mug down, causing drinkers at neighboring tables to stop talking and look over.

"Then I go home and find Jessie in Cooper's arms. I never liked Cooper, but he is 'The Angel Gabriel' in this town and has connections." Silvio sighed and looked at the patient Carla. "So, how did it go with your day?"

Carla knew Silvio didn't care how her day had gone, but relied on her to keep her ear to the ground for useful information. "Just the usual night of sliding beer and beef stew to the dining elite, and listening to their woes."

Realizing she might have been singling out Silvio, she added, "But I know you're under a lot of pressure and need to talk to someone. Why do you stay with Jessie? Buy her out and live with me. I'll get your mind off of Mario *and* Gabe."

"So, it's *Gabe,* is it? Has he charmed you too?"

"No. He's just a regular who stops in, drinks a lot, and pours out his soul. He still has feelings for Jessie. Maybe this is your chance to lose Jessie and be with me."

"Jessie is my wife. I can't lose her to someone. Mario already thinks I'm too weak. If I lose Jessie to Cooper that would just convince him more."

"Listen Silvio, you're a feared and respected member of Long Harbor. You also bring in good money for Mario. The man is no fool.

He'll cut you some slack."

Silvio wasn't ready for reason. "What did Cooper say to you? Is he thinking of moving in on me with Jessie?"

She knew she should have stopped there, but she was getting angry with Silvio. "He wants to move in on Jessie *and* Rico. He thinks you're a lousy husband and father."

Silvio took another sip and shouted. "Fuck." He looked around but the other patrons kept their heads down, pretending not to notice. "Cooper needs to keep his feelings to himself. I know what it takes to build up respect in this community. People know that I can be reasonable as long as I'm not messed with. There's no way I'm allowing Cooper to make me look like a fool." Silvio took one final swig. "Forget the food. Let's get out of here. Is your shift over?"

"Honey, you own a chunk of The Wharf. I'm sure I can end my shift whenever you want. Let's go home and work out some of that anxiety."

Meeting Silvio in the parking lot, she slid into his Explorer and they took off towards Carla's apartment. After flipping through his CDs, she picked out a jazz compilation, which seemed to sooth him. Deciding to get a head start on further relaxation, she gently rubbed her hand between his legs, having an immediate effect on Silvio's focus.

Gabe, walking on the shoulder of the road ahead, heard the approaching SUV and turned just in time to see it bearing down. He jumped and yelled "Asshole." as Silvio realized he was driving half on the road and half on the shoulder and was about to hit someone. He swerved to avoid the pedestrian and came to a stop. When he composed himself after the near miss, the "asshole" remark registered.

Gabe emerged from the ditch, brushed himself off, and glared at the driver who was glaring back. He realized it was Silvio, with a woman at his side. He couldn't identify her, but it wasn't Jessie. Gabe collected himself; he needed to calm things down.

"Silvio, let your friend drive next time. You almost ran me over."

"So I'm an asshole, am I?" Silvio bent forward and appeared to be reaching for something.

Just then the woman said to him, "Silvio, let it be. Don't make things worse."

He thought for a second, then put down the object. "Cooper, we'll discuss this and other things that happened today very soon. You're screwing with the wrong guy." Putting his Explorer into Drive and speeding off, he left Gabe to wonder why that woman's voice was so familiar.

- - -

On this Saturday afternoon in St. Augustine's church, the sun's rays filtered through the stained glass providing a guiding light to those seeking reconciliation. Father Jim sat in the confessional going over his Divine Office. These prayers inspired him and he viewed them not as repetitive drudgery, but as a way of communicating with the Holy Spirit.

Pulling a folded slip out of his prayer guide, he studied the football spreads for the week. Overall, he lost more often than he won, and was now running a consistent losing streak. He raised his entry stake each week in hopes of catching up.

Silvio had been understanding about Jim's inability to pay up; maybe because the weekly interest rate was exorbitant, or because Silvio was trying to influence Jim to legitimize Fortunato Brothers in the community.

The door to the confessional opened and Silvio came in. "Silvio!" exclaimed Jim. "It's good to see you here." He opened his arms and looked around the small room, not much larger than a closet. "The confessional is God's way of expressing his compassion and forgiveness. Have a seat."

The big man was confused; he came to threaten Jim and now he was getting spiritual guidance?

"So Silvio, how long has it been since your last confession?"

The bookie thought this over. "When did Rico make First Communion?"

Jim drummed his fingers on his bible. "Let's see, Rico is 20. Typically, people receive First Communion around eight. So twelve years."

"Twelve years then."

This wasn't going to be easy. "Let me walk you through this.

"Do you believe God is our only God, and renounce other gods?"

"You bet. No pun intended, Padre." Silvio smirked as he nodded towards the betting slip.

Deciding to ignore this, Jim continued. "Have you used God's name in vain?"

"Do you mean 'God Damn,' 'Jesus Freaking Christ,' things like that?"

Jim sucked in a breath, thought a second and let the crudities pass. "Well, yes. When was the last time you attended Mass?"

"Like I said, twelve years," shrugged Silvio.

"Do you honor the memory of your mother and father?"

Silvio considered this, then turned red. "My mother was a saint. I light a candle for her every year. But my father was a real prick. Enrico and I could never do anything right in his eyes."

"Maybe, then, you have a chance to make sure you don't act the same way with young Rico," Jim said, hoping to reach the man on a paternal level.

Silvio rose up and turned redder. "Rico is weak, Padre. He needs to toughen up or this world will push him around."

He paused. "Hmmm, maybe that's what my Dad thought."

Sensing progress for this sinner, Jim pressed on. "Have you ever killed anyone?"

"Are we back to the commandments? No, I've never killed anyone—personally. I believe in leaving conflict resolution to those who specialize in it. Do you have a problem with that?"

"Just asking," Jim hurried. He paused to see if Silvio's color would return.

"Have you committed adultery? That is, have you slept with another woman since you married Jessie?"

"What?" asked the reluctant penitent. "Maybe you should ask your brother Gabe about adultery the next time he wanders in here.

"I'm done confessing," shouted Silvio. "Maybe we'll do this again some other time when I'm not here on business. You owe two thousand bucks to Fortunato Brothers. You have three days to pay up."

"Silvio, you know that I pay up—eventually," Jim pleaded. "I've just been on a bad streak. Please. I'm paying you a hundred fifty just in interest every week. I don't make much here. You have to give me more time."

Silvio flashed a toothy grin. "Jim, I like you, but this is business. I need to bring in revenue and make sure that no one is short-changing me." He dropped his smile. "And frankly, your problems are not my problems."

Jim sunk into his chair. "Maybe I can ask Gabe for a loan. I'm going to have to explain the situation, but I'm sure he'll understand."

"Gabe. It's always Gabe," exploded Silvio "He's a pain in my ass, and he's horning in on my wife. When you talk to him, tell him he's pissing off the wrong guy."

Taking a breath, Silvio continued. "Jim, there's a way you can get better terms on your debt. You know about the zoning meeting coming up on classifying parts of Long Harbor as residential. This means an opportunity for Fortunato Brothers to offer their services to a whole new set of customers." Silvio nodded towards the betting slip.

"There's a lot of money out there, Jim, and we don't forget our friends. I've spoken to you before about talking up Fortunato Brothers, and that helped. Now, you need to ratchet things up. I need you to talk up the zoning from the pulpit and in your dealings in the community. Mention that good corporate citizens such as Fortunato Brothers can help Long Harbor to thrive with this boom. You're a man people listen to."

Jim sat up and raised his hands in supplication. "Please, Silvio, don't make me turn my pulpit and community works into a commercial for gambling interests."

Silvio pushed back the chair, stood, and brushed the wrinkles from his slacks. "Either that or come up with two thousand in the next three days. It's your funeral." He folded his hands in fervent humility and bowed his head. "Now, give me my absolution. I'm a busy man and have to see other clients."

– – –

St. Augustine's was an acoustical wonder. On Sunday mornings, you could hear every creak of a kneeler, every cough and sneeze, and every sigh when the congregation was bored.

Jim stepped up to the pulpit knowing he was going to compromise his standing with the faithful. These folks came from humble roots but knew when they were being played.

He leaned on the pulpit and glanced towards the pews. From that vantage point, he could also see outside and note the cold December morning. Maybe there will be decent football games today, he thought. Anything to get his mind off this task. He looked out at the congregation and noticed Gabe by himself. Silvio and family were there also; Silvio was smiling. Boy, this wasn't going to be easy, Jim thought.

"My brothers and sisters in Christ, we first meet David as a young man, called in from the fields and selected by God through Samuel to be a future great leader. God did not find favor with his more worthy and learned brothers, but with this humble man of toil."

Not unlike the Coopers.

"David becomes a court servant to King Saul who finds much favor with David for his sweet music. David rises in power and eventually slays the great warrior Goliath, a threat to Saul's power."

Now you're messing with Goliath, Gabe. You'd better have one heck of a slingshot to ward off Silvio.

"Saul is jealous of David's rising influence, even attempting to kill David while he's playing the harp."

Are you hearing this, Gabe? Don't mess with Saul, er, Silvio. Man, is Silvio Saul, Goliath, or both? Either way, brother, steer clear.

"But David is human as are we all. He uses his power to seduce Bathsheba, the wife of a soldier."

Gabe has no idea where I'm going with this.

"But David rightens his path, rules his people with might and justice, produces a son, Solomon, who becomes a great king himself, and continues to find God's favor."

Gabe, you're no David, and your luck is going to run out. Find a nice, quiet, uncomplicated girl and leave Jessie alone before your head ends up on a stake.

"So what do we take from this, my brothers and sisters? We're all

human. Capable of great and terrible things. It is our relationship with God that will steer us from danger if we repent our shortcomings, endeavor to make things right as well as we can, and follow His straight paths."

Jim shuffled his notes and closed the bible; when he looked up he met Silvio's annoyed glance. Well, no way to avoid this, he thought.

"Oh, and one other thing, my brethren. Our community is at a crossroads, not unlike those met by David."

Boy, that's lame.

"We have an opportunity to expand our beloved Long Harbor and build housing and businesses for a throng of young, upwardly mobile Christians looking to enjoy the beauty and tranquility of our town.

This will be a great opportunity to employ our youth suffering from the economic downturn, while enabling our fine tradesmen – such as we have here in our midst today – to expand their many offerings. People are going to need plumbing, landscaping, home construction and other services. Let's improve Long Harbor, put people to work, and expand our Christian community. Forget the naysayers concerned with water runoff, pollution, traffic, crime, and other misguided concerns."

Boy, Silvio looks mad. Did he just mouth motherfucker?

"Let's go to the zoning meeting Tuesday and show how much we support this change."

That was painful and inappropriate, he thought, but I hope it buys me some time with Silvio. Hmm, 12 minutes; there will be some grumbling when I meet the faithful after Mass, but at least then it's out of these garments—which I have truly soiled today—and off to watch the pre-game at The Wharf. I wonder what the analysts think of my picks.

– – –

Chapter 3

Goliath and the Philistines

Detective Mark Porfino came to Long Harbor six months ago, replacing Tony Wagner who had resigned suddenly citing health reasons. Mark had earned a Criminal Justice degree from the state university and joined the Cambria police force. After three years walking a beat, he passed the detective exam and applied for the Long Harbor detective position when it became available.

On reviewing the Long Harbor case log, he was surprised at the lack of any real prosecution for gambling-related activity. The one open case that drew Mark's attention was the mysterious death of Enrico Fortunato. Enrico was co-owner of Fortunato Brothers Plumbing with his brother Silvio. Both were suspected of being involved with the street gambling trade. Enrico was found floating in Long Harbor inlet a few days after being reported missing by his brother.

The autopsy listed the cause of death as drowning. There were no apparent signs of blunt force or other marks that might indicate foul play. Still, the investigation was dropped too quickly in Mark's mind. Detective Wagner's made few notes and interviewed no one; maybe he was already planning on getting out and didn't want complications.

Police Chief Gene Benson walked into Mark's office, and flopped onto the visitor chair. The Chief was a nice guy and a good boss. Mark couldn't figure out how he'd gotten along with Wagner who'd seemed short-tempered and solitary.

"Mark. I want you to attend the zoning board meeting tomorrow night. Normally, these are snooze fests, but there's a lot of talk over the zoning change to allow residential permits for the old factory area.

It might get pretty tense, and I want a police presence to make sure things stay civil."

"Sure, Chief. It'll give me a chance to see all elements of Long Harbor interacting at once. Fourth of July parades don't really give a picture of who likes who and who can't stand each other."

Benson glanced at the papers on Mark's desk. "The Fortunato case, huh? It's closed you know."

"I know. I just can't get over why there was such a short investigation. I want to look into this and make sure it wasn't a murder."

The chief stood. "Maybe it was. Look Mark, a bad guy died, let's focus on the living." Benson turned as he walked towards the door. "Don't forget about the zoning board meeting."

– – –

The function room was filling and it was only 7:30 p.m. It seemed to warm a few degrees in just minutes. Chairman John Fox peeped between the drapes and knew that this would be a long night. Along with the regular senior citizen attendees, there were those with a stake in the factory zoning matter: environmentalists from the community college reading and discussing the study released last week, school board members, and members of the business community.

And, also in attendance, Silvio Fortunato and his plumbing thugs, Gabe Cooper, the model citizen, and even Father Jim Cooper, the former champion of the downtrodden who has now converted to supply-side economics apostle. Thank God the cops are here, Fox thought.

The proposal to rezone the Hillside factory area was good in theory but required a lot of study, especially on the environmental impact. That study had been done at the request of the board and was performed by a firm recommended by board members Willet and Robbins, both close associates of Silvio. It raised more questions than it answered, but the board decided that it be presented as is.

The members took their seats precisely at eight. Normally, they came out early and chatted with the audience, but tonight was different. No niceties tonight. Fox positioned the microphone and tapped to make sure it was on.

"The zoning board will come to order. We have many things to go over tonight and I see we have a large, civic-minded crowd. This is a bit unusual for an early December meeting. I would have thought everyone would be Christmas shopping and not focused on zoning issues."

This met with a low laugh from the crowd. "If you have a comment on any matter before this board tonight, please stand at the microphone when the issue comes up. You will be recognized."

Joan Grey, the board secretary, read each item before the board. All except for the Hillside factory zoning were minor disputes between neighbors or small businesses. A few of these brought input from speakers in the audience. As each speaker voiced their opinion on a matter, each met with grumbling from the audience. It was clear they wanted to get to the rezoning.

Fox took the microphone from Joan Grey. "The last item will be to entertain discussion and come to a vote on the zoning of the Hillside factory area to residential. As I can see from the audience, the environmental study has been well scrutinized. The board feels that the study is complete and gives us enough information to determine how to proceed on this matter. If anyone has comment, please step to the microphone."

Professor Amos from Cambria Community College stepped forward. While he was certainly scholarly, he was also known for his short temper and impassioned defense of the environment. "Mr. Chairman and board members, we at the community college—and outside parties interested in this issue—have indeed read the environmental study. Frankly, it was completed in too short a time for a matter of this import, and was severely lacking in detail. There was only passing mention of asbestos and other dangerous materials, with the conclusion that the materials could be removed easily.

"Some of these factories are almost 100 years old. We believe that these buildings are rife with hazards, not to mention possible mercury. We demand that the board conduct another study, this time with a state-certified company, not some hand-picked local crew with minimal experience, and give that company enough time and freedom to conduct a thorough study."

The community college contingent—mostly students, including young Rico Fortunato—applauded. Chairman Fox waited for the applause to subside and said, "Professor, the board subcommittee has reviewed the study with our consultants and feels that the study is complete. Is there anyone else?"

"But Chairman Fox..."

"You've had your say, Professor." Fox looked around. "Anyone else?"

Bill Harrington, president of the Long Harbor school board, stood.

"Mr. Chairman, the school district of Long Harbor is facing the same constraints being experienced by other districts across the country. We have insufficient funding and a dwindling tax base. We've had to use layoffs to balance budgets.

"While the addition of these 1000 residential units will dramatically increase the tax base eventually, there are already rumblings of tax incentives being given to the buyers. There was also mention of funding from the Long Harbor government to help set up the clearing of the site and, indeed, paying for the removal of the dangerous materials. It will be several years before the school district realizes the revenue increase from the expanded tax base."

Harrington turned towards the audience. "In the meantime, we'll need to build new schools for the expected increased enrollment. This'll be a burden that the community cannot undertake. We ask that the board reconsider this ill-advised zoning change. It's obvious that the only ones who will benefit from this zoning change will be the business community represented here. We need to consider the impact on our children. We need to insure that we maintain our quality of life in Long Harbor and not sell out to those looking to get wealthy on the backs of the rest of the citizenry."

More applause now, from school board members, teachers, and the environmentalists. Silvio did not appear to be sympathetic.

Fox cleared his throat. "Thank you, Bill. We on the board hear your concerns and sympathize. Is there anyone else?"

He was hoping for some miracle that would prevent others from approaching the microphone. He knew this wasn't going to happen.

Silvio lifted himself from his overmatched folding chair and stepped to the microphone. "I'm Silvio Fortunato. I own Fortunato Brothers Plumbing." Everyone in the room knew Silvio. Most in the room wished they didn't. Many owed him money for non-plumbing services.

"The business owners in Long Harbor know that this zoning change will put us on the map and bring a new set of people into our community. It will provide jobs and revive the town. We've all seen the environmental impact study. It says everything will be fine."

He looked around the room, then back at the board. "Why are we even discussing this? My men and I look forward to the increased work this will bring into Long Harbor. We provide a much-appreciated service to the community and a happy, busy workforce keeps everyone happy. Believe me; we want to keep our skilled workers busy and happy."

No argument from the audience there. Most of Silvio's skilled workers were parolees who walked the legal line and stayed out of jail through Silvio's influence with the police.

He stepped away from the mic and looked at Jim, who stood and approached the podium like he was walking to his execution.

"Father Jim. It's rare that a man of the bible speaks on zoning matters. What do you have to say?" asked Fox.

Jim coughed. "I understand the concerns of everyone over this rezoning. No one wants the environment threatened with polluted ground water and no one wants the noise and inconvenience of the construction with no real guarantee of success for the housing project."

Silvio was staring a hole into Jim's back, and he felt it. "But we need to move forward with this. The expansion of the community—with the hopes of good paying jobs and the increased trade that will develop—means that we need to take this opportunity and run with it. I feel that the passage of this zoning change will lift a burden off many of my fellow townspeople. Let's do this and go home."

Fox was somewhat bewildered by this speech, as was most of the audience. The community college and school board folks appeared confused and angry. Father Jim had undone a lot of good will.

"Thank you, Father Jim, for your input. The board has heard

enough and, I believe, is ready to vote." He looked over to the other members who nodded. "Secretary Grey will poll the board."

Joan Grey leaned into her mic. "On the matter of the petition to rezone the Hillside factory area as spelled out in petition 1765 for residential use, how votes the board?"

"Mr. Willet?"

"Yes."

"Mr. Fox?"

"No."

"Ms. Wagner?"

"No…Never!"

"Mr. Robbins?"

"Yes."

"Miss Gillek?" There was a pause. She seemed to be nervous. "Yes."

Chairman Fox leaned forward. "The vote being three Yes and two No, the petition is approved."

There was loud murmuring in the crowd and angry glances at Silvio and Father Jim.

Professor Amos walked mid-way to Silvio. "We're not beaten, Fortunato. This rezoning is a terrible idea and threatens the safety of the whole community. You may have used your influence on the stooges you control on the board, but we will appeal this, seek an injunction, and stop this whole farce. You may think that you and your thugs control Long Harbor, but the day will come when we're rid of the likes of you."

Silvio stopped shaking hands with his crew and turned to Professor Amos. He held up his hand to stop some of his crew who wanted to separate Amos from his incisors. He grinned. "Professor, I appreciate your zeal, but it's no good now. This is a done deal. Long Harbor will be a different community because of this change and you, and your academic nerds, will have to look for a greener world somewhere else. Long Harbor is going to become the next Cambria, and you can't stop it."

"Fortunato, you will get what you deserve, sooner or later."

Mark stood and stepped between the two men. "Please, gentlemen. Let's be civil here. We heard the arguments and the board voted. Professor Amos, if you plan to appeal, that's your right. There is still time before any shovel hits the dirt. Mr. Fortunato, maybe you should leave with your men. You've gotten what you came for."

Fox took a moment to gain his composure, slammed his gavel on the podium, and faced the crowd that looked ready for further argument. "We are done for the evening, folks. I ask Detective Porfino and our guests from the police force to assure that everyone leave peacefully. Good night, everyone. Have a safe trip home."

- - -

Silvio wedged himself into his Explorer and drove to The Wharf. Before getting out, he dialed Mario. "This is Silvio. The zoning petition passed."

Silvio paused to hear Mario's reaction. "No," he answered. "There was no real question of the petition passing. Willet and Robbins voted "Yes" as expected, and Fox and Miriam Wagner voted "No." Miss Gillek thinks Father Jim walks on water. She'd follow him into hell. Once he spoke in favor, it was a done deal."

Silvio listened some more, then spoke. "There was some anger, and Professor Amos promised further action. He also threw a few threatening remarks at me and my men. I'm trying to decide if I should straighten him out." Silvio listened to the angry response. "Okay, Mario, I'll let him slide this time, but I don't like being threatened."

Chapter 4

David and Goliath in Battle

The next morning, Gabe was having coffee and eggs at Lucy's Eat and Go Diner. This was an unfortunate name, really, as Lucy's had a reputation for greasy food and questionable sanitary conditions. Gabe liked Lucy's, though, because it was cheap and on the way to his office. It was also a hangout for the community college students and faculty who liked the 24-hour convenience; it was a good place to cure a hangover while preparing for classes.

Gabe was shoveling runny eggs onto rye toast and reading the story of last night's zoning meeting when Rico entered and ordered a large take-out coffee. Turning, he spotted Gabe, walked over and sat across from him.

Looking up from his Long Harbor Press, he smiled at the young man. "Rico, I was just reading the summary of last night's meeting. While I support the chance for new business, I do agree that the environmental questions need to be cleared up. Let me tell you that it should never have passed without more study. And Jim? That beats me. He has suddenly become a venture capitalist."

Rico removed the lid and took a sip of coffee. "I appreciate your concern, Gabe. My dad's pushing this project because he's being pressured by the Cambria office. That whole crew makes me nervous. On top of that, Dad's rarely home and I think he has someone on the side. I want to be more sympathetic towards him and want him to treat me and mom better, but I think it's too late to change."

Gabe put down the paper. "I'll try to talk some sense into him, but I can't promise anything. Your father and I rarely agree, but I'll try."

"I appreciate that, Gabe. Do what you can."

Rico extended his hand to Gabe, who shook it. "Things will get better, Rico. I promise."

Silvio, who happened to be at the counter buying a bear claw and newspaper, took this in and left.

- - -

Professor John Amos had been teaching Environmental Studies at Cambria Community College for five years. When he walked into his Wednesday class, he was surprised to see all of the seats filled and a few unfamiliar students standing in the rear. There was a small round of applause. He nodded with a slight smile. A pretty coed in the front row said, "Professor, you were very courageous last night standing up to Fortunato and his men. What can we do to stop this project before we have a disaster?"

Amos took a second to study the young lady. There was a nice crop this year. "Thanks, Janie, and thanks everyone for your concern. I haven't given up the fight. This is too important for Long Harbor."

He walked behind his desk, opened his portfolio, and pulled out a map of the Hillside factory area, which highlighted buildings containing asbestos and land parcels having measurable amounts of mercury and other chemicals. These areas rose above a Long Harbor residential area and a middle school.

"This ruling was made in haste, and I daresay was a done deal before the meeting ever started. Fortunato and his backers are influential in this town and zoning boards can be bought." He stopped as many students turned towards the middle row. Sitting there was Rico. Amos realized he hadn't thought of Rico when he'd made his statement.

"Rico, we all know the position you're in. I consider you a friend and well- respected student. I have a strong disagreement with your father over this issue and I'm going to have to say and do more about this matter. Just know that nothing I say or do is meant to harm you or your mother."

Rico stood. "Professor, my father is involved in things that I find repulsive. I have talked to him about what he is doing to the town. I doubt if it has sunken in." He sighed. "Do what you have to do, Professor."

– – –

Father Ray Langley had been pastor of St. Augustine's parish for 10 years. He previously served at St. Mary's in Cambria, and thought he had traded in an urban, street-tough community for a more idyllic one in Long Harbor. But, the same unemployment, delinquency, and petty crime had followed him.

Fortunately, Ray shared parish responsibilities with Jim, who had grown up in Long Harbor and seemed to know everyone in town.

Jim was a godsend. He had been at the forefront of the parish outreach to identify those in need and to create programs to help them, but now Jim was involved in zoning matters, of all things. He had chosen to come down on the side of business on a matter in which the environment might be damaged, and schoolchildren short-changed for funding. Ray asked Jim to meet with him this morning to discuss what was happening and why.

Jim entered Ray's office, clearly uncomfortable. "You wanted to see me, Ray?"

The pastor waved Jim to a chair, took a sip of coffee, put down the St. Augustine Knights mug, and took a second to study Jim.

"Jim, I need to talk to you about this business lobbying, for lack of a better term. This is so uncharacteristic. You have been on the side of the needy and disadvantaged, and now you're shilling for Fortunato and the other business owners. What's going on?"

Jim shifted in his chair. "Ray, Long Harbor needs growth. We are a dying community. The young people are leaving as soon as they can, and there are a lot of unemployed men and women wondering what's next. I'm just trying to do my part by promoting the redevelopment of Long Harbor."

Ray frowned and shook his head. "And you're not worried about the pollution and potential health impact on the community? That environmental study was a sham and you, for one, should know that. I'm all for growth too, but we need to make sure it's done so that we can all benefit and be safe."

Leaning in closer, he said, "Jim, what's the deal with you and Fortunato? He's crooked and everyone in town knows it. Mario Gallante owns his business, and *he's* even dirtier. Gallante's in the forefront of the sports gambling that is plaguing Cambria and is spreading into Long Harbor. Is this why you're doing this? Are you gambling again?"

"I'm doing some sheets and having a run of bad luck. If I can just get a good run, I can be rid of Silvio."

Ray turned red, started to shake, and leaned face to face into Jim. "What the hell, Jim. You're betting with a bookie? God, what else are you doing on the side?"

Jim cleared his throat. "Well..."

Ray stood straight and held up his hand. "Don't tell me—not yet. I don't want to strangle my associate pastor."

He sat down and pulled his chair closer. "It doesn't work like that with betting, Jim. You have an addiction and winning here and there just draws you in further. How much do you owe Silvio?"

"Two thousand, after last weekend. I can't pay that, Ray, and Silvio's putting the screws to me. He's also pressuring others. That's why the zoning passed."

Ray put his face to his hands. He seemed to laugh for just a second. "And you're abetting him."

He sat back and studied his associate. "Here's what's going to happen. I'm going to cash a check out of my own money for $2,000. You're going to see Silvio tonight and give him the money. You're going to tell him that you're done with the gambling and that you're going to withdraw your support for the rezoning. It's not too late to stop this thing."

Taking a breath to calm himself, he continued, "I like you, Jim. You're good for the community. But get this done and get Silvio off your back or you're gone. One call to Bishop Reilly and you'll be tending sheep elsewhere—get it?"

"Okay, Ray."

"And I'm going to dock your pay until I get my two thousand back. I'll leave you enough for a few bad meals at Lucy's and some gas money. But if I hear about you buying as much as a lottery ticket, you're through." He paused to think for a second and then showed his wry smile. "Oh, and you're on confession duty for the next month."

– – –

Gabe was preparing to leave the office for the day. He planned to go to his apartment, nuke something quick, drink a few beers and fall asleep in front of the television. The phone rang. It was Jim.

"Gabe, what are you doing tonight? How about we grab something at The Wharf? There's someone I need to meet there and I'd like you along."

Gabe sighed. "Only for my brother. Okay, drive over here and we'll go over in my car. You have to promise that if I drink too much, you'll drive me home."

"Done, Gabe. I'm not going to drink much either. I need to be clear headed."

The Wharf was hopping for a Wednesday night. Silvio was holding court with his work crew and celebrating the zoning victory. His workers, while lousy tradesmen, were good at running betting slips and collecting from deadbeats. Silvio paid his men well for their work *and* their discretion. This rezoning would mean more work for the crew. There might even be some plumbing work coming out of it.

Gabe entered, wiped his hand from the sticky doorknob, and sat himself at a table. Jim had been collared outside by a parishioner. Imagine meeting your priest going into a crummy bar, Gabe thought. That could only happen to Jim.

He ordered chili over rice and a draft for himself and Jim. The chili at The Wharf was well thought of by the bachelor clientele. It was hot and meaty.

Taking a long pull of his beer, he took in the customers that evening: the usual blue-collar tradesmen, including some of his own. He also noticed Professor Amos from the community college who was downing a draft, plowing into a plate of chili, and looking towards Silvio's table while trying not to be conspicuous. You're out of your element here, Professor, Gabe thought.

Silvio and his men were enjoying themselves. A lot to celebrate after last night's victory. Gabe had just finished his first draft and ordered another, when Silvio spotted him and walked over. He sat without being invited. Eyeing Jim's chili, he picked up the spoon and tasted. "Hey, not bad. Listen, Cooper, I saw you with my son this morning at Lucy's. You and him appear to be pretty chummy. What's going on? First you're hugging my wife in my own home, and now you're being Daddy to Rico?"

Silvio picked up Jim's draft and took a few gulps. "Why don't you get your own family and leave mine alone? Maybe find some sweet girl who'll put up with your holier-than-thou attitude, and drive you home from The Wharf when you're too screwed-up to drive."

"I had a sweet girl years ago, but I let her go. Now she's married to a thug."

Silvio turned red, then smiled. "Cooper, this is a good evening for me, and I'd hate to spoil it by having to kick your ass. We're adults, you and me. I'm going to keep smiling and forget what you said. Just know that I can make you disappear as easily as you can make that draft disappear. Leave me and my family alone, before you end up in the harbor."

He stood, wiped his mouth on Jim's napkin, and started to walk away. Carla had taken in the whole encounter. Silvio waved to her. "Hey Carla, another draft for my friend Gabe." He turned to Gabe. "And by the way, your sweet girl is cheating on me. I always suspected you, but could never prove it. Now I think that you're too weak to turn her head."

Gabe took this in. Maybe Silvio was right. Jessie had this simmering sensuality about her that she wasn't afraid to flaunt. Maybe he wasn't enough for Jessie after all, he thought, except as a friend.

He signaled Carla for another spoon and napkin, and a new plate of chili for Jim. A few minutes later, Jim entered, wiped his hand from the doorknob, and spotted Gabe. He sat and looked at his draft; it didn't appear to be completely full. He picked up the mug anyway. Gabe, realizing that Silvio had drank from it, raised a finger. Too late. Jim downed half of the remaining beer. "Sorry about that. I got into a discussion on Sunday music of all things."

He looked down at his Chili. "It looks hot and filling. What else does a man need?" he said as he picked up his spoon and dove in.

Gabe was feeling no pain. "Ah, my brother the Father. How the hell are you? So, are you here to save the wretched, or to kiss Silvio's ass?"

Jim realized that Gabe was half in the bag.

"Gabe, I'll explain later. I'm here to get Silvio out of my life and the lives of those other dopes, like me, who owe him money and a pound of flesh. I'm done with gambling and I'm done with creeps like Silvio destroying people's lives. It's time Silvio got what's coming to him."

He drained the rest of his beer, stood, and walked over to Silvio's table. He said something that Gabe couldn't hear, but which got a rise out of Silvio's men, especially Sal. Silvio stood, waved off his men and walked with Jim over to the corner of the bar. Jim was angry and reaching into his pocket; Silvio was smiling.

"Here's your two thousand. I'm done with gambling and I'm done with you and your threats." Jim shoved the money at him.

Silvio appeared ill at ease and looked around. "Jeez, Jim, don't do something like that here. I'm glad you're paying up, but actually I was going to cut you a break after your fine endorsement last night. You've done a good thing for Long Harbor, Fortunato Brothers and Gallante Supplies. Why don't you go home to your cathedral? Tomorrow, mail fifteen hundred to Fortunato Brothers. Then we're square."

Jim leaned into Silvio's airspace. "Silvio, I'll mail you the two thousand, and then I'm going to write a letter to the editor of the Long Harbor Press saying that I retract my endorsement of the zoning change. Don't worry, I'm not stupid enough to implicate you. I'll just say that the environmental concerns, including air and water pollution, caused me to rethink the overall benefit. All rather civil, I would say."

Silvio moved nose-to-nose with Jim. "Not a wise move, Padre. I have as much dirty laundry on you as you have on me. Gambling, sneaking around with Miss Gillek—those alone would cost you your residency and probably send you back to Cambria to serve the Bishop in whatever hell-hole position he can find."

He put his hairy hand on Jim's shoulder. "Believe me Jim, we can all benefit by letting this situation play out. When you come to your senses, you'll see this. And, who knows? In a few weeks, if you miss the thrill of pissing money away on point spreads that you don't understand, maybe we can do business again."

Jim started for his table, but turned around and said in a too-loud voice, "Silvio, everyone's crimes catch up with them. You will learn that soon enough. It won't be long before this town is rid of you and your band of thieves."

"Padre, you've had a long day. Why don't you go home and sleep on things. Sal will drive you home." Silvio chuckled. "Or to wherever you want to get off."

Jim waved off Sal. "Just watch your back, Silvio. Things happen in this town."

He walked past Gabe and out the door. Gabe waved at Carla to pay his bill.

Silvio walked over. "Leaving too, Gabriel? Not a good night for the Cooper clan. Both of you should stay out of my life. It's better for everyone."

Handing Carla two twenties for the chili and drafts, Gabe was about to walk out when he realized she had been the one with Silvio when he almost ran him over. Gabe winked at Carla. He knew this would piss Silvio off. "Good night, young lovers, sleep tight."

Leaving The Wharf, he found Jim standing in the corner of the lot staring at the harbor. He was next to Silvio's parked Explorer, which was taking two spaces. "Are you okay, Jim?" Gabe asked.

Jim turned towards Gabe. "You know, Gabe we're…"

"Hold that thought," Gabe said, and walked over to the driver's side of Silvio's explorer and relieved himself onto the front tire. "Now, you were saying?"

Jim turned to Gabe after looking at the wet tire and puddle. "You know, Gabe, except for a few physical characteristics, you and I aren't very similar. You're the hard-working, no-nonsense upright citizen who can always be counted on for help. I'm a parish priest who can't write a decent sermon, has a gambling problem, and will sell out his town. Face it, you're the good brother, and I'm the bad."

Gabe sobered enough to respond. "Jim, you're admired in this town by people of all beliefs. You've done good things. You're human, though, like the rest of us. I'm not sure how deeply you've stepped into things lately, but it looks pretty nasty and involves Silvio. Now it looks like you're trying to make good. Just be careful around Silvio. He's not the kind to forgive and forget. As for being the good brother, maybe I haven't taken advantage of the opportunity to be bad. But I'm tempted, like everyone else."

He belched and continued. "I hope I can continue to do the right thing by folks, but I have my demons. Drink, for example, and my desire for Jessie. I just hope that if I stumble like you claim to have done, that I can right myself and get on with my life."

He laughed loud enough to make Jim look around to see if they were being overheard. "You know, Jim, this whole good and bad business—I'm not so sure I can make the distinction sometimes. Maybe there are times you have to do something people think is bad, in order to make things better. Who's to say?"

"Gabe, let me drive you home. You're in no shape to drive, and I still have a few things to do tonight."

Jim paused. "And at the end of the day, I'm just a man myself; with flaws that make me question life as well." He smiled at his brother. "Maybe we both need to sober up."

Gabe took one more admiring glance at his artwork on Silvio's tire and said, "I need to walk home. Maybe the air will do me good. Take my car and do what you need to do. Then drop it off at my place later on and leave the keys in my mail box."

He handed Jim the keys to his Prius and started walking towards his apartment. Two miles, but not a bad evening. If only the scenery would stop moving around.

Jim got into Gabe's car and honked as he drove by. He seemed on a mission.

- - -

Jim drove out of town and found himself behind an older woman doing about fifteen under the limit. He followed her for a mile or so, hitting light after light. He didn't recognize her as a parishioner. The opportunity finally came to pass her and he pulled in front and had to slam his brakes not to go through the next red light. This caused the woman to have to jam her brakes. She honked at Jim. He returned a single finger salute and drove off as the light turned green.

The woman was shocked but had the presence of mind to record the license number. She pulled over and called the police. Detective Porfino was working late and answered.

"This is Claire Woodward from Glen Heights. I want to report a reckless driver. He pulled out in front of me and I had to jam on my brakes. Then he flipped me the bird and drove off. I got his car type and his license."

Mark stifled a laugh and took the car make, yellow Prius, and license. "Did he appear to be drunk, Mrs. Woodward?"

"I couldn't tell. The bastard was sober enough to flip me off."

Porfino realized that he'd never want to get on her bad side. "Okay ma'am, what did he look like? Was it a kid?"

"No, actually a dark-haired man, around 40 or so."

"Okay. We'll have the patrol keep an eye out for him. Thanks for calling."

Porfino relayed the information though the dispatcher. He ran the license against the DMV database. It came back *Gabriel Cooper, 280 Jackson Circle, Long Harbor.* Well, well, he thought. I would never have expected that.

Jim pulled onto Longshore Drive, in The Willows section of town. He parked at the end of the street and walked to number 118. He knocked lightly after looking around to make sure he wasn't being observed. Jan Gillek answered the door and dropped her jaw. "Jim, what are you doing here? We agreed that we would only meet away from Long Harbor. This is dangerous."

Jim walked in. "Jan, we need to talk."

- - -

Silvio left The Wharf about 45 minutes after Gabe and Jim. He was feeling pretty good; he had a buzz on and had handled the Coopers. Saying goodbye to his men, he was about to open his Explorer when he noticed that his front tire was stained and that he was standing in a puddle. It has rained earlier, but this didn't look like water.

Silvio's realized what had happened. What kind of drunken low life would do this? Then it dawned on him. "Cooper. That's it. I'm gonna find that guy and kick his ass." He looked around. Gabe's car was gone, but it wasn't like him to drive drunk. He guessed the good Father Jim, his sainted brother, poured him into his faggy Prius and took him home.

Silvio slammed his hand onto the door of the Explorer, shouted "That bastard," climbed in, amped up his Jazz CD, and took off towards Gabe's apartment.

At the same time, an unobserved acquaintance started his pickup and followed at a distance. Silvio followed Harbor Drive and plotted how to make Gabe regret his actions. He saw a dark figure slowly making his way along the harbor walkway. He was heading east towards the Jackson Place apartment complex. Gabe. Perfect.

Silvio pulled into a parking area at the dock and slipped into a handicapped spot. He jumped out and slammed the door with the engine still running. "Cooper," he called. "You're a dead man!"

Silvio. Shit, Gabe thought. I should run but my feet wouldn't cooperate. Time for negotiating skills. "Silvio. Thanks for thinking about my safety, but I really don't need a ride. The walk will do me good. Thanks, anyway."

"Cooper, you pissed on my tire and I got it all over my shoe."

Gabe suppressed a laugh. "Sorry, Silvio, I thought I was relieving myself on a stranger's tire. No harm meant."

Stomping over, Silvio stood in front of his inebriated nemesis. Grabbing Gabe by the shirt collar, he shook him violently back and forth like a rag doll. He clenched a fist and prepared to punch Gabe. Unfortunately, the shaking caused Gabe's body to seek relief wherever possible, so Gabe simultaneously shit himself and projectile vomited onto Silvio.

As he surveyed the combined beer and chili on his shirt, Silvio fumed. However, he unclenched his fist as he saw no spot to hit Gabe where he wouldn't be landing on vomit. Instead, he threw Gabe towards a pile of debris.

There was a yelp as Gabe landed. He had fallen on a small dog in the process of relieving itself. The dog ran away barking its displeasure at the inconvenience of having his constitutional interrupted. Gabe sat up and realized that his shirt and pants were covered with mud and crap. Perfect.

Silvio laughed. "Now you know how it feels. Here's some number one to finish your experience." With that, Silvio kicked Gabe in the ribs and shoulder with his urine-soaked boot.

"Get up, Cooper. We've just started."

Holding his side and gasping for air, Gabe stood. "Silvio, you got in your shots. Leave me alone."

The man laughed and started forward. Gabe remembered his recent attempt to learn kickboxing and landed a weak kick at the lunging Silvio. It hit pay dirt in the testicles. Not very hard, but effective. It was painful enough to get Silvio doubled over. Gabe fell over from the momentum and the pain in his side.

"Now we're even," gasped Gabe as he stood up on two unsteady feet. "Now let's both just go home and sleep this off."

Silvio struggled to stand and walked back to the dock while reaching into his coat. He turned towards Gabe. "Not before I do something I've been planning for a long time, Cooper."

As it reappeared from his jacket, Silvio's hand revealed a black metallic object. Gabe, fearing Silvio had a gun, ran headlong into Silvio's chest, driving him stumbling backwards towards the edge of the dock. He kicked him for good measure. "How's that feel, Silvio? How's it feel to be on the receiving end?"

Silvio stood slowly, holding his side. He again reached into his coat. Gabe ran at Silvio and pushed him off the edge of the dock. The black object fell out of Silvio's hand as Silvio fell sideways off the dock. His head made contact with a piling and with a cry of pain, he belly-flopped into the water and disappeared underneath.

"Silvio!" Gabe called out. Silence. He took off his shoes and jumped into the murky water. "Silvio!" he repeated. Gabe soon realized that he wasn't going to find Silvio in the darkness. He swam to the dock and pulled himself out. He lay on his back catching his breath and thinking about what just happened. God, I just killed him. Should I call the police? I have to. It was a fight that went too far. He'd pulled a gun. It was self-defense.

He pulled out his cell, but then saw the black object that had fallen from Silvio's hand. It wasn't a gun. It was Silvio's cell.

He put his phone back into his pocket. Silvio didn't have a gun after all. How could Gabe explain this? He picked up Silvio's cell and looked at the recently called numbers. Was he calling Jessie to lord his victory over him? Was he calling for someone to finish Gabe off? Uncertain what to do next, but feeling that he had to report the death, he dialed 911 from Silvio's cell.

The operator answered "9....1.....What is...name, loca...and the nature of....emergency?"

Gabe looked at the cell. It must have been damaged when it fell from Silvio's hand. When I killed him, he thought. Gabe heard "Hel..," as the operator sought an answer.

I have to think this over, he thought, and hung up. He started walking in the direction of his apartment, making sure to stay in the shadows. Silvio's Explorer sat in the handicapped spot, waiting for its master and using up the remaining gas.

Suddenly, the theme from The Sopranos rang out. Gabe looked

around for any sign of a television or radio. He then realized that it was the ring tone from Silvio's cell. He looked at the incoming ID: 911 CALL CENTER.

He almost dropped the phone. They must have caller ID. Of course. He took a deep breath and answered, saying a cautious "Hello."

"This is ...911 call cen.... A call just came ...this number. Is there ...emergency?"

"No. Everything is OK now, thanks." He hung up, turned towards the harbor, and threw Silvio's cell as far as he could into the murky water.

- - -

In a side parking lot about a quarter mile from the fight, a man standing by a pickup had taken in the exchange between Gabe and Silvio. He considered driving over when Silvio fell in the water, but then thought better of it. Silvio was out of the way, and all he had to do was watch. Sometimes, the breaks come your way, he thought. And to think, mild-mannered Gabe Cooper did him in. He pulled out his cell and dialed '1' on his speed dial. A female voice answered. "Mission accomplished," he said and hung up.

He'd seen Gabe make a call and then throw the phone into the bay. Who had he called, the police? It was time to leave.

As he walked towards his pickup, a yappy terrier ran by, making the man lose his balance. The dog barked and growled as he shoved it away with his shoe. "Get away, you filthy mutt."

The dog barked again and struck a defiant pose. He reached into his truck, pulled out a baseball bat, and struck the ground near the dog, forcing it to retreat. He started his truck and drove away as the dog issued more challenges.

He drove home towards Cambria, put on Bruce Springsteen, set the cruise control and relaxed. He didn't see the red light he drove through as he left the Long Harbor city limits, and also didn't notice the accompanying flash of the red light camera. He went to bed and slept like a baby.

- - -

Jim drove home from Jan's house after breaking things off. What had started as mutual enthusiasm in helping the less fortunate had turned to thinly masked flirting and then into a serious relationship.

He was ashamed that he caused her so much pain, but when the gambling caused him to further betray his ideals, he realized he had to turn his life around or condemn himself to a deepening spiral of deceit. Time to sink or swim; time to swim back to shore while he still had the strength to save himself and Jan.

Pulling into the parking lot of Gabe's apartment, he settled next to his own car. He pulled the envelope for Silvio, addressed the front to Fortunato Brothers Plumbing, but realized that he didn't have a stamp. He would have to go into Gabe's and take one out of his desk drawer.

He opened the car door and swung himself out. Old Mr. Richardson was about 100 yards away, looking around as if he had lost something. He spotted Jim. "Hi, Gabe. Looks like it was a late night. Did you happen to see Reggie in your travels? He ran out the door before I could put the leash on him."

Jim was going to identify himself but decided not to. Mr. Richardson's mind was failing anyway, and he wouldn't make the distinction. "Hi, Mr. Richardson. No, I didn't see Reggie. I'm sure he'll be back. Good night." Mr. Richardson heard this and was quiet for a moment. Did he notice a difference in Gabe's voice?

"Okay, take care, Gabe. This December weather can be tricky. It may be raining lightly now, but it could just as easily be snow. You don't want to be caught out in bad conditions with that putt-putt of yours."

"Good advice. I'll watch myself." He walked to Gabe's doorway. His porch light wasn't on, but there was enough indirect brightness from the street light to find the lock. Jim entered, closed the door behind him, and turned on the hall light.

Meanwhile, Mr. Richardson continued his search for Reggie. Good night, Gabe, he thought. Get some sleep. You don't seem yourself.

Eventually finding a stamp, Jim left the apartment, placed the envelope and Gabe's keys into the mailbox, and raised the flag. He started walking to his blue Miata. No Mr. Richardson around. Jim started the engine, turned on the radio, and heard *Gimme Three Steps* from Lynrd Skynyrd. He pulled out singing and drove towards the rectory.

- - -

About fifteen minutes later, Gabe approached the door of his apartment. Jim's car was gone. I have to talk to Jim first thing tomorrow, he thought. He looked at his torn clothes and winced at the pain in his ribs. First thing tomorrow. Boy, am I soaked. At least I wasn't seen.

He looked around: no Mr. Richardson walking his defecation factory, no Mrs. Reynolds looking out from her shades. He opened his mailbox and fished out his keys. He saw the letter addressed to Fortunato Brothers and felt a chill. He unlocked his door, entered his apartment, took off his soaked and soiled clothes, and bagged them. Tomorrow, he would toss them in a dumpster far away.

He took a long, hot shower, hoping to wash off Silvio. He thought about the 911 call and the fact that they had called him back. As he was toweling off, he looked at his bruised, and possibly broken, ribs. That's going to hurt like hell in the morning. Maybe I should call Lou tomorrow and tell him I'm sick, he thought. He took two extra-strength painkillers and lay down, hoping for some sleep, though he doubted it would come. Tomorrow would be here eventually and he would have to decide what to do next.

- - -

Chapter 5

Sins are Washed Clean

Thursday morning was rainy and cold. Typical early December weather.

At least it isn't snow, thought young Patrolman Ted Hanson. Hanson had been on the Long Harbor police force for three years now and idolized Detective Porfino. He took every opportunity to ask him for advice and bounce ideas off him. Porfino liked Ted and enlisted him in his study of the Long Harbor cold case log—and the death of Enrico Fortunato three years ago.

Now, Ted was on normal patrol of the commercial dock area and the Long Harbor business area. He was driving through when he noticed an Explorer parked in a handicapped spot, without handicapped tags. Out in the driving rain, he looked for a temporary handicapped placard or visor attachment. Not seeing either, he wrote a ticket and shook his head. People think they can park anywhere they want. Well, here's your $200 ticket, whoever you are. I hope you enjoyed your expensive view of the waterfront.

- - -

Jessie awoke to find no Silvio next to her. She had gone to bed before he came home so thought she'd missed him completely. Probably out late, drinking and screwing around. She walked to the kitchen. Rico was downing a cup of coffee and munching on an English muffin. He looked up from his sports section, nodded and mumbled a nook-and-cranny filled "Good Morning."

"Did you see your father this morning—or even last night for that matter?"

Rico shook his head. A missing Silvio was not unusual and, given the relationship between the three, even disturbing. "Mom, how can you stand this? You deserve better. Dad doesn't show you any respect. He's never around."

She poured herself some coffee and thought a moment. "Rico, when I met your father, I had just gotten over thinking Gabe and I had a chance. Your dad moved to town and he's was this hulking, confident man who knew what he wanted. He was what I needed at the time. He was a good husband and father when you were young."

Jessie sighed. "Then your Uncle Enrico died, and he became a different man. He was distrusting, quick to anger, and aggressive. He told me once that Enrico's death wasn't accidental and he had an idea about who killed him. He told me he wasn't going to let the same thing happen to him."

Putting her cup down, she continued. "Whoever he suspected was connected enough to prevent Dad from confronting him directly. I thought it might be Mario, or his organization, or maybe even someone with the Long Harbor police. Whoever it was, from that point on, Dad was a different man. He trusted no one and seemed determined to make sure that he could always protect himself.

"We've become a low priority in his life. He seems to be spending a lot of time with his new girlfriend. I think I know who that is now, but at this point maybe it doesn't matter any more."

Jessie took a long gulp and seemed to be thinking about her next step. "Anyway, I'll call your Dad today to make sure he's coming home tonight. He owes us some semblance of a family life even if it's only for appearances."

Rico stood, wiped his mouth, and hugged Jessie. "Mom, you deserve better. Think of yourself. There are better men out there than Dad. You don't owe him a thing."

Jessie returned a weak smile. "Rico, I still love him and he loves us both, in his way. And no matter what, he will always be your father."

Grabbing his car keys, Rico sighed. "I guess so. I have to go to class now, Mom. I'll see you later."

Jessie stood to wash out her cup. "Be careful out there. It's been raining and it's cold. Accidents happen in this weather."

- - -

Gabe tossed in his bed replaying what had happened until he finally fell asleep. When he awoke, the pain in his side had worsened; he could barely stand without doubling over. He took two more painkillers and examined himself in the mirror.

What do I do now? Maybe I should have reported it to the police. It was a fight and I defended myself. Silvio slipped, fell, and hit his head. No chance to save him.

He decided that it would be a bad idea to call in sick, since he never missed work and didn't want to arouse any concern in Lou. He dressed, avoiding any movements that would put pressure on his ribs, pulled an overcoat from his closet and picked up his keys.

Outside, in the steady rain, he started to unlock his car. Just then, Mr. Richardson walked by with his mongrel. He had an open umbrella protecting himself. Reggie wore a vinyl raincoat tailored for his short body. "We meet again, Gabe. Twice in just a few hours. I hope that you've recovered after your long night."

He almost dropped his keys and wondered what Richardson knew. Composing himself, he smiled. "Some nights are better than others, Mr. Richardson. You and Reggie better get in from the cold and rain. This looks like it's gonna be a bad day."

He drove slowly to Lucy's, as every movement hurt. He could barely get out of the car without sharp pains in his side. Taking off his wet coat, he found a seat at a nearby booth, and asked Lucy for a large coffee and some scrambled eggs. He took a sip of the bitter brew, loaded it down with sugar and cream, and tried again. Better this time. He drank some more, plowed into his runny eggs and felt even better. He looked out the window. Where is Silvio now, he wondered. God, I hope he's at the bottom and stays there. Maybe this will all just go away – eventually.

Detective Porfino walked up to Gabe and smiled. "Can I join you,

Gabe? I wanted to talk to you about what you did last night." Gabe blanched. Man, he thought, even in cheap murder tales, the killer gets away with it for a while. Who else knows besides Mr. Richardson and Porfino? Reggie probably even suspects.

He waved the detective to an opposite seat. Mark nodded to Lucy for coffee and then looked at Gabe. "Look, Gabe. We all have bad days and we all have a few too many sometimes. What you did last night wasn't right, but I'm not sure if I wouldn't have done the same thing."

Gabe was startled. "Are you saying it was okay, what happened?"

"Gabe, I feel like flipping off slow drivers sometimes, too. Claire Woodward was upset though. Let me propose a solution to all of this. Send her some flowers with an apology. Then, no ticket and it will be like nothing happened."

I didn't even know *this* happened, Gabe thought, but breathing a painful sigh, he nodded. "Good advice, Mark. Can I call you "Mark?" I guess we all do things that we wish we hadn't. I'll go over to Harbor Florists and take care of that right now."

He stood, left a five-dollar tip, and walked to the counter. Porfino noticed his slow pace and thought that it must have been a rough night for Gabe. Gabe paid and said "Great breakfast, Lucy. My compliments." Lucy was not normally on the receiving end of such praise. She smiled and said she looked forward to seeing Gabe again.

He left the diner and started to walk across the street to the florist. Porfino watched from the table. He smiled at the man and thought "Saint Gabriel. If flipping off a driver is the worst thing you've ever done, you're not likely to meet me again on a police matter."

Walking into Harbor Florists, he told the clerk he wanted to send something nice as a means of making amends. She suggested roses and asked for delivery instructions. Gabe pulled over a phone book on the counter, realized that this might be suspicious, and explained that he had just met his flower recipient and wasn't familiar with her section of town. After flipping to the Ws, he found Claire Woodward and gave the address to the smiling clerk.

"Any card?"

Gabe thought, "Thanks for the alibi" but decided on "Sorry for my bad behavior last night."

"Any name?"

"Better to keep that blank. She'll know who they're from." The clerk gave a knowing smile.

"A dozen roses, fifty dollars, sir. Money well spent."

- - -

The lone human witness to Silvio's death awoke the next morning and slid out of bed. He put on the local morning news and started the coffee. No news on Silvio's demise. Looking out the window at the rain, he thought it would probably wash away any evidence of a fight. Gabe lucked out too.

Tony Wagner sat and propped up his feet and thought about what had happened. There he'd been ready to kill his second Fortunato, when fate dealt him a better hand. His cell rang. He looked at the display; she must want more detail. He pushed Answer.

"Hi, Sis." Rapid speech on the other end.

"Whoa. I can't talk about it now. Don't worry; there are no tracks to cover up. Let's just say that Silvio won't be a problem for either of us anymore. I gotta go now."

He actually had nowhere to go; he just didn't want to listen to his nervous sister. He had a lot of spare time on his hands, now that he was retired and on a nice pension. He stirred his coffee and grabbed a packaged sweet roll. He looked at the nutrition label. Man, 600 calories. This stuff will kill me. Then he laughed. Well, at least I won't kick off under water in Long Harbor. I hope Silvio isn't chewed up too bad by what's under there. He laughed again. I hope he doesn't poison anything in there, either.

- - -

Father Jim awoke early, feeling like a new man. He had squared things with Silvio and ended things with Jan. He felt bad about how he left her, but was now relieved that he could start anew. He read his Divine Office and brewed himself a cup of coffee. The first day of the rest of my life, he thought. Things will get better from here.

He pulled out his vestments for 8 a.m. mass. As he was walking from the rectory, he saw Father Ray with his car hood raised, looking at the guts of his 10 year-old Corolla. He had his rain hood raised but was wet anyway. Looking up, he saw Jim. "I think I have a dead battery. I really should keep better track of things like this."

Jim smiled. "Not a problem, Ray, let me give you a jump."

He threw his vestments into his car to keep them dry. He didn't seem to care about getting wet himself. He went into his trunk and pulled out jumper cables. As he connected the cables, he was whistling. Ray couldn't help but notice Jim's happy demeanor.

"So things are square with you and Silvio, huh?" he called out through the increasing rain. Jim jumped into his driver seat, started his engine, and signaled Ray to do the same. The car started up. Jim got out of his car and signaled an ok to Ray.

"All square with Silvio, Ray. He won't be controlling me anymore. I took care of that. I did what I had to do." Jim reached into his car and picked up his vestments. "Ray, go to your dealer and get a new battery. I'll cover here. It's a new day."

He went into the sacristy to change and in a few minutes walked up the center aisle and called out to those attending early mass. "Good morning everyone. What a wonderful day."

Mrs. O'Reilley, a consistent attendee at morning mass, looked out the side window and thought, what day is he talking about?

Jim went through the mass in a more deliberate fashion than normal. Instead of the rote steps he followed week after week of daily masses in front of usually the same ten or so regular attendees, he took in the steps with a new appreciation for what was taking place. He continued to smile as he went through the readings and prayers. Most of those assembled were in their 70s and 80s and were world-weary. They weren't used to Jim's near giddiness and smiled weakly back trying to figure out what was going on.

After the Gospel, the assembly awaited what was normally a short weekday sermon. No doubt something about it being another day in Advent preparing for the coming of the Lord. Jim closed the bible, took a breath, and stepped away from the pulpit and to the front steps of the altar area. This took everyone by surprise. They were used to the separation that the pulpit offered. Actually, they preferred it.

"My dear friends in Christ. What a beautiful day. Oh, it might be rainy and cold but inside I feel warm and comfortable. For I was blind but now I see, lost but now am found. My dear brothers and sisters in Christ, we are all troubled with the burdens and temptations of this world. We are all faced with problems that seem insurmountable. We are all confronted with demons that block our paths to more righteous pursuits.

What are we to do? I say confront your tormentor no matter what the cost. Walk up to your demon and tell that wretched creature that his hold over you has ended. Cast him into the sea so that he may sink to the bottom and no longer cause pain and suffering.

Our Lord was confronted by the demon when he fasted in the desert. The demon offered earthly comfort to our lord in exchange for his very soul. But the Lord rose up and said "Be gone Satan. I do my Father's will." And Satan left. He was rejected and cast out by the Lord.

Well, my friends that is what we must do with those who would destroy our lives. I say, destroy the devil before he can destroy you. Cast the devil into the darkness that he deserves. Then we can rise again in our new lives. We can know that we will never have to face the devil again. We can know that we will never again need to face such hardship. Cast the devil away. Let him drown in his own evil."

He returned to the pulpit and signaled the congregation to stand for the Profession of Faith. The congregants were bewildered by Jim's sermon; he was not a fire and brimstone preacher, but here he was, whooping it up. Boy Father Jim, you must have had some night, thought Mrs. O'Reilley.

After Mass, Jim stood in back, greeting the attendees. They shook his hand but were unusually quiet. They were still taking in his sermon. He went into the sacristy and changed, walked out of St. Augustine's and towards the rectory. He flipped open his cell and checked his voice mail. There was a message from Jan.

"I can't understand what happened last night. Things were going so well with us and then suddenly you decide to break it off? I need a better explanation. Let's talk again, anywhere you want."

Damn, he thought. I shouldn't have expected things to end so easily. I'll call her back later. Maybe she'll come to her senses. This is the last thing I need.

- - -

After he left Harbor Florists that morning, Gabe went to the office. Not much of a business office, really, but there was enough room to muster his work crew for the day. He examined the work log and dispatched his men to the various indoor assignments scheduled for the day. Outside work would have to wait until Friday because of the rain and wind. He put Lou in charge of overseeing things claiming that he needed to do some paperwork, but Lou knew that Gabe had a long night and probably drank more than he should.

He went through the motions but couldn't concentrate. Besides the pain in his ribs—which hurt almost every time he breathed—he felt a tightness in his chest that he suspected was not only from pain, but because he had just taken someone's life.

Turning on the small office TV to listen for local updates, he expected to hear breaking news about a body being discovered in the harbor. Instead, there were mostly reports on the rain and chilly conditions. By mid-afternoon, Gabe realized that he had gotten nothing done. He left for the day, went to his apartment, and started drinking. He passed out on the couch and didn't wake up until 5 a.m.

- - -

Chapter 6

He arose on the Third Day

The next morning, Friday, Patrolman Hanson drove through the harbor parking lot and noticed Silvio's Explorer still parked in the handicapped spot, the ticket still pinned to the windshield, soggy. He looked through the driver side window. No sign of activity since yesterday. He wrote another ticket and placed it next to the original. Maybe this guy thinks this is his permanent space, he thought. Tomorrow you're towed, pal. Maybe then you'll come to your senses.

- - -

Jessie awoke and looked across her shoulder. Still, no Silvio. This is the last straw, she thought; at least come home at night. She picked up the phone and dialed Fortunato Brothers, getting voice mail. "Silvio, you better call me. This has been two days now. If you're off screwing someone, then it's over. Do you hear?" She slammed down the phone and decided to dress and go for a run to clear her head.

Half an hour later, Silvio's foreman Sal called and got her voicemail. "Jess, this is Sal. We haven't seen Silvio since Wednesday night. I thought he might be home sick or sleeping it off. Let me check with the men to see if anyone knows where he is. Maybe he has something going on. Don't worry, Jess. We'll find him and get him to call you."

- - -

Dave Ulstead was a retired accountant from Cambria. A widower with no family ties to Cambria, he'd moved to Long Harbor for the slower pace and more scenic surroundings. He had a small apartment in Jackson Place and got along well with his neighbors. He enjoyed his quiet bachelor life.

This morning he'd switched on the TV for the local weather. "A good day" said the anchor "to be outside and enjoy the harbor and bay." He decided to rent a small sailboat and ease his way into the harbor. Maybe do some fishing. Dave wasn't much of a fisherman but believed in the adage that "a bad day fishing was better than a good day at work."

He hired a twelve-footer and motored out to the sailing lanes in the harbor. After adjusting the sail to pull in the light wind, he turned off the motor and set his sights on Key Bay, five miles away. He looked around at the scenic harbor and took in the warmth of the sun. Not bad for a December morning, he thought. Maybe this global warming has its benefits.

After a few minutes, Dave was jolted forward as the boat hit a solid object and listed. He steadied himself and looked over the side. Oh boy, I hope it's not a tree stump, he thought. The last thing I need is to have to pay for damage to a rental. He noticed a silhouette in the water, still murky from the full day of rain. He grabbed an oar and gingerly pushed on the obstruction. It was massive. He stood and pushed some more on the dark object to gain some distance and make out what it was. This caused Silvio's body to rotate face up. Dave dropped the oar, shouted a "holy shit" and almost fell in. He grabbed for the metal seat and settled onto it. He took a minute to calm himself and wondered if he had imagined what he'd seen. He snuck a glance over the side. Silvio was looking back, eyes glazed.

Reaching into his pocket and pulling out his cell, he flipped open the cover and shook so much it fell from his hands. It landed on the railing of the boat and fell over the side, right into Silvio's floating lap. Dave held onto the railing and reached gingerly to Silvio's pants. As he grabbed the cell, a small Channel Catfish surfaced and swam over to Silvio's face, bit off a small piece, and submerged. He juggled the phone again but this time held on.

Deciding not to get any closer to Silvio and his new companions, he moved to the center of the seat and dialed 911.

"911. What is your name, location and the nature of your

emergency?"

"This is Dave Ulstead. I live in Jackson Place. Right now I'm in a sail boat in the Long Harbor channel about two miles from the Bay."

The operator said "Okay. And what is the nature of your emergency?"

Dave took another breath. "I just ran over a dead man."

– – –

The 911 operator explained that the police and Coast Guard would be on the way. Dave was to stay on the line and try to maintain his current position. If need be, he would have to set off a flare.

The Long Harbor police had worked with the coast guard from Key Bay on Search and Rescue missions and on investigating criminal matters in the harbor and the adjacent bay. There hadn't been a dead floater to contend with since Enrico. Detective Porfino joined the coroner and two officers and set off in a police patrol boat towards Dave's location. They would meet the Coast Guard there; Chief Petty Officer McWilliams would be present, with a crew.

Mark was not into water sport. In fact, he could barely swim. He had always dreaded the day when he would have to climb into a patrol boat on a police matter, and today was the day. The officers assigned with him, though respectful of his authority, sensed his lack of ease and smiled to each other. Doctor Adam Wakefield, the coroner, waved Mark to take a seat beside him, but he preferred to stand since he didn't want to lose his grip. He kept one hand on the side railing and one on the upper cabin railing. He weighed the benefits of vomiting over the side versus maintaining the respect of the officers.

Steadying himself and peering towards the horizon, he hoped to project the actions of a thoughtful detective preparing for a crime scene, not someone close to losing bodily fluids from multiple locations.

After about three miles, the police pilot slowed and signaled that he spotted Dave's sailboat and the Coast Guard cutter. He set off two blasts from the boat's horn. While this was to signal CPO McWilliams, it also served to cause Mark to lose his grip on the cabin rail and fall ungracefully onto the side bench. The coroner moved over to give Mark some room while the officers attempted to stifle a laugh. Mark noticed, and laughed "Go ahead, let it out. I'm not Popeye, okay?"

The patrol boat edged alongside the Coast Guard cutter. The captain waved and directed his men to lower a walkway at the stern and to help Mark, the coroner, and the two officers climb aboard. Standing next to the captain was Dave, holding a cup of coffee and shaking. His small boat was tied to the cutter.

Once Mark climbed aboard, he introduced himself to Dave.

"Good to meet you, Detective. This is something, huh?"

The Coast Guard had already secured Silvio's body with netting to prevent it from floating away or sinking. With Mark and Wakefield's approval, McWilliams directed his divers to jump in and guide the body to the stern. The coast guard seamen and police officers pulled on latex gloves and lifted Silvio on board and onto a tarp that had been laid out.

Dave put down his empty cup. "Boy, I expected a quiet day of sailing and instead I bump into a dead body. It was enough to throw me forward and get my attention. I couldn't have killed him, could I?"

"Too early to say," said Wakefield. He, McAdams, and Mark put on gloves and knelt next to the swollen body. Mark went through the pockets and pulled out car keys and a wallet. He looked at the name and picture and then back to the face of the dead man. It was swollen and lacerated from being fed on by the fish. Even so, there was no mistaking. "That's Silvio Fortunato from Long Harbor. How the hell did this happen?"

Wakefield looked over Silvio's body and paid close attention to his face. "He has obviously taken in a lot of water. He also has lacerations. Look at the right side of his forehead. There's a deep wound, irregular in pattern. Maybe he hit a tree trunk while floating. Maybe it occurred before he fell in." Wakefield looked at Mark. "There don't seem to be other injuries."

Wakefield stood and removed his gloves. "I'll need to bring him into the morgue to do a full examination." He looked up at Dave, who appeared to be getting faint. He smiled and said, "Don't worry. This was no boating accident."

- - -

Gabe had woken up early. He switched on the TV and searched for local news. Instead, he was bombarded with Cialis commercials, infomercials on butt improvement exercises, and reruns of 1980's sitcoms. When he did find news, it was more about how Thursday's rain and wind had changed over to a nice and sunny Friday. "A good day" said the anchor "to be outside and enjoy the harbor and bay."

He scrambled a few eggs and considered what to do next. He studied his reflection in the teakettle on the stove. What a wreck. A tired, aching, confused wreck. He had to tell someone, not just continue to drink the problem away. He had been determined to tell Jim yesterday, but couldn't muster up the courage. What would he say if he did face Jim? Instead, Gabe decided to go into the office and put off the inevitable as long as he could.

He got there around 7:15 and started the coffee, took a sip, and turned on the TV. His cell rang, but he let it go to voice mail. He stared at the TV, then checked the message. "Gabe, this is Jessie. Silvio hasn't been home for two nights. He must be shacking up with his waitress from The Wharf. This is it, Gabe. The last straw. If Silvio doesn't pop up soon, I'm going to divorce his ass and move on. I need my own life without worrying about what he's going to do next."

He heard a sigh. "I'm so mad I could wring his neck. He's screwing with me and Rico. My son needs a father he can look up to. Not someone who isn't around when he needs him."

What could Gabe say? Don't worry, Jessie. Silvio's not shacking up, I killed him Wednesday night and he's floating in the bay. He'll pop up soon enough. He stood, searched for a piece of paper, and scribbled a note for Lou saying he was going to be out for the day. I have to see Jim, he thought. I need to talk to someone who can help me sort this out.

- - -

Jim and Jan had agreed to meet this Friday morning in Carson, about an hour west of Long Harbor. Jan suggested the Starbucks at Barnes and Noble. Jim agreed to ten-thirty. He thought that would be a good time since it would precede any lunch crowd. He had no duties scheduled for this morning and left a note for Ray telling him he was meeting a friend for coffee and would be back around one.

Jan was already seated and drinking a large cup of coffee. Jim, wearing his glasses to disguise his appearance, grabbed a book from the nearby Relationships section, got into line and looked down—a perp look if there ever was one. A small flat-screen TV sat in the corner nearest the counter. The weatherman was praising the beautiful day.

When he was second in line, Jim looked over the menu. He was stymied. It was in a European language, possibly Italian. Macchiato, Dolce Latte, Cappuccino. The harried mom in front of him struggled with her toddler. She ordered a Nantucket grape juice for him and a Grande Caramel Frappuccino for herself. Jim ordered the Frappuccino also, since it looked harmless. He parted with five dollars and change and walked around the room pretending to seek the perfect table. The room was about a third full, with a half dozen empty tables.

He approached Jan's table and motioned to the seat across from her. "Excuse me, miss. Is this seat taken?" Jan sighed, and said, "Help yourself," as Jim smiled and sat.

Taking a sip from his Frappuccino, he gagged from the sweetness and spewed brown fluid on the table. His rarely used glasses slid down his nose as he coughed. Jan handed him a napkin. He wiped his mouth and then the table. "Thanks," he smiled at Jan and to those close enough to have seen the spectacle. He still had a dot of whipped cream on his nose. Jan first decided to let it be, then, out of pity, pointed to the tip of her nose. Jim looked puzzled, then rubbed his nose and removed the cream.

He looked at Jan's drink. "What are you having?"

"A Grande Americano."

Jim gave the brew a studied look. "Looks like a large coffee to me."

Jan laughed. Jim's humor was one of the things she loved about him. He opened his book to a random section, "Being Gay in a Macho World," and pretended to read. He looked up and said "Okay. What now?"

Jan put her Grande down and said "Like I said in my message, I want a better explanation of what's going on. Things were going so well. We were being discrete and you seemed comfortable with the relationship."

"Look Jan, what we had was great and I hated to end it. But I'd lost my moral bearing. There I was gambling, drinking more than I should, and then sneaking around with a parishioner. I had to put the brakes on or I was going to lose the most important part of my life."

He leaned forward and whispered. "What we had was important to me also, but I had to make a decision: priesthood or you. The priesthood is my life, Jan. It's how I help people and connect to them. I decided to continue with that." Jim sat back. "I hope you understand."

She fumbled with her coffee while holding onto her emotions. A small tear formed and trickled down her cheek. She took a moment to compose herself, calmly dabbed at the tears and looked at Jim. "I guess I was expecting this sooner or later. I thought we had something, Jim, but maybe I was fooling myself."

Jim knew there was not much to say. "Jan, you made me a better and more feeling person. You let me know that I was important to you on a personal level. I never expected to experience such a thing. For that, I am grateful. I will never forget our time together. It just wasn't the right life for me."

They sat in silence for a moment. There was a movement of chairs as people stood and moved towards the front of the café. Jim saw that they were circling the flat screen. The barista who'd served him pressed the remote control and raised the volume. This made those not already focused on the TV turn and pay attention.

A reporter was standing on the southern dock on Long Harbor and nodding towards a police boat. Officers were transporting a large body bag off the boat.

Jan turned towards the TV when she realized that Jim was watching closely. The reporter said, "To repeat, the body of Silvio Fortunato, a local businessman with suspected connections to the Cambria crime organization, surfaced in Long Harbor channel two hours ago, just a few miles from the bay. Police suspect that he has been dead for days. He was last seen Wednesday night leaving The Wharf. Police also confirm that Fortunato's Explorer was found not far from here. They had been ticketing the SUV since Thursday morning because it was parked in a handicapped spot. This also has police believing that the local man may have fallen into the harbor Wednesday night. Police have ruled out neither accidental drowning nor foul play."

Jim turned towards Jan. "Well, how about that? What made him stop on the southern docks? I wonder if he was meeting someone."

- - -

Gabe had his car radio switched to the all-news station as he drove to see Jim. He was thinking about what he would say, when he heard Silvio's name. He turned up the sound and heard a recap of the discovery of Silvio's body and the believed timing around the death.

He almost went through a red light, seeing it at the last moment. He stopped partway through the intersection, receiving a disapproving shake of the head from an elderly man who had to walk around Gabe's Prius to continue his crossing.

He realized that he had to think this out. Noticing a strip mall a block down, he drove to the entrance, turned and looked for a place to gather himself. "A Starbucks, good." Gabe parked in front and walked into the café.

As with the Starbucks currently serving Jim, people were standing around a flat screen TV. The anchor was recalling details of the recovery of Silvio's body, causing Gabe to became woozy and fall back. He steadied himself on a nearby counter and looked around to see if anyone had noticed his reaction. He pretended to ignore the TV and walked to the register. The barista spotted him, and walked to the counter from the TV.

"Give me the largest coffee you have." He walked to the farthest point from the TV and sat down. He could still hear the news report. He wasn't going to be able to drown out the top story that easily.

- - -

Mark put Ted Hanson in charge of having the body sent to the morgue. He gave a hurried "No comment" to reporters as he walked to his cruiser.

What a day, he thought. It's bad enough finding a floater who's been dead for a couple of days. Now, it turns out to be the most hated man in town. There must be dozens of people in Long Harbor who wanted him dead. Now I have to make the call to his wife, have her come downtown, and officially identify him. Shit.

He would have preferred to speak to Jessie in person but, with the press already getting wind that a body surfaced, it would just be a matter of time before speculation got around to who it was. He called Jessie but there was no answer. At the voice mail prompt, he left a brief message asking to meet him at the station. He couldn't tell her in a voice message that her husband died.

Mark told an officer to drive to the house and wait for her return. After a few minutes, he drove to the station, and avoided camped out reporters by pulling into the restricted parking area and having an officer close the gates. He sat in his car for several minutes turning the event over in his mind. My first homicide in quiet Long Harbor; and it's a big one, too.

He left the cruiser, entered through the back of the station, and walked down the corridor. He pushed the door to the stairway planning to walk down to the morgue as he saw Jessie and Rico Fortunato walking in accompanied by an officer. Mark took a breath and walked over.

"Mrs. Fortunato, Rico. I'm Detective Porfino. Please sit down." He cleared his throat. "I'm sorry to tell you this, but we found your husband. He drowned in the harbor." He sat and waited for Jessie to compose herself. Rico stared at his mother, unsure of what to say.

Disturbing the silence, Mark spoke up. "The body is being brought to the morgue for autopsy. We'll need you to make an official identification. As it stands now, we don't know if this was an accident or something else. We'll know for certain in the next day or so."

Jessie dabbed her eyes and looked at Mark. "Detective Porfino, Silvio—despite his size—was an excellent swimmer. If he fell in somehow, and even if he was drunk, he would have been able to swim to a pylon or step. Do you really think this was an accident?"

"Mrs. Fortunato, we will investigate this thoroughly and if this was foul play, we will get to the bottom of this and arrest whoever is involved."

Jessie let out a derisive laugh. "You know, Silvio's brother Enrico died in a similar manner. He fell in not far from where your boat brought back Silvio. Detective Wagner assured Silvio that they would investigate thoroughly and determine if it was an accident or murder. Then, after a few days, they declared it an accident. Accident, my ass. Enrico was killed and so was Silvio. I think the police knew that all along."

Mark knew Jessie was right. The more he had investigated Enrico's death, the more he knew the investigation concluded in haste with loose ends never explained.

"Mrs. Fortunato, I cannot speak for my predecessor. I can only say that if this was murder, I'll find who did it and make sure they come to justice."

- - -

Mark brought Jessie and Rico into the morgue and introduced them to Dr. Wakefield. "Call me Adam, Mrs. Fortunato, Rico. I am sorry for your loss."

He led Jessie to the table, as Rico followed. "I have to warn you that his face is scarred from being exposed to the elements."

Mark felt it was pretty thoughtful to put it that way, rather than saying Silvio had been chewed on by harbor sea life. Adam looked at Jessie. "Are you ready?"

She took a breath and nodded solemnly. Adam pulled back the sheet enough to expose Silvio's face. Jessie examined her husband for a few seconds and nodded. Starting to walk away, she stumbled. Rico bear-hugged his falling mother, guided her to a chair, and sat next to her.

Mark gave them a few moments, then cleared his throat. "We need to do an autopsy to determine the exact cause of death. We'll also need to send fluid samples out for toxicology. This could take a few days. We'll have a clearer picture then. We can release the body in a few days. In the meantime, we have folks who can assist you with setting up funeral arrangements."

Jessie looked up and smiled at Detective Porfino. "Thanks, but we're getting experienced with these things. We'll call Danzetti's. They took care of Silvio's brother."

"Let me drive you and your son home. This is a shock and neither of you should have to drive in this state. I'll have an officer follow us in Rico's car."

They walked to the elevator and Mark pushed the button for the main floor.

"I don't want to expose you to any press. We'll go out the side entrance and through the restricted gate."

As they approached Mark's car, reporters shouted from the gate. Mark motioned an office over. "Clear the gate. Tell those leaches to stand back at least fifty feet."

As the car idled, waiting to pull into the street, Rico looked out the window and tapped his mother on the shoulder. "Mom, there's Professor Amos in his car. I wonder what he's doing here."

She looked over and made eye contact with the Professor, who looked down. Mark waved over the officer. "Ticket that creep over there. Tell him he's illegally parked. In fact, pat him down. Make sure the press sees it."

Mark looked at Jessie. "That creep's going to regret coming here." Jessie smiled, but seemed confused.

– – –

Chapter 7

One Dying for the Many

On the ride back to Jessie's, Mark took the opportunity to ask a few questions.

"Sorry, Jessie, but I have to ask. When was the last time either of you saw Silvio?"

Jessie nodded that she understood. "Wednesday night, before he went to The Wharf to party with his crew. He was celebrating the zoning victory, which would mean more work for his business interests."

"I was at the zoning meeting," Mark said. "It was pretty contentious. Looked like a lot of hard feelings."

Jessie looked straight ahead. "Silvio usually got what he wanted. He didn't make a lot of friends in the process."

Mark turned to Rico. "When was the last time you saw your father?"

"Wednesday morning at Lucy's. We didn't really talk. I saw him leave; I was talking to Mr. Cooper. He looked at me like he was mad. I should've talked to him, I guess, but I didn't. I was mad at him for the whole zoning situation. Now he's dead and my last memory of him is…" He trailed off and looked out the window.

Jessie started to cry. Mark handed her a tissue. "We'll talk again later when you've had a chance to collect yourselves. We'll find out what happened."

He said his goodbyes to Jessie and Rico and instructed the officer who followed them to make sure they had everything they needed.

Returning to the morgue, he walked in as Wakefield was examining Silvio. Body parts sat in trays and Adam was weighing what appeared to be the heart. He nodded as he saw Mark. "So, do we have anything yet?" Mark asked.

Adam recorded the weight of the heart, and put it on a table. "I'm just about done with the body. I sent samples out for toxicology. That will take a few days."

He motioned Mark closer. "Take a look at this. There is an irregular contusion on the forehead. I pulled out a splinter, which was pretty deep. I don't think this happened while floating. My guess is that the wound occurred before he hit the water. Maybe it knocked him out. It must have certainly made him woozy at least. The splinter seems to be coated in a heavy resin."

Mark looked at the splinter. "Maybe to make it waterproof. So maybe he fell on the dock, got up and either fell into the water… or was pushed."

Adam looked at the splinter. "Look how dark this is. I don't think it came from the dock. Maybe from a pylon. Maybe he hit the pylon when he fell in."

"Or was pushed," Mark repeated.

"Or was pushed. I guess that's your job. One other thing. There is a circular bruise in the middle of his chest. Fairly symmetric."

Mark looked where Adam was pointing. "Could it be from a fist?"

"No, it's too large. It could have happened when he fell in or maybe while he was floating. I don't think it was from the boat."

Adam picked up Silvio's shirt. "I also found some interesting items from his shirt. First of all, it's stained with what appears to be vomit. We'll test the contents and run the DNA. The water soaking may prevent any identification, but we'll see what we get.

"Also, and this is really odd, I found this in his shirt pocket. A bit waterlogged. Chili beans and some rice kernels. Both partially digested."

Mark looked at the discolored residue. "So, maybe Silvio had Chili as his last meal and vomited it during whatever happened?"

Adam put down the shirt. "Or someone vomited on him."

– – –

Mark left Wakefield to finish the autopsy and remembered that he had skipped lunch. He had an iron stomach; talk of vomit and head contusions did not get in the way of packing it away. He thought of picking up fast food but decided to visit The Wharf and kill two birds at once. Grab something that would stay with him through the rest of this long day and maybe check on what happened Wednesday before Silvio died.

Opening the door to The Wharf, he walked in, then reached into his rear pocket and retrieved a tissue. He wiped off his hand and thought, Man, if that doorknob could talk. He saw Carla on duty and she waved him to a table. Carla gave Mark a menu that must have socialized with the doorknob. Out again came the tissue for another wipe.

Carla grabbed a cloth from her back pocket, took the menu from Mark, removed all evidence of recent use, handed it back, and wiped the table.

"So, what's good?" Mark asked.

Carla smiled and said, "Detective, we have a decent pork sandwich, burgers, and the chili is a big favorite. We also have a page full of beers, each guaranteed to make you forget why you came here."

"I'll have the chili, and a Coke. I'm still on duty."

She returned in a few minutes with both items. The chili was steaming and there was a side of rice. Mark mixed some rice in and took a taste.

"Hey, this is pretty good."

"You appear shocked. The food's actually pretty good here. We could stand to be cleaner, but the crowd we get is used to the ambiance. As long as they can get a load on and cheaply, no need for spic and span."

Mark put down his spoon. "Carla, I heard that you and Silvio were very close. I'm looking into his death. I'm sure that you're interested in getting to the bottom of this also." He signaled Carla to sit down across from him.

She pulled out the chair, wiped an unknown substance with her towel and sat. She looked Mark in the eye. "The reporters are saying it's a mob hit. Maybe some retribution for stepping out of line. I don't believe that. I think someone local killed him."

Carla was silent for a moment. "You know, this is a lot like what happened to his brother, Enrico. Maybe it's the same guy. That investigation, as brief as it was, didn't turn up anyone." Carla started to cry. She dabbed her eyes with her dirty towel.

He gave Carla a few moments, as he took a few spoonfuls of the chili and sipped the Coke. When Carla steadied, he put down his spoon. "I intend to look at all possibilities, Carla. First thing I need to do is retrace his steps from Wednesday night onward. Who was here that night?"

Carla studied the dingy ceiling and thought it over. "Everyone, it seemed. Wednesdays are usually busy. The workweek is half over and the locals are starting to loosen up. Silvio was partying with his men over the zoning change. Other tradesmen were here. The usual crowd. The Cooper brothers came in. Gabe is a regular, but his brother Jim came also."

She thought for a few moments. "And Professor Amos from the community college was here. That seemed odd. He was nervous, like a fish out of water. But he really put away the chili and had a few Buds."

The creep who was parked outside the station, he thought. Mark took a few more spoonfuls. "This is really good. Was the chili a big hit Wednesday? Did Silvio have a bowl?"

Carla turned this over. "No, he had a pulled pork sandwich and about a pound and a half of fries." She thought some more. "Come to think of it, he did have a few spoonfuls of Jim Cooper's chili."

Mark laughed. "That's unusual. Were Jim and Silvio that close?"

"You could say they were business associates. No, Jim was outside. Silvio ate the chili to intimidate Gabe. Show him how macho he was. After Silvio went back to his men, Gabe had me bring a new bowl for Jim."

"So Jim had the chili?"

Carla seemed puzzled. "Yes and Gabe, and half the people here. I even had a bowl. As I said, it's very filling and very popular. It goes down good with a few beers."

She stood. "What's all this about chili? Are you suggesting that it somehow did Silvio in? Are you saying he was poisoned?"

"No. It's just one of many things we're looking into." He put down his spoon into the empty bowl and looked Carla in the eye.

"How was Silvio that night?"

"He was in a good mood from the zoning vote. He had a few too many beers, but he was feeling pretty good."

Mark took out his notebook. "Did he have words with anyone besides Gabe Cooper?"

"Yes, he and Jim Cooper met for a few minutes at the end of the bar. Then suddenly they're shouting at each other. Jim was mad at Silvio. There was a lot of back and forth." Carla frowned. "Jim couldn't have killed Silvio. He wouldn't hurt a fly."

Mark wrote these details into his notebook. "I need to cover all of the bases." He closed the book. "You know, for someone close to Silvio, you seem to be holding things together."

She straightened up. "I need to work. I need to put on a game face here and keep people happy, or at least, drunk. I'll cry at home when I have a chance to let this sink in. Detective Porfino, you can drop the kind talk. Silvio and I were lovers. I kept asking him to leave Jessie. He wouldn't do it. Not so much out of love as out of comfort and standing in Long Harbor. My world is shattered right now. With Silvio, I was someone special, even if just a good lay and a diversion. Without Silvio, I'm just another waitress in another bar in a small town going nowhere."

Placing one arm on the chair top, she leaned towards Mark. "Find the bastard that killed him. And don't worry about mob hits. They wouldn't make it look exactly like Enrico. This was personal. A lot of people in Long Harbor hated Silvio. A lot of people are happy that he's dead. I'd start looking right here in town."

\- - -

Jim returned from Carson soon after seeing the news report. He hoped he wouldn't have to deal further with Jan anytime soon. He also hoped that Silvio had kept his knowledge of his affair with Jan to himself. On the way back, he listened to details of Silvio's discovery on his radio; it was all the local stations could talk about. Reporters were speculating on a crime hit. Jim wondered if that was possible. He also wondered if they would look into Silvio's books and discover details of his involvement in sports betting.

Entering the Rectory, he attempted to tiptoe past Father's Ray's office door. No luck there. "Jim. Come in, have a seat," called Father Ray, who was leafing through a magazine. "I'm glad you're back. How was the coffee klatch with your friend?"

He looked at Ray for any sign that he knew Jim had been meeting with Jan. Ray looked sincere; no attempt at a subtle probe. "It was nice. We went over old times. So, how was mass this morning?"

"Same old, same old." Ray paused. "You know, Mrs. O'Reilley said that you gave a corker of a sermon yesterday. Something about being lost and now found, blind but now you see. Is this from breaking your ties to Silvio?"

"Yes. I feel like a new man."

Ray looked at Jim as if trying to read his mind.

"Did you hear that Silvio was found dead this morning? He was found floating near the bay. You got out just in time Jim, or that may have been you later on. You were screwing around with the wrong people. The press is already talking of Silvio's death being a mob hit."

"I know, Ray. I saw the body unloaded off the boat on local television. I just hope they don't look at his books."

Ray frowned. "I hadn't thought of that. Well, you made a clean breast of things. We'll have to see what develops. I'll back you, Jim."

The young priest felt a burden lift. "I appreciate that, Ray. I'm trying to put my entire life back in order."

Ray closed his magazine—the Sports Illustrated Swimsuit edition. Jim saw and smiled at Ray, who blushed. "Just window shopping, Jim."

Opening his lower drawer, he deposited the magazine, twisting his head to get one last glance at the cover model before the drawer closed.

"Look, there's something else. They're going to want to bury Silvio with a lot of flourish. Just like his brother, Enrico. It will be crowded with a lot of his associates from Cambria. I want you to say the funeral mass and do the burial. Maybe give another corker of a sermon."

This was not what Jim needed. Frankly, he wasn't overly upset that Silvio died. He was sad for Jessie and Rico maybe, but not for the deceased.

"Jim, you're well respected in this town and considered to be a leader. It would help if someone who knew Silvio and his shortcomings could put a perspective on his life and maybe, at the same time, point to the consequences of leading a criminal life. There's no need to go into your own participation, and no need to beat up Silvio; just leave people from Long Harbor and Cambria something to think about."

Jim squirmed. He needed to get out of this.

"Won't the Cambria and Long Harbor associates, as well as Jessie and Rico, want the pastor to say the mass?"

Ray smiled. "Nice try. Screw the Cambria folks. As for Jessie and Rico, you'll have a better chance of consoling them than I will. They respect you, Jim. Think of this as part of your penance and as a chance to start making things right for yourself and the community."

Ray picked up a newspaper lying on his desk, folded to an article called *Best Local Beers*. "Now, start writing that corker. Let's get people thinking about what's next."

- - -

Gabe drove back to his apartment that afternoon and sat in the car for a minute. Would he be arrested soon? Was there anything on Silvio that would point to him? God, I barfed all over him, he thought. I hope that came off in the water.

There was a tap on his window, followed by a growl. Gabe jumped and expected to see a cop with a police dog. Instead, it was Mr. Richardson, holding his growling mongrel.

"Are you okay, Gabe? You were just sitting there."

He got out and smiled, then attempted to pet Reggie, who returned an aggrieved bark. In that instant, Gabe could have taken a second life in less than a week.

"I'm ok, Mr. Richardson. I've just had a rough week and was trying to relax for a minute."

Mr. Richardson stroked Reggie's head and neck. "Well, as they say, you can't burn the candle at both ends. You got home late Wednesday and were out early Thursday. A man needs his rest. Did you hear about Silvio Fortunato? Turned up dead in the bay. Well, good riddance to him and his kind. Whoever killed him did us all a favor."

"Do you really think so?"

"I know so. I bet most people in town would like to take the killer's hand,"—he grabbed Gabe's hand with his free right hand—"and give it a firm shake."

Mr. Richardson let go of Gabe's hand and leaned in. "Hell, I'd even buy him a beer at The Wharf." Reggie growled as Mr. Richardson continued.

"Odd thing is that Reggie loved Silvio. He would run up to him, bark, and wag away." Mr. Richardson looked at Reggie. "Oh well, who can account for these things?"

He noticed that Gabe had turned pale. "Hey Gabe, you really are all shook up. Your hand was clammy. Let me take you to The Wharf and buy you a beer. Maybe that will settle your nerves." Reggie growled again.

Gabe looked at Mr. Richardson. Is this guy psychic? Does he know I killed Silvio? Or is he just some crazy bastard? I need to find out.

"I'll take a rain check on that, Mr. Richardson. I wouldn't be good company. I might have a few here and then turn in. Maybe I can buy you a beer at The Wharf sometime and we can talk some more."

Mr. Richardson smiled, showing perfect teeth. "That sounds like a deal, Gabe. Reggie, say goodbye to Mr. Cooper." Reggie growled louder.

- - -

Mark returned to his office after his lunch at The Wharf. He called Ted Hanson and asked to meet him at the dock to secure the area. He also told him to check the pilings for any damage or blood. Mark would meet him there later.

He sat and pulled out the file on the death of Enrico Fortunato. He started to look for similarities to Silvio's death.

Gene Benson was passing by Mark's office. He spotted Mark, walked in, and flopped into the guest chair. "Mark. What a day, huh? Silvio Fortunato found floating in the bay. What does Wakefield have to say?"

Closing the folder, he sat back. "Chief, he thinks Silvio hit his head or was hit with a wooden object with a rough surface. He showed me a long splinter he took from the contusion. Looks like he fell into the water after hitting or being hit by the object and drowned. He may have hit a piling—or he was bludgeoned with a club-like object. I'm going out to the dock area in a few minutes, but first I want to look over Enrico Fortunato's file to see if the situations are similar."

Mark sat up. "Oh yeah. And there was vomit on Silvio's shirt, and remnants of chili and rice."

Gene leaned forward. "It sounds like his last meal was at The Wharf. That chili is damn good. And he spat it up just before dying?"

"Or someone vomited on him. Anyway, the rain on Thursday may have washed away anything substantial. Let's hope we can find either some blood or signs of a struggle."

Mark leaned forward. "Gene, I have to ask you something. When we talked before the zoning meeting, you indicated that maybe Enrico had been murdered. Yet, the report from Detective Wagner concluded that it was an accident. Why do you think it might've been a murder?"

Standing and then closing the door to Mark's office, Gene took a breath.

"Mark, Tony Wagner conducted a short, and in my mind a half-hearted investigation. He hardly interviewed anyone. Coroner Rollins also came to a quick conclusion. The toxicology showed some alcohol, but nothing else. Wagner declared it a drowning and no one objected, not even Silvio. I wondered about that, but reopening the investigation seemed pointless. There was no evidence that it was anything more than an accident, and there was no pressure to investigate further. I suspected that the Cambria family knew more than they let on and that they wanted to handle the matter themselves."

Mark closed Enrico's folder. "So, you think Wagner yielded to some outside pressure and closed the case?"

Gene picked up the folder. "I think Wagner killed him, maybe on orders from Mario Gallante, maybe not. He leafed through the folder. "A good detective can make a murder look like an accident."

- - -

Mark found Tony Wagner's home phone number in the department records. It was a Cambria exchange. He dialed and after a few rings connected to voice mail. "Tony. This is Mark Porfino from the Long Harbor police department. I guess you heard that Silvio Fortunato was found dead this morning. Drowned in the bay. There are similarities to Enrico Fortunato's death, so I wondered if you could come in so I can speak to you about your investigation. I can also meet you at your home if that's more convenient. Call me at 800-555-7296. Thanks."

Tony had been listening from his sofa. He stood, walked to the phone, and replayed the message. Well, here we go, he thought.

He dialed a Long Harbor number and after a few rings, Miriam answered. "Sis, I just got a call from Detective Porfino in the Long Harbor department. Silvio's body turned up. He wants me to come in and discuss the investigation of Enrico's death."

"Tony, I don't like this. Be careful. Porfino has a reputation for being thorough."

"Don't worry, Miriam. I was a detective there for ten years. I can handle Porfino. I'm more concerned with Benson. He always seemed uncomfortable with how Enrico's investigation finished. I'm going to go in and offer any help they need. Better to know from the inside exactly what they have."

"Just keep me out of this, Tony. Neither of us needs to dredge up old memories or suspicions," she answered, loudly.

Tony fumed at the tone, but took a second to calm himself. "I got your back, Miriam. As always. And I hope you have mine."

- - -

Mark put on his coat and drove to the dock. The afternoon had turned cold and windy. Patrolman Hanson was taking pictures of everything in sight. He also had crime scene tape everywhere, but half of it had blown away. Mark expected to see the dock cats running around with yellow tape on their backs. He walked up to him. "Hi Ted. Find anything?"

"Hi Detective. You were right. I looked over the pilings and there was blood on one of them."

He pulled out a baggie containing slivers from the piling. He also had tubes containing swabs, which would turn out positive for blood.

"Send them to the lab. And you took close-ups of the piling itself?"

"Twelve of them. I was hoping I could keep a few."

Mark smiled at this odd statement. "Maybe, after the case is closed. For now, they are very important evidence. Good work, Patrolman."

Ted beamed. "My pleasure, sir. This is a lot more interesting than writing out tickets."

"But Ted, even the tickets tell us something. I heard that you wrote up Silvio's Explorer." Mark pulled out his notes.

"I did. Thursday morning and Friday morning. He'd parked in a handicapped spot and I was going to have it towed if it was still there Saturday."

Mark looked over to the Explorer. "Then good luck for us that Silvio turned up on Friday."

He put his arm around the young patrolman. "Ted, I can use an extra set of hands, eyes, and ears for this case. I'm going to ask that you be assigned to me for a few weeks. Is that okay?"

Ted's eyes widened as he smiled. "Of course. That would be great. I can't wait to call my mom. Boy, this turned out to be a great day."

He realized that Mark had stopped smiling. "Except for Silvio, of course."

\- - -

Mark and Ted went through Silvio's Explorer before turning it over to Forensics. The key was in the ignition, in the "On" position. Mark turned the key, but there was no sound. The battery was dead. Silvio must have left the motor running when he got out. Had he been in a hurry? There was little else unusual on first glance except for an odd pattern on the front driver-side tire. Whatever caused the two-tone aspect of the tire hadn't washed off in the rain.

Mark instructed Ted to take a swab of the tire, drop off the evidence he had collected, follow up with Forensics, check for any 911 calls logged since Wednesday night, and write a report of what he found.

Ted was thrilled. Mark had never seen someone so anxious to write out a crime report. He returned to his office and went over the notes from his talk with Carla at The Wharf.

Opening his notebook to a new page, he wrote: The Wharf on Wednesday night looks like the center of things. Maybe the chili list is a good place to start. Let's see. Gabe and Father Jim Cooper, Professor Amos. Can't even rule out Carla, or for that matter, Silvio's crew. Plus, persons yet unknown.

He peered out his window and took in the afternoon activity outside. He glanced at his notes. One person at a time I guess. I'll start with Father Jim. Let's see what the argument was about. Then Gabe Cooper, though he seems to have a built-in alibi since he was clear across town flipping the bird at an old lady around the time Silvio was killed. Then Professor Amos. Where does he fit in? Is he carrying a grudge from the zoning vote, or is something more going on?

He smiled as he thought of Ted's joy at being involved with a murder. He made an additional note: Have Ted go over the minutes of the zoning meeting. Maybe something there will shed some light. There were a lot of angry people there. Let's see if someone was angry enough to kill Silvio.

He noticed that his voice mail light was red. He dialed the access number and selected the new message. "Mark, this is Tony Wagner. It's good to hear from the department. I'm living in Cambria these days and bored to death. I'm even thinking of becoming a mall cop. Don't need a good ticker for that."

After a pause, Tony continued. "Anyway, I'll be happy to come over on Monday and discuss Enrico's death. Not much there really. The man was drunk, and drowned. But anything to help. Plus, it will be good to meet again with the old crew. How does ten a.m. sound? See you then."

He made a note of the ten a.m. meeting and left a message for Chief Benson to see if he wanted to join in. Should be just like old times, he thought.

- - -

Mario had been surprised by Silvio's death and angry that he hadn't been informed earlier of Silvio's disappearance. He would talk to Sal and decide what to do next. Sal was Mario's man inside Fortunato Brothers. He hadn't trusted Silvio so had always relied on Sal to report back to him.

He packed a suitcase and drove to Long Harbor on this Saturday morning, deciding to stay a few days, look into Silvio's death, and take a closer look at the gambling operation. He'd left Cambria early and was now hungry for breakfast. Spotting Lucy's Eat and Go Diner, he pulled his Caddy into the lot. Lucy's looked like a typical east coast diner. It had that blue-collar feeling along with the requisite pick-ups and old model cars parked outside. A good center of operations, he thought.

He walked in and was waved at by Lucy herself, indicating that he could sit anywhere he wanted. A fiftyish bleach-blond approached the table with a menu and smiled. "Hi, I'm Sheila. I'll be your waitress."

She handed him the menu, which was larger than most newspapers and included selections for breakfast, lunch, dinner, and late night. He asked for coffee and proceeded to leaf through the menu; so much to choose from.

She returned with the coffee. When he asked for a recommendation, she looked over the page Mario was on. "Try the creamed chipped beef on toast. It will stick to your ribs." She leaned in closer. "The old timers call it 'Shit on a Shingle.'"

Mario laughed. "Well, you only live once. I'll take it."

She seemed pleased with the order and walked away. Mario sat back and looked over the diner. A lot of folks were looking back at him, although their eyes darted away when he made eye contact. He smiled to himself. Maybe they know me already, or maybe they just haven't seen many people in here wearing $1500 suits.

Smiling back at whoever dared to glance his way, he thought to himself. Well, folks you'll soon know who I am. Who knows? Maybe one of you killed Silvio.

Sheila returned with the creamed chipped beef and a refill of coffee. He looked at the imposing entrée: there had to be two pounds of food, and most of it looked like it'd been partially digested already. He grimaced.

Sheila smiled. "Bon Appetite," she said and walked away.

Bottoms up would be more appropriate, Mario thought. He slid his fork under a mound of red beef, lifted and placed into his mouth, expecting the worst. Not bad. He could get used to this. He picked up his coffee and looked back at those waiting for a reaction. He lifted his cup in a mock toast. "Bon Appetite." This place would do just fine.

Sheila stopped by a few minutes later to pour more coffee. Mario had consumed almost the entire plate.

"Looks like you enjoyed it."

He started to talk before realizing that he had a piece of beef wedged in his front teeth. Waiving his finger to indicate that he needed a second, he removed the piece with his napkin. "It was excellent. Not deserving of the nickname at all."

"Good to hear. You're pretty adventurous for a first timer."

"Is it that obvious?"

"I make it a point to know everyone who comes in here. I've worked in this place for fifteen years and I've met everyone in town."

She leaned forward and whispered "And I know their innermost secrets, and who's screwing who."

\- - -

Mario left the diner and walked across the street to Harbor Florists. Mrs. Galley, who had waited on Gabe, was on duty. She greeted Mario with a smile. He asked for a dozen of the best roses. "Oh my," said Mrs. Galley. "You men are keeping us in business. Not another love spat like Thursday, I hope. A nice man ordered a dozen beautiful roses sent to a lady he had obviously wronged. I hope you are not in the same boat."

He smiled. "No. Sadly, these are for condolences. I'm here to see Mrs. Fortunato, whose dear husband Silvio was found drowned just yesterday."

The clerk turned serious. "I heard about that. Very sad. Though people say that he and his brother were always up to no good and connected to those bad apples in Cambria. Something about gambling. Some people are even saying that the Cambria mob killed Silvio."

He looked at the clerk's nameplate. "Mrs. Galley, I knew Silvio and his brother since they were little boys. He may have had a few rough edges, but he was a loyal friend. I hope people are gracious enough to mourn him and comfort his family."

He smiled. "And I'm sure that the fine Long Harbor police department will get to the bottom of Silvio's death, be it accident or by someone's hand."

"Well said, sir. Please be assured that no slight was intended. I shouldn't be repeating idle gossip. I hear so much I'm starting to take it for truth." With that, she finished wrapping the flowers and handed them to Mario.

He paid cash for the roses and tipped Mrs. Galley ten dollars. He smiled as he remembered Pilate's observation during the passion: "The truth. What's that?"

Returning to his Caddy, he tossed the roses onto the back seat, belched once in honor of the cream chipped beef, and slid behind the steering wheel. Well, between Sheila and Mrs. Galley, he thought, people will know I'm in town. Maybe they can be my eyes and ears as I figure out what happened to Silvio. No one in my organization killed him. It was someone in this sleepy town did him in.

- - -

Gabe walked out of his apartment and headed for his car. He was about to slide in when he saw Mr. Richardson and Reggie standing at the end of the parking lot, speaking to a large, disheveled man. He decided to make sure that Richardson wasn't sharing his suspicions to this stranger. As he walked towards the three, Reggie spotted Gabe, spun around, and started barking. The large man bent down and petted Reggie, who seemed to calm from the touch, but continued to growl at Gabe.

He reached the three and said a cheerful "hello" to Mr. Richardson, who appeared somber. The large man turned around and faced Gabe. It was Silvio.

He had a large swelling on his forehead with a jagged cut, and bite marks on his face. His clothes were water logged and stank of fish. "Good Morning, Cooper. You're looking well. Please excuse my appearance. I was just telling Mr. Richardson that I took an unexpected dive off the dock Wednesday night and hit my head going in. It knocked me out and I drowned. Looks like I'm dead."

Gabe was speechless. Mr. Richardson spoke to Silvio: "The wages of sin, Silvio. We reap what we sow."

"I could stand a cigar," Silvio said as he reached into his jacket pocket. His screwed up his face and struggled with the object. He pulled out a small fish and laughed.

Mr. Richardson turned towards Gabe. "And now, Gabe, you have crossed over into this darkness. It's not too late to make this right. Confess your guilt. Tell the police. Atone now, before it eats you up and destroys everyone around you."

Shaking, Gabe took a moment to steady himself. He started to respond when the sun, appearing through his window, woke him up.

Soaked and out of breath, he sat up and looked around for Mr. Richardson, Silvio, and Reggie. He lay back down and thought about the dream. Richardson's right. This will kill me. I have to tell someone.

He looked at the clock; almost eleven. He dressed and made a cup of decaf, took a few sips and tossed the rest away. He needed to see Jim, needed someone else to know what happened, and help him sort this out.

Gabe left his apartment—for real this time—and had started towards the parking lot when he saw Mr. Richardson and Reggie. He got into his car and drove closer, stopping far enough away to avoid Reggie, whom Mr. Richardson was restraining.

"Good morning, Mr. Richardson. How are you this lovely December morning?" Mr. Richardson picked up Reggie and stroked his head. This calmed Reggie, who still emitted a low growl.

"I'm fine, Gabe. It's a beautiful day. This is a great time of year: Advent, Christmas, people preparing to celebrate the holiday, people making things square with God and their neighbor. It's never too late to start over and renew your life. Isn't that right, Reggie?" Reggie growled at Gabe.

- - -

Mario checked into the Holiday Inn for a week. The motel was mostly empty; Long Harbor was not a tourist destination—not yet anyway. Mario had plans for Long Harbor, though. Once the new homes were built in Harbor Overlook—Mario's pet name for the residential development of the Hillside factory area—Long Harbor would become a desirable location for young, wealthy buyers. The type of folks with disposable income and a desire to piss it away on gambling and adult pursuits.

He inspected his room. Clean enough to not make you want to check out immediately, but not flashy enough to spend more than sleeping time here. This is a good location, he thought. Maybe I can turn this place into something.

He stopped unpacking and hurried to the bathroom. He dropped his trousers and landed on the toilet just in time to part with the cream chipped beef from Lucy's. He sighed with relief. Well, that's a lesson. Next time, just ham and eggs.

- - -

Mark slept in this morning, though sleeping in for him was eight a.m. After a quick bowl of cereal and some juice, he went for a jog down to the harbor; a mile each way, just enough to get his pulse running. He sat on a bench when he reached the harbor, not far from where Silvio had fallen in. His cell rang: Ted Hanson.

"The forensic folks found only Silvio's prints on the steering wheel. Other prints were found elsewhere but could be from family. They're checking. Found a .45 in his glove compartment. Loaded, safety on. For whatever reason, he left it there Wednesday night. I guess he wasn't planning to shoot himself, or anyone else, that night.

"I also checked 911 calls and calls to the station Wednesday night. There was a 911 call around 11 p.m.; too quick to get a GPS fix, but they got the number from caller id. Caller didn't identify himself, and said there was no emergency. You'll never guess whose phone it was."

He stopped for effect, and Mark waited for him to continue. After a few seconds, he said "Ted, I'm not going to guess. Whose phone was it?"

Ted coughed. "Sorry, Detective, I guess I was getting dramatic."

"Who was it, dammit?"

"It was Silvio Fortunato's phone."

Mark sat up. "Do we have the 911 tape?"

"We do, but it's scratchy. Almost like the phone was damaged."

Mark met Ted in his station office a few minutes later. He walked in and saw Ted sitting in a guest chair, beaming. He shook his head, but had to admit he admired Ted's enthusiasm.

"Now, about this 911 call."

Ted waved towards Mark's workstation. "Want to hear it?"

Mark never logged off, so his computer was constantly running. The screen saver showed Oreo cookies pursued by a lustful Cookie Monster. He motioned for Ted to take control.

The officer sank into Mark's padded chair, let out an inadvertent blissful sigh, sat up, and signed onto the evidence lab. He selected 911 calls and entered Wednesday night. He selected the call at 11:10 p.m.

"There are actually two calls. One came from someone on the docks, but whoever it was hung up. The second was the 911 operator returning the call."

Ted turned up the volume "Hello, this is the 911 call center. A call just came in from this number. Is there an emergency?"

The caller replied "No…thing is okay...anks."

Ted looked at Mark. "It's scratchy and there are gaps. Can you tell anything by the voice?"

"Well it's a male. It's hard to catch any accent or speech anomaly. He was courteous, at least. Sounds like he said thanks."

– – –

Mario stopped in the lobby and bought a pack of Lifesavers. He put two into his mouth to kill the taste of the creamed chipped beef, which had attacked on all fronts. He got into his Caddy, entered Silvio's address into his GPS, and pulled out of the lot.

Silvio and Jessie lived in the Willows section of town, a modest bedroom community. Silvio could have afforded a nicer accommodation but true to his simple roots, found life in this community just fine.

The caddy stopped about a block away from the house. Mario grabbed the roses and got out. He was about a hundred yards from

Silvio's when he saw the door open and Jessie come out with a middle-aged, bearded man. They hugged. Must be a family friend, Mario thought.

The man tried to kiss Jessie; not a consolation kiss. He was going for full mouth. Mario stepped back and stood behind a hydrangea. The widow pulled back and was clearly annoyed. She looked around to see if they had been observed. Mario ducked down.

Jessie spoke to the bearded man, clearly advising him to keep his emotions to himself. The man appeared to be embarrassed and left. He got into a blue Focus and drove away without looking back. Jessie checked her appearance in the glass of the screen door then went back inside.

Mario waited a few minutes and thought over what had just happened. Had Jessie been cheating on Silvio? Or was this creep just taking advantage of her? He would check on beardman later.

Hearing a squeak, he looked down to see a young girl looking at him. "Whacha looking for mister? You look like you're lost."

"Hello, young lady. I'm looking for the Fortunato house. I'm a friend of the family."

The girl examined Mario and pointed towards Silvio's. "It's over there mister, but that man died yesterday. Mommy said he was a gangster. Are you a gangster, mister?"

"No, little girl. Just a friend. I'm in the plumbing business."

"Mommy says plumbers are thieves. Are you a thief, mister?"

Mario grimaced, then decided that a smile might be better. "No, young lady. I'm one of the honest ones."

"OK, mister. If you say so."

He took out his Lifesavers and popped two more onto his mouth. He looked at the little girl. "You want a Lifesaver, kid?"

Her jaw dropped. "My mommy said I should never take candy from a strange man. She said they are bad men who want to hurt little girls. Are you a bad man, mister?"

Mario was overmatched. "No. I'm not a bad man. I have to go now. Have a nice day."

On walking towards Silvio's house, he looked back. The girl was still watching him. Great, he thought. Made by a five-year-old girl on training wheels. Mario, you're slipping.

After what seemed like minutes of ringing the chime, Rico opened the door. "Uncle Mario. Please, come in."

The mobster glanced back to see if his young interrogator was watching, then stepped inside as Rico walked into the next room to tell his mother. Mario heard "He is?" and felt even more uncomfortable.

After a few minutes, Jessie walked into the room. "Mario. Thank you for coming. I didn't expect such an early visit."

He pushed the roses forward to Jessie, who appeared to jump back a bit. She composed herself and handed the roses to her son, asking him to put them into water.

"Jessie. I was surprised and saddened to hear what happened to Silvio. He was a valued friend and employee. I still can't quite believe it."

She smiled weakly. "He didn't come home Wednesday night. I called his office Thursday and Friday but they didn't know where he was either. He's disappeared for a day or so before, usually due to a woman, but never this long. I was about to call the police when I got the call from Detective Porfino."

"I had no idea he was missing," said Mario. "I know that he had his moments where he forgot about his responsibilities to you, Rico, and Fortunato brothers, but he always seemed to snap out of it and make things right."

She appeared to be ready to rip into him. Rico, meanwhile, had come back into the room and noticed the tension.

"Uncle Mario, mom is tired and needs to rest. Maybe we can talk later."

"You're right, Rico" Mario said as he turned towards Jessie.

"I'll be going. I guarantee you that I'll look into this and figure out what happened."

She nodded, looked down, and mumbled an "okay."

He stepped towards Jessie with arms open to hug her, but she recoiled. He dropped his arms to his side, and coughed. "I'm staying in Long Harbor for the week, to make sure things continue smoothly with Fortunato Brothers, and to look into Silvio's death. We will not rest until we determine what happened."

A small tear trickled down her cheek. "Detective Porfino gave me the same promise." She paused and smiled. "Maybe you both can meet and compare notes. I'm sure you have questions for each other."

"Jessie, we will work with the fine Long Harbor police force to make sure we come up with an answer."

She looked up with the same pique she had shown before. "Oh, like you looked into Enrico's death? He died the same way. Yet everyone was happy to call it an accident. Do you think his death was an accident?"

He hadn't expected this but thought a second, and decided to make the best of it. "Jessie, the police concluded it was an accident. No evidence came out to prove otherwise. If he was murdered, the killer covered his tracks well."

Jessie's dropped her glare but spoke up. "Mario, I think they were both murdered. Maybe by the same person and maybe with the same help to cover up the crime. Whoever did this to Silvio, and to Enrico before him, was either extremely lucky or had someone on the inside making sure it looked like an accident."

"As I said before, we will look into this. Enrico was reckless and probably played both sides of the street. Frankly, it didn't surprise me that he came to the end that he did."

This wasn't helping. "Silvio, on the other hand, was very measured in what he did. He could lose his temper, and he wasn't the ideal husband, but he was steady and, despite his shortcomings, loved you and Rico. Silvio didn't deserve what happened to him. We will find out who did this."

He walked towards the door and turned around. "Oh, when I was walking up, Jessie, I saw you speaking to a man at the door. Another mourner, I am sure, expressing his condolences."

Rico stepped forward. "That was Professor Amos from the Community College. He's my Environmental Sciences professor and has been very kind to me and mom. He delivered flowers and sympathy from the college community."

Mario looked at Jessie. "I'm sure he can be very consoling. Maybe I'll catch up with him this week, thank him for his concern, and have a chat. Maybe he can even tell me what he thinks happened to Silvio. This is a small town. I'm sure everyone has their opinions."

"Goodbye Mario," Jessie replied. "Thanks for the roses. I'm sure we'll see each other soon. Don't forget to have a nice talk with Detective Porfino. I'm sure he'll want to hear *your* opinions."

- - -

Mark drove home and thought about the 911 call from Silvio's phone. It was a male voice, middle aged. Well, maybe that excuses Carla, Jessie, or another female. But, then again, maybe an unknown "she" hired someone or convinced some poor schmuck to kill Silvio. Or maybe we're still at square one, he thought.

He decided to stick with his original plan: interview those who hated Silvio and were in the vicinity the night he died. Still, that didn't make for a small number. He settled on Father Jim first: there had been an intense argument around a suspected gambling debt; maybe the good Father decided to turn Silvio into Jonah for his sins. No whale this time, though. Just a lot of hungry catfish not too choosey about the main course.

Easing into his ten-year-old Beemer, he started the engine and heard the comforting purr. He smiled. Boy, those Germans can make a car; 150,000 miles and going strong. And it takes off. Not like some wimpy Prius, like Gabe Cooper drives. Maybe if he had a man's car, he wouldn't feel the need to flip off old ladies.

Stopping at McDonalds, he undid all the good his morning run had done for him. He'd have a salad later, he lied to himself. Chili at The Wharf seemed more likely.

He knew the way to St. Augustine's, not because he was religious, but because he had attended a few funerals, a wedding for a distant cousin, and even spoke in the basement meeting room on police procedure for a senior group get-together. Mark recalled his experience: man, those seniors were tough. Mostly questions on tasing. Where does it hurt the most? Where is it most effective? I wouldn't want to meet any of them in a dark alley, he laughed.

He pulled up to the rectory. It was two p.m. and the parking lot was deserted. Two hours before the throngs arrived for Saturday evening mass. He knew this from being caught up in traffic on Saturday afternoons, finally training himself to take an alternate route to do his shopping.

A grown man going to the mall every Saturday afternoon to do his shopping and to see other people socializing. Boy, do I need a life, he thought. And boy, do I need a woman. But, that would have to wait.

As he rang the rectory bell, "Amazing Grace" chimed out. Pretty Cheesy.

A few minutes and several Amazing Graces later, Father Ray came to the door. "Ah, Detective Porfino. Sorry about the delay in answering. Watching a British soccer match. Boring stuff, but you keep hoping something will happen. Somebody has to score eventually. Come in, Detective. What brings you here on a Saturday afternoon?"

"I need to talk to Father Jim."

Father Ray nodded and motioned Mark inside. He wiped his feet on the mat that read "Bless You," and felt sacrilegious cleaning off his shoes. He walked into a hot, stifling foyer. It must be 80 degrees in here, he thought, and the old man has a sweater on. I'd better not go to Hell, he thought. I'd never survive.

Ray offered Mark coffee and pulled out a chair. Mark asked for a glass of water instead, feeling parched already from the hothouse he had walked into.

"Jim is in the church at this moment, Detective. He's hearing confessions. Is there anything I can help you with?"

He took a sip of the cool water and emitted an unintended "Ahhhh."

"Father, as you know, Silvio Fortunato was found dead in the bay on Friday morning. It looks like he fell or was pushed into the harbor. Probably around 11, —Wednesday night. I'm investigating the circumstances surrounding his death. I understand Father Jim had a recent argument with Silvio and, from all accounts, it was an argument that didn't end well."

Ray took a sip of coffee, put the cup down, and shifted in his seat.

"Detective, I've known Father Jim for five years now. He is a good priest, respected in both the parish and the Long Harbor community. He may have his shortcomings like the rest of us, but I assure you that he could not perform an act of violence."

Another sip of water and opening his top shirt button made Mark feel even better. He was already sweating.

"Father, I'm sure Jim is a credit to the parish and community. However, I need to track down all leads and determine what happened. It's no secret to the police or yourself, I would guess, that Silvio was involved in illegal gambling. From the argument they had on Wednesday night, it sounds like Jim was tied up in it. You don't get into an argument in a bar over a plumbing bill."

Ray finished his coffee and stood up. He walked towards the door and opened it.

"Detective, Jim would never act violently toward another human being. Any gambling he did is over now. He was cutting ties with Silvio. He had no reason to get in deeper. If you'll excuse me, I have to get ready for evening Mass."

Mark stood. "I'll make this easy on both of you, Father. When did Father Jim get back on Wednesday night? If you say that he was tucked in snug, or reading vespers at 10 p.m., maybe there's no need to go anywhere with this."

"Sorry, Detective, I turned in around 10:30. Jim must have come in later."

"Thanks, Father. I'll need to speak to Jim himself. You say he's in the church?"

"Hearing confessions. If you must speak to him, please be discrete."

"I'll do my best to not disturb anyone. I just hope Father Jim cooperates."

Ray closed the door and watched Detective Porfino walk across the parking lot and enter the church. Well Jim, he thought, maybe we need to talk again.

- - -

Jim was having an easy time manning the confessional this afternoon. Not much serious sin in Long Harbor. At least none that anyone was confessing. Maybe folks were getting into the Christmas spirit and practicing peace on earth. He disposed of the few contrite visitors who entered the confessional with a penance of three Hail Marys and wishes for a happy and holy season.

Between confessions, he planned to fill his time writing the sermon he'd give for Silvio's funeral. I'm stuck, he thought. How do you mourn a man who did the world a favor by dying? I need an angle that pays him a level of respect but doesn't make him out to be a saint. Maybe I'll use some gibberish about him being a child of God taken from his loved ones in the prime of life. He chewed his pencil. No. No one's buying that. Silvio was hated by more people than loved. Except for maybe Jessie and Rico, Carla his girlfriend, and Mario Gallante, no one cared much for Silvio. Plus, a lot of people owed him serious money.

He wrote: *One man dying for the many. Silvio died so that others may live. He wasn't our Christ, but he sure was our Barabbas. He was an insurrectionist and probably a murderer. Pilate let the wrong man go. Maybe this time we got it right.*

Not quite sure how to sell that, he knew he needed to work on it. To make the point that Silvio got what was coming to him while putting a redemptive spin on it. *We should always be ready to meet God and account for our actions. We reap what we sow.* He shook his head and tapped his nose with the eraser. How true for all of us. *However, the quality of God's mercy is not strained.* Not a bad theme. *We are all sinners who must trust in God's mercy and love.* Even pricks like Silvio. Maybe I'll throw in some Shakespeare. *I'm here to bury Silvio, not to praise him.*

The confessional door opened. Jim put his notes inside his bible, adjusted his cassock, put his bible on his lap, and waved the visitor in. "Please, have a seat. How can I be of help today?" Mark walked in.

Jim was surprised but smiled and said, "Detective. How good of you to come. I guess we must all unburden, even guardians of the law. I must say that I didn't even know you were Catholic." Jim motioned towards the padded chair. "Don't worry. The love of God extends to all members of his church, even those who don't participate as often as they should. How long has it been since you last confessed?"

Caught off guard by this, Mark paused, then said, "Father Jim, I'm not here to confess. I just have a few questions for you."

Jim shifted in his seat "Not to worry, Detective. I am happy to be of service. What's troubling you today?"

"I heard that you had a heated argument with Silvio on Wednesday night, just a short time before he died. That true?"

Jim put his bible on the table. He was angry but tried to appear composed.

"Detective, this is the time of week when Catholics can come and unburden themselves to God. It is not a time to conduct a police interrogation. I may have people outside now waiting to come to confession."

"Sorry, Father. I've been sitting outside the last fifteen minutes getting a feel for the surroundings and formulating what I would ask you. During that time, an elderly lady came in here and was out a few minutes later. People aren't exactly beating down the doors to come in."

"Still Detective, I must ask you to maintain the sanctity of the setting."

He leaned forward, his voice almost a whisper. "You're right, Father. No need to make a scene here. How about if you stop by police headquarters on Monday morning? Say around 11? We can have a long talk then about your actions Wednesday night. Maybe you'll also share your alibi."

Leaving the confessional, he entered a pew about ten feet away, slid towards the middle, and looked around. The church was filling for afternoon mass. An elderly woman approached the confessional.

Jim had been sitting, realizing that he was going to have to explain where he went after leaving The Wharf on Wednesday night. This would bring Jan into the discussion and expose them both. He stood up and started to leave just as Mrs. O'Reilley was coming in. "Father, confession isn't over yet, is it?"

He sighed. "No, Mrs. O'Reilley. Please come in." Jim kissed his eccleastical stole, and sat down thinking: she's here every week. Some nun in her grade school must have put the fear of God in her.

Mrs. O'Reilley confessed a small set of minor indiscretions. Jim listened politely, issued his standard three Hail Mary sentence, and wished her a good day.

After she left the confessional, she entered the pew in front of Mark and was joined by another septuagenarian. They started to chat. Mrs. O'Reilley was extolling the virtues of Father Jim.

Mark leafed through the hymnal, pretending not to listen.

"...and you should have heard his sermon on Thursday morning.

All full of righteous vigor, about confronting your demon and casting him into the sea. "*Cast the devil away. Let him drown in his own evil,*" he said. "They were powerful words, *I'd* say."

Well, those are powerful words, Mark thought. I'll have to discuss these with Father Jim when we talk on Monday.

Jim peeked out the door to see if anyone else was waiting. There stood Gabe, looking anxious. Jim straightened up.

"Hi, Gabe. Look. Mass is starting soon and I've got something I really need to take care of. Is there any chance this can wait?"

Gabe frowned and mumbled a low "okay."

Jim realizing Gabe was troubled, extended his arm, palm up, and motioned towards the chair.

"Step inside my office. There's always time for my brother."

Gabe took a seat and sat in silence for a few minutes. He smiled and said, "Jim, this is going to take a while. Maybe now is not a good time. Like you said, mass is starting soon. I'll need to talk to you sometime soon. I'm just not sure I'm ready yet to say what I have to say. I'll call you tomorrow, or in a few days."

The priest studied his brother. "Okay, Gabe. I'm always available when you want to talk."

Gabe walked from the confessional and into an adjacent pew, two pews up from Mark, who had seen Gabe enter. Gabe sat and sighed as the detective slid lower in the pew.

Jim left the confessional and saw Gabe sitting in a trance. He walked over and leaned into the pew. "Gabe, let's talk after I say the 9:30 mass tomorrow. There's nothing you can tell me that we can't work through."

"I hope so, Jim. I'm in a real mess." Jim didn't know what to say. He and his brother seemed to each have their problems.

He put his hand on Gabe's shoulder. "We'll both get through our difficulties, Gabe. I have faith that God will give us the strength to do what is right."

Mark heard all of this and thought: looks like I'm going to 9:30 mass tomorrow. What's up with them? Neither seems likely to kill anyone. Yet they both seem anxious. Well, where there's smoke...

- - -

Chapter 8

Let He Who is Without Sin

Jim genuflected towards the altar and turned towards the side exit. This took him past the sacristy where Father Ray was dressing for mass. He tiptoed, but Ray spotted him.

"Come in, Jim. Close the door and have a seat." Jim stepped in and sat on the edge of a padded folding chair. He couldn't mask that he was nervous; he felt like an elementary pupil about to be scolded.

"Detective Porfino stopped by. We had a nice little chat. He's investigating Silvio's death. Apparently, he thinks it might be murder because he's checking out persons known to have been with Silvio on Wednesday night. Specifically, he wanted to know what you were arguing with him about. He also wanted to know where you were around 11 p.m. He thinks this is when Silvio died. I told him that I was asleep by then and didn't hear you come in."

Looking Jim in the eye, he said, "Jim, tell me if you had anything to do with Silvio's death. I have your back on the gambling, but if you killed someone or know who did, we need to get this cleared up. So, what do you know about this?"

Jim sat back in the chair. No time like the present to come clean.

"I didn't kill Silvio and I don't know who did. I was visiting someone Wednesday evening. We have been involved romantically for six months now. Silvio knew and threatened to expose me. I went to her house to break things off between us. First, there was the gambling, and then this. I've made a mess out of my life Ray, and I was trying to put things back together.

"She isn't taking this well at all. That's where I went Friday morning, to talk with her one more time and try to end things on some sort of peaceful note."

Ray, who had been standing like a principal ready to chastise a wayward pupil, pulled out a padded folding chair, sat down, and thought for a minute.

"You should have talked to me sooner. You need to come clean with Detective Porfino. He's a man of the world. He'll understand your liaison, but won't understand any attempt to cover it up."

"I know, Ray. I just need to talk to her and let her know what's happening. She's still upset and exposing her to scandal would make a bad situation worse. Can I ask you to keep this to yourself until I talk with her? Detective Porfino has me coming in for an interview on Monday morning. I have until then to try to make things right."

Ray picked up his vestments and started to put them on. "Okay, Jim. You have until then. Take tomorrow afternoon off if you have to. I just don't want this to linger. It isn't good for you, me, your friend, or the parish."

"Thanks, Ray."

Leaving the sacristy, Jim walked to the rectory, nodding his greetings to the parishioners arriving for Saturday afternoon mass. He entered his office and dialed Jan's number. *"Hi. This is Jan. If you're not trying to sell me something, then your message is important to me. Please leave your name and number and I'll get back as soon as I can."*

Jim waited for the beep. *"Jan. This is Jim. We need to talk again. We need to talk about Wednesday night. Please get back to me. I'm free tomorrow afternoon. Let's meet somewhere."* He put down the phone, swiveled in his chair and looked out at the arriving parishioners. He was scheduled to say the 9:30 mass on Sunday morning. He looked at the notes on his desk. Crap, he thought, I need a sermon for tomorrow.

\- - -

Mark flipped open a small notebook and made some notations. He thought over the events of the last few days and wondered if the brothers Cooper were knee-deep in Silvio's demise.

Suddenly, everyone stood and started singing. He repeatedly whispered, "Excuse me." as he worked his way to the end of the pew. The pew mates shared confused stares but allowed him to slide by. Mark turned towards the back of the church with his head lowered, and walked flush into two altar boys who were solemnly walking in front of Father Ray. This caused the singing to stop as Mark helped one of the altar boys to his feet.

Ray at first appeared angered by this, but smiled and brushed off the back of the altar boy's robe. "Detective Porfino, how nice of you to join us today. I hope you can stay and participate in the mass."

He addressed the parishioners. "How about it, everyone? Should we invite Detective Porfino, a visitor today to our parish, to join us in our celebration?"

The congregation let loose with a vocal and sincere "Yes, Father."

He turned towards Mark. "Please have a seat and know that you are welcome here." He turned towards a parishioner in the adjacent pew. "Mrs. James, please make room for Detective Porfino and hand him a hymnal. It's number 286, Detective, *How Great Thou Art*."

Looking towards the congregation and then the choir loft, Ray called out. "Now let's do this again from the top. Hit it, Gloria. Play it loud enough to make the Baptists down the street hear it."

Mark moved into the pew and was handed a thick hymnal by Mrs. James, already opened to Hymn 286. He jumped as Gloria stomped the treadle and started *How Great Thou Art*. The parishioners broke into song as Mrs. James pointed to the lines and encouraged Mark to join in.

Ray turned with the altar boys towards the front. The boy who Mark had knocked down gave him a decidedly unchristian look. Ray smiled at Mark as he sang out and continued towards the altar. Mark accepted his fate, and picked up on the words. Mrs. James smiled and nodded.

- - -

Jim awoke on Sunday morning and noticed the message waiting light on his cell. He had silenced his ring function during the confession hour, then forgotten to set it back to on. The message was from Jan. She was still angry about how their relationship had ended, but agreed to meet Sunday afternoon at their secret Barnes and Noble.

He had a quick breakfast of toast and coffee and leafed through the daily paper, *The Long Harbor Press*. There was more news of

Silvio's drowning and the police investigation. Marie Collier, a recent grad of the community college with an associate's degree in journalism, was the investigative reporter for the paper. Most of her articles dealt with small matters, but now she was reporting on the biggest story in town.

Her front-page article stated that Mario Gallante, Silvio's employer, was in town to take control of Fortunato Brothers. The article also hinted that he appeared to be conducting his own investigation into Silvio's death. Detective Tony Wagner, retired from the Long Harbor police, had been called in by Detective Porfino to discuss Silvio's death and its similarities to that of his brother Enrico, years earlier. Detective Wagner had been chief detective at the time.

He put the paper down and thought of Jan and the situation they were in. He needed to remove any suspicion that he might be involved.

Walking to his office, he picked up his notes for his sermon and read them over. This will start the ball rolling, he guessed. I need to start coming clean now. I hope that people will understand. He walked over to the church and greeted the parishioners he passed on his way. As he entered the sacristy, he saw Gabe enter the church. He waved, and Gabe raised his hand in greeting and smiled.

He dressed in his rose vestments. This was Gaudete Sunday, the third Sunday of Advent. Rose vestments were also worn on Laetare Sunday, the fourth Sunday of Lent; they represented Christian joy during these reflective seasons.

He left the sacristy and directed the altar boys to the back of the church. He signaled Gloria to start the entrance hymn, *How Great Thou Art,* and he and the altar boys proceeded. There's quite a crowd today, he thought. I hope they're ready for some good old-fashioned contrition.

He spotted Detective Porfino at the end of a pew. Mark smiled at him as he bellowed forth the hymn. Jim nodded back and thought, for a non-Catholic, he sure spends a lot of time in church.

Walking further down the aisle, he saw Jan standing near the front, dressed in that tight skirt that drove him wild. Geez, what else can happen? I wonder if the bishop is here.

He ascended the altar steps, continued to the presidential chair, and stood, singing the second verse of *How Great Thou Art* and waiting for Gloria to finish playing. But Gloria played on, so Jim continued singing. Finally, she ran out of verses and ended the hymn after a few final seconds of organ hum.

He greeted the congregation, made the sign of the cross, and began the opening prayer. He then gave way to the lectors, who recited the first reading, the response, and the second reading. Jim stood and signaled the congregation to do likewise.

Proceeding to the pulpit, he opened his bible to the Gospel, and read a passage from the apostle John. It dealt with John the Baptist announcing the coming of the Lord, denying any special position for himself in salvation, but, rather, preparing the people for the Savior who was to come. *"But there is one among you whom you do not recognize whose sandal strap I am unworthy to untie."*

Jim closed the bible and signaled for the congregation to sit.

"I guess you're wondering why I am wearing pink. Priests wear pink on this third Sunday of Advent and the fourth Sunday of Lent to show Christian joy during these solemn seasons. Plus, I look good in pink, don't you think?" The congregation laughed and nodded their assent. Good. Start with a little humor to make them forget that they're hungry and want to get out of here.

"My brothers and sisters in Christ. As we read in John's gospel, John the Baptist, a man of good standing in his community, made clear that he was but a servant of God and an unworthy one at that. It is our unworthiness that links us to the great saints of the church.

Our patron saint, Saint Augustine himself, was a notorious sinner. But his mother, Saint Monica, prayed for his conversion and never lost faith that her son would turn his life over to God and forsake his wicked ways. St. Augustine was fortunate to have such a loving mother and, also, the guidance of Saint Ambrose.

We are all sinners, my brothers and sisters. Whether we are sitting in a pew or standing at the pulpit, we all do things in our lives that challenge our relationship with God. Usually these actions are destructive, to not only ourselves, but to those around us."

Gabe and Jan each straightened in their pew and wondered if this sermon was directed at them. Mark thought that he'd hit the lottery. Was this a confession in front of an entire congregation?

"I can tell you personally that these pink robes don't shield me from sin any more than your faithful attendance at Sunday mass, and the moral teaching that you received growing up, shields you. We all need to face up to what we have done and whom we have harmed."

Mark took out his notebook, opened it within his hymnal and started writing. He also looked over at Gabe, who seemed to be slinking down in his pew after having sat up just a minute earlier.

This was getting good, Mark thought.

"Some of us pay the price in this lifetime. We will bury someone later this week whose shortcomings may have gotten him killed. Before we judge such a man, however, let us judge ourselves. Let's ask whom we have harmed, whom we have deprived of the happiness and humanity that we all deserve.

My brothers and sisters, I stand before you as a wretched sinner myself. In the coming weeks, those sins will be revealed to all. Just know that I am attempting to make things right with God and right with you, my fellow travelers, on our journeys to heaven.

I ask your forgiveness and understanding and promise to extend the same to you as we all reconcile with God in this Advent season and prepare for the birth of our savior, Jesus Christ."

He closed his bible and stepped away from the pulpit. From the front pew came a single set of hands applauding. Then, like a contagion, the applause spread to a few nearby congregants, then carried over to the entire assembly. People stood as they applauded. A man cried out "We love you, Father Jim, we've got your back." Others smiled and mumbled in agreement. Jan was crying.

Jim smiled and started to tear up. He nodded to the congregation and took in the wave of love he was receiving. "Thank you all," he said nearly choking. "We are all in this vale of tears together, and together we will help each other achieve the great reconciliation for which we strive."

He finished the mass and stood at the entrance to greet those leaving. Most of the time, this was a pleasantry only for those not rushing out to beat the traffic jam in the parking lot. Today, people stopped and shook Jim's hand.

Gabe smiled at his younger brother and gave him a firm hug. "That was terrific, Jim. Can I stop by the rectory later this afternoon so that we can have that talk?"

He studied his brother. "OK, late this afternoon is better. I have to run out earlier."

As Jan stepped up next, he flinched, then offered his hand. She embraced him instead, the hug lingering with perfume and emotion. Mr. Richardson, waiting to shake Jim's hand, wondered about the effect the sermon had on her. Jim thanked Jan for her kindness and she smiled and replied "Anything you need Father. Just ask."

He nodded and thought of St. Augustine. This was to allow his thinking to stay on track and to quell the erection, which was disquieting his vestments.

Mark was waiting for Mr. Richardson, who held onto Jim's hand and seemed to be examining him closely. "You know, Father, you're a dead ringer for your brother. I wonder why I never noticed before."

Mark looked at Jim and realized Mr. Richardson was right. Stepping up to Jim, he said, "Powerful sermon, Father. Don't forget that we are meeting tomorrow. Who knows? Maybe I can help you with your problem. Like they say, confession is good for the soul."

– – –

Mark left the church and drove into downtown Long Harbor. He was hungry and spotted Lucy's Eat and Go. He pulled into the lot and looked at the row of cars; quite crowded for a Sunday. He had decided to skip Lucy's when he noticed Mario Gallante wolfing down some eggs.

Lucy herself wasn't working today, but a chipper twenty-something welcomed him.

Mark nodded towards the back. "I see a friend of mine. I think I'll join him." The hostess smiled and handed Mark a menu. He walked down the long row of booths on his right and counter stools on his left. He stopped at Mario's table and cleared his throat, but Mario spoke first.

"Detective Porfino. Here this morning for a nice breakfast? I recommend the scrambled eggs and sausage. Everything looks good actually, although I'd skip the cream chipped beef. It has a delayed effect, if you know what I mean."

"Can I join you, Mario? I believe we are both looking to answer the same question."

He waved Mark to the opposite padded bench. Mark sank in and found comfort in the soft pleather. Mario smiled. "The King of Queens once said that booths are a vacation for your ass. I agree."

Sheila appeared with a coffee pot and an extra cup. She refilled Mario's cup. She placed the extra cup in front of Mark and poured the coffee without asking. "Your breakfast will be up in a minute, Detective," she said with a voice gravelly from too many cigarettes.

Mario smiled at Mark. "I saw you coming, Detective. I took the liberty of ordering for you."

She winked at Mario and walked away. Mark poured too much sugar into his cup and took a sip. He grunted in approval, looked at Mario and said "Just right. You know, I still can't get over how everyone knows everyone else's business in this town."

Mario looked back at his plate, balanced a forkful of eggs and a quarter of a thick sausage link onto a section of toast and popped the combination into his mouth. He chewed carefully and swallowed.

Starting to say, "We need to talk," Mark was interrupted as Mario raised one finger, picked up his coffee, and with an audible slurp, washed down the remnants. He dabbed his mouth and belched. "You were saying, Detective?"

"It's clear to me that you're in Long Harbor to look into Silvio's death. That's your prerogative, I guess. Just don't inhibit the police investigation."

Sheila brought over Mark's breakfast as Mario was about to answer. Mark looked at his plate. "There's enough home fries to feed an army."

Sheila smiled. "Want some ketchup?"

"Why spoil a masterpiece?"

Mark picked up a saltshaker and attacked his home fries like he was trying to put out a fire. Mario waited. "Detective, I was Silvio's friend and business manager. I'm here to comfort the family and see to it that Fortunato Brothers continues to function smoothly. I'll stay through the funeral. If I come across some information pertaining to his death, I'll deal with it in the manner best for Silvio's and my own interests."

Putting down the shaker, the detective eyed his booth mate. "Your best interest would be to inform the police in a timely manner. You're too smart to do anything foolish, Mario. If more bodies start showing up, I'll know who to look for."

Mario waved for the check. "Detective, I'm a business man. I weigh cost versus return. You're right that we both want this issue dealt with and with certainty that the right result has been gotten. I'll make sure that we both end up with what's best for everyone. Now if you'll excuse me, I need to go to Fortunato Brothers and check on the activities for the coming week. Faucets don't fix themselves."

He stood up and walked towards the register. And gambling debts don't collect themselves, Mark thought.

When he finished his breakfast, Mark waved to Sheila for the check. She smiled. "It's been taken care of already, detective. Your nice gangster friend picked up the tab."

- - -

Jim changed into jeans, a blue golf shirt, and loafers. He waved to Father Ray as the pastor was preparing to leave for mass. "Good luck Jim," Ray called out. "Let's get this whole affair behind us."

He slipped into his car, waved to a few parishioners arriving for mass, and drove off towards Carson and his meeting with Jan. He mulled over what he would say. As he was leaving the Long Harbor city limits, he had to come to a hard stop as he realized he was running a red light. Half into the intersection, he cautiously reversed back to behind the white pedestrian crossing lines. He looked up and cursed to himself; one of those camera red lights. That's the last thing he needed.

An elderly woman in a late model Nissan driving in the cross lane glared at Jim as she drove through the intersection. She snorted something about impatient men—as if stopping at a red light is going to make them late for some important get together. Wait a minute, she thought, isn't that the man who gave me the finger last week? It's not the same car, though.

Jim nodded and mouthed "sorry." Where have I seen her before? Is she a parishioner, he wondered.

Claire Woodward then remembered the beautiful roses this young man had sent last week as an apology. She smiled and signaled all was okay.

He waved back. Busted; where do I know her from? He was brought back to the moment when the loud blare of the car behind him indicated that the light had turned green. Jim started to raise his hand in a single-fingered salute when he thought the better of it.

Driving through the intersection and out of the Long Harbor limits, it hit him that the woman in the Nissan was the slow driver that he had flipped off on Wednesday night. Oh, my God. I might have my alibi he said aloud. Maybe he didn't need to pull Jan into this after all. He still had to meet with Jan though—just in case.

- - -

After mass, Gabe stopped for gas, bought a newspaper, a bear claw, and a 24-ounce coffee. He drove back to his apartment. He left his car, balancing the coffee, claw, and thick Sunday paper, when Mr. Richardson walked by with Reggie on the leash. Reggie barked and growled at Gabe. What's with that dog? Gabe thought. What did I do to him? And why does he constantly have to be walked?

Mr. Richardson smiled. "Hello, Gabe. Don't mind Reggie. He'd rather be inside gnawing on a rubber bone than interacting with us people. I don't think he entirely trusts us."

Gabe nodded and tightened his elbow grip on the sliding newspaper. "I don't blame him."

Mr. Richardson looked up at the sky. "It's a glorious Sunday, isn't it? Makes you glad you're alive. Poor Fortunato isn't around to appreciate the fine weather, and this time of year. Oh well, as they say, 'One man's loss is another man's gain.'" Reggie growled again and snapped his teeth.

Gabe wished Mr. Richardson a good day and entered his apartment after fumbling for his keys. He walked into his kitchen and pulled orange juice from the refrigerator. He noticed that he had a voice mail, and played it back. *"Mr. Cooper. This is Mark Porfino. It occurred to me after mass that I didn't invite you in on Monday to discuss Silvio Fortunato's death. How about coming in around one? Just want to check on a few things. Thanks."*

Gabe listened to the message again. Here we go, he thought.

- - -

Jan had driven directly home after mass. She had a light breakfast of yogurt with fruit, and thought over Jim's sermon. Well, I guess things break for good today. He's going to ask me to forgive him and then tell me that he's coming clean to Father Langley. I guess I always knew that this was headed for an unhappy ending. If only something would happen to hold off this moment. I'm not sure I'm ready for this yet.

- - -

Jim entered the Barnes and Noble, went to the Puzzles and Games section and selected a book of crossword puzzles. He smiled to himself; better than the alternate lifestyle book I grabbed last time. He looked over to the Starbucks Café but didn't spot Jan. He went through the coffee line and decided to skip the Frappuccino. "Just a large, sorry *Grande*, coffee," he said to the barista.

"Americano?" Jim was stymied. "Coffee…I just want coffee, please." The barista, barely 18 Jim guessed, frowned and poured steaming black liquid into a thin cup, and set it on the counter as she reached underneath for something. Jim put his three dollars on the counter and picked up the cup as the barista started to say something. The cup burned Jim's hand. He was about to mutter words best not heard on Sunday when she handed him a coffee cup sleeve. "I was about to tell you that you needed this. This stuff can get pretty hot."

Jan walked into the bookstore and headed straight for the Cafe. She ordered a Grande Caramel Macchiato and biscotti, paid, and turned towards the tables. She spotted Jim and started to walk over. Jim admired her ability to order in Starbucks lingo without a translator.

Dispensing with any pretense of a chance meeting of bibliophiles, Jan pulled out the chair opposite Jim and sat down. Jim looked around. No scandalized reaction. So far, so good.

She looked at Jim who stared intently at the crossword. "CHASTITY," she said in a voice loud enough to be heard at nearby tables. Jim was startled. He looked around and whispered, "What?" Jan pointed to the puzzle. "CHASTITY. Twenty-six across, eight letters. Abstention from sex."

Jim looked at the puzzle and filled in the boxes. "Thanks. Got it."

He smiled at a woman at the next table who had turned when Jan spoke out. He pointed to the answer in the puzzle. "She's better at this than I am."

Jan was enjoying this. "Last time we met, you were reading a book on gay relationships. How's that working out for you?"

The woman at the next table looked up. Jim grimaced, and said, "Do you mind?" to the woman.

The woman stood up, picked up her coffee and plate, smiled at Jim and as she was moving to a table farther away, said, "It's alright son, we all have our secrets."

He waited until the woman was out of earshot. "Jan, this is serious. I am being questioned about Silvio Fortunato's death."

"You're not involved are you? I'd never be able to believe that."

"No, of course not. I would never lay a hand on anyone. I wasn't raised that way. It's just that Detective Porfino wants to know my whereabouts on Wednesday night, around eleven."

She frowned. "And that would be me. If you tell Porfino where you were Wednesday, we're exposed. I guess that's what you were referring to in your sermon today."

"Yes. I haven't told anyone yet about you. I did tell Father Ray that I was seeing someone and broke it off. I also told him about Porfino wanting an alibi. Jan, I don't want to expose us. I would rather this ended quietly. There might be one way out, but it's iffy."

He explained that he saw a woman Wednesday night and then just now. He didn't mention the birding. If he could just locate her, he could have her vouch for his whereabouts on the fateful night.

"But I still need to have the ability to mention you as my alibi if I can't figure out who she is. Are you all right with that?"

Jan thought. "Jim. Ending our relationship and then exposing it would be very painful. Just make it a last resort. I have to live in this town, too."

- - -

Gabe watched about an hour of pro football; the local favorite, the Predators, had a bye week. The network choices for fill-in games were of little interest to him. He wondered how Jim got so obsessed with all of this.

He'd been preoccupied anyway, by how he was going to explain to Jim what happened on Wednesday night. He switched off the television and decided to go over to the rectory now, even if he would be too early for Jim. He thought he might talk to Father Ray in the meantime and see what advice he could offer.

Leaving the apartment, he spotted Mr. Richardson and Reggie passing by, again. Stop feeding that damn dog, he thought to himself.

Mr. Richardson waved to Gabe and wished him a good day. "No real football today, eh Gabe?"

"No. Anyway, I have to meet someone."

"Your brother gave a corker of a sermon today. I hope whatever he was talking about works out. He's such a nice young man to have such heavy worries."

Gabe nodded and fiddled for his keys. "Jim's problems will straighten out, I'm sure." He started to slide into his car. "Thanks for asking, Mr. Richardson, I'll pass on your kind thoughts to Jim."

He nodded in Reggie's direction. "Maybe you should return to your apartment in this cold weather. Reggie appears to be shaking."

Mr. Richardson looked at Reggie. "He's made of pretty tough stuff. I think he's seen enough of this world in his long life to cope with discomfort. Funny thing, though. He seems to have taken a dislike to you recently. If only we could figure out what he's thinking."

"Maybe it's better we don't," Gabe said.

- - -

He drove to the rectory mulling over what he was going to say to Jim. How do you say that you killed someone? What a God-awful mess, he thought. I should have reported this right away. Now I'm in deep.

Pulling into the empty lot, he parked next to Father Langley's ten-year-old Corolla. He studied the car. Minor dents in the side panel, could use a wash. Well, Langley wasn't in it for the money that was for sure.

He rang the bell. "Amazing Grace" tolled out. He laughed despite his anxiety. No answer; he rang again. He heard a "Hold on, I'm coming," and in a minute, Father Ray answered the door. He saw Gabe and smiled. "Jim's not here Gabe, he's off on a personal matter," he said, then saw how serious Gabe looked.

"Come in from the cold, Gabe. You can wait in the living room with me if you want. I was just watching some football. Pretty dull, with the Predators not playing. At least they won't lose today." Father Ray laughed at this and said, "Sounds like a glass half-empty approach. Oh well, we must take the good with the bad."

He waved Gabe towards a stuffed chair, turned down the volume on the game, and offered a beer. "Flying Dog," he said. "Pretty smooth." Gabe declined.

"If you'd rather, I have coffee. It's not Starbucks but it'll warm you up."

Gabe smiled, but declined again.

"Do you mind if I finish my beer? It's my one real indulgence of the week. My Sunday afternoon collar tossing escape. That and the Predators, of course."

Gabe nodded his okay. Ray drained the last of the bottle and gave an appreciative "ahhhh." Gabe sat forward on the cushion. "Father, I need to talk to Jim on an urgent matter. But it's going to be difficult to discuss. I've done something that's not easily explainable or forgivable."

Ray put down his empty bottle and thought for a moment. "Would you rather discuss it with me? Would that be easier for you than talking with your brother?"

"No, this is something brothers need to discuss. It's personal and affects us both."

"I understand. I hope you know, Gabe, that we all have our issues. We all have things that we've done that we regret. I'm no exception, and neither is Jim, as you well know."

Ray eyed his bottle and continued. "Brothers have a special bond best unbroken by outsiders. All I can assure you, Gabe, is that Jim will listen and be understanding. That's our job as priests and his obligation as a brother. If he can't help, then I'm still here. Whatever you've done Gabe, be assured that you'll get through this. We're all in this life together. The only way we get out of our difficulties is if we help each other."

Picking up the empty bottle, he waved it at Gabe. "Now, how about that beer? Man does not live by bread alone."

Gabe nodded, mumbled a "thanks" and sat back. Ray went into the kitchen and brought back two cold ones. "I can't have a parishioner drink alone."

- - -

An hour later, Jim pulled into the rectory lot, cheered by his encounter with the mysterious Nissan woman. This was a chance to establish an alibi and spare Jan. As he climbed the rectory steps, he noticed Gabe's car and remembered he was coming over. He smiled and thought, I hope Ray has some Flying Dog left. I could stand a cold one. I bet Gabe could, too.

He walked into the living room. The second Sunday football game was on. Gabe was sitting in a lounge chair polishing off what appeared to be his third Flying Dog. Father Ray was snoring in his barca lounger. Three empty bottles were next to him.

Whispering a hello to Gabe, he went over to Ray and removed the beer balanced between Ray's hand and the seat cushion. He looked at Gabe. "Let me grab one for myself and we'll go into my office."

Gabe struggled out of the lounger and stood unsteadily. "My brother Jim. The good brother. Always to the rescue."

"In my office Gabe, okay? Ray needs his afternoon siesta."

Seeing one remaining Flying Dog in the refrigerator, he popped the cap and took a swig. Man, that's good, he thought as he studied the label. He broke out of his Nirvana as he wondered what Gabe might be there to talk about. He couldn't be in a bigger mess than Jim was now, could he?

- - -

Jim walked into his office, but Gabe was not there. He heard him recycling his beer in the hall bathroom. Sitting down, he swung ninety degrees in his leather swivel chair to face the couch, took another swig and waited for the sound of urine hitting water to stop.

There was a hopeful pause and then a continuation for a few seconds. Finally, after all appeared lost, came the sound of a flush and water running in the sink for a brief period. Another thirty seconds and Gabe walked into Jim's office. Jim waved him to the couch. He tried to sit down, but it was more of a flop.

"So Gabe, how are you? What's up?"

Gabe straightened himself and looked at Jim.

"Jim, I did something terrible and I've been living with it these last few days and I need to get it out. It's driving me crazy. I've made a real mess of things and they will just get worse if I don't come clean."

Jim rolled over to Gabe. "What is it, Gabe? Let's work though this. Now, what did you do that is bothering you so much?"

"I killed Silvio."

The beer slid from Jim's hand but he caught it between his knees. He placed the bottle on the desk. "What was that? You killed Silvio? Are you drunk?"

"It was an accident, I guess. Silvio pulled over, shouted my name, parked his Explorer, and jumped out. He was pissed. He came storming over yelling about pissing on his tire and how he was going to tear me apart. He grabbed me and started shaking me."

Jim rolled forward. "What did you do then?"

Gabe thought for a moment and smiled. "I threw up on him. Chili, beans, and beer. He was covered; boy, was he mad. He shouted and threw me into the bushes. I landed on dog crap and a dog yelped and started barking."

His mouth formed an "O" as he came to a realization. "Come to think of it, it was Reggie. Anyway, Silvio walked over and starting kicking me in the ribs. He was enjoying himself. I got up and kicked Silvio in the nuts. Boy, that felt good. I figured we were done. Silvio staggered back to the dock. I stood up as best I could and faced him. Silvio reached into his jacket and said that he was going to do something he'd been thinking about for a long time. It looked like a gun. I ran at Silvio and head-butted him in the chest. He fell over. I started kicking him like he kicked me."

Now drained of all color, he continued. "He stood up and reached into his pocket again. When I saw the black object, I ran towards Silvio and pushed him. He dropped the object and fell off the dock, hitting his head on a piling as he fell in. He let out a cry of pain and went under. I was hurting from the beating and half-drunk. Still, I jumped in and tried to find him. The water was too dark and I could only go under for a few seconds at a time. After a few minutes, I realized that Silvio was gone. I swam to the dock and pulled myself out."

Jim sat there stunned. Gabe was staring ahead in silence. "It was self defense, Gabe. Silvio pulled a gun on you and you reacted."

He covered his face. "It wasn't a gun. It was his cell phone. I killed a man who was attacking me with his cell phone. How will that sound to the police?"

Jim was silent. Gabe removed his hands from his face. "I thought of calling 911. I picked up Silvio's phone and dialed. When the operator answered, I hung up. I was confused and scared. How do you tell someone that you just killed a man?"

Gabe sobbed. "I threw Silvio's phone into the harbor and walked home. I've been living with this since then, popping pills to put up with the bruised ribs, and wondering if anyone knows. I swear Mr. Richardson knows. Maybe Reggie told him. I can hardly sleep, and when I do, I dream of Silvio and that night."

Walking to the couch, Jim sat next to Gabe and put his arm around him. Gabe buried his head deep into his hands and started to cry. "What do I do now, Jim? This is a living hell."

"Call Detective Porfino. Explain what happened. Better to do this than to live with it or, worse, have him drag it out of you. He's probably going to question you anyway. He'll wonder where you were that night."

Gabe looked up wearing an odd smile that disturbed Jim. "I have an alibi, believe it or not. An old woman, Claire Woodward, claims I flipped her off in traffic clear across town around the time of the killing. Porfino told me that himself. He's interviewing me tomorrow but I'm probably not a suspect."

He took a breath. "In the meantime, Mario Gallante is in town. If I confess, how do they stop Mario from having me killed? I have to keep with my alibi until Mario gives up the search. Maybe things will calm down by then."

Damn, Jim thought. Bad enough his brother confesses to killing Silvio, but now his ability to keep himself and Jan from scandal meant he'd have to refute Gabe's alibi.

Jim sighed. "Do what you think is best, Gabe. I still think you should come clean with Detective Porfino. It will chase your demons, give some closure to Jessie and Rico, and spare others from the investigation. Porfino will keep Mario at bay."

Gabe was unconvinced. "Mario has friends. I think I'm going to wait this out. If things get too screwed up, I'll call Porfino. Otherwise, I'll hope for a miracle. Thanks for hearing me out, Jim. A brother really is a friend in need."

- - -

Chapter 9

Truth. What does that mean?

Mario walked into Lucy's on Monday morning. He exchanged greetings with Sheila, ordered coffee and read the menu. Looks like a pancakes day, he thought. She returned with the coffee and took Mario's order for a short stack with sausage. He poured enough sugar into the cup to change the chemical composition, and looked around.

The usual morning crowd, he imagined. Men on their way to blue-collar jobs, older women chatting and laughing. He spotted a couple in the corner, then looked closer. Wait a minute, that's Tony Wagner...and his sister, Miriam. I thought he moved to Cambria. Funny, turning up after Silvio's death.

His staring caught Tony's eye, but Tony looked away, pretending he hadn't seen Mario. He said something to Miriam who glanced over. Mario stood up and walked over.

"Detective Wagner, long time no see. What brings you to Long Harbor?"

He put down his fork and took a breath. "Hello, Mario. I believe you know my sister, Miriam?"

Mario bowed. "Pleased to see you again, Miriam. When was the last time? Oh, yes. It was at Enrico Fortunato's funeral. How have you been?"

She nodded a hello. "I'm fine, thanks. My brother is in town and we're catching up over breakfast."

Mario smiled. "It's good that brothers and sisters stick together."

He turned to Tony. "So Tony, are you in town on business or pleasure? I'm sure you heard that our dear friend Silvio turned up dead on Friday. Similar circumstances to how Enrico died three years ago. Pretty eerie, huh?"

Just breathe, Tony reminded himself. Don't give him the satisfaction.

"Mario, actually, I'm in town at the request of Detective Porfino. He wanted to question me about the investigation of Enrico's death. Not much to say. It was an accident."

Miriam picked up her coffee cup and Mario noticed a slight tremor. "Oh, I'm sorry, Miriam. You dated Enrico, didn't you? Silvio's death must bring back memories."

He turned to Tony. "I'm in town to run Fortunato Brothers in Silvio's absence. I'm also here to determine what happened to Silvio. I'm not leaving until I find out."

He nudged Miriam, who had to shift over to let him sit down.

"Porfino's a good man, Tony. He's sharp. I would be careful around him. He has his doubts about Silvio's death being accidental. I bet he has already come to the same conclusion about Enrico."

He turned to Miriam.

"Sorry Miriam, but I have to be blunt here. Enrico was no damn good. I'm sure you knew that. I didn't agonize over his death because, frankly, he was a thorn in my side. It was convenient for me to accept the accident angle."

Tony slammed his fist. "I closed it as an accident and the coroner agreed. We have nothing else to discuss, Mario."

"Have a good breakfast, Tony. Maybe we'll see each other again soon. Miriam, it's been a pleasure to see you again. Take care of your brother while he's in town. It's nice seeing family stick together."

He returned to his table in time for Sheila to deliver the pancakes and refill his coffee. Nodding towards Tony and Miriam, he said something to Sheila. She smiled and nodded. The brother and sister sat for a few moments unsure what to say next. Finally, Tony looked at Miriam and said, "Let's go. I have to meet Porfino. Don't let Mario upset you."

Tony waved Sheila over. "Can we have the check?"

"No need, Detective. You breakfast has been paid for by that nice gangster over there."

They looked over at Mario who waved his fork full of a syrupy pancake wedge and smiled.

"Have a great day, you two."

- - -

Mark walked into his office and saw Silvio's toxicology report on his desk. On the folder was a yellow Post-it reading: Nothing unusual. High alcohol content as we expected. No other drugs. Stop by if any questions. Should I release the body? Wakefield.

Adam was right. Still, it didn't rule out that a drunken Silvio fell into the harbor on his own accord. It also didn't rule out he was pushed.

Patrolman Hanson rapped on the door. Mark waved Ted in and motioned towards a chair. "The toxicology came back," Mark said. "He was drunk. That's about it."

Ted, plying a manila folder in his hands, cleared his throat. "I know that we ran the 911 calls on Wednesday, and looked over the police blotter. I thought I would also check the red light cameras to look for anything unusual. There was a red light infraction caught on camera about 11:45 p.m., just a few minutes away from the harbor."

Ted handed Mark the folder. "Maybe it's just a coincidence."

Mark opened the folder and looked at the picture. Ted appeared uncomfortable. "The license and make are on the bottom. I ran them. There's no mistaking it."

Mark looked again at the picture. There was Tony Wagner, driving through a red light, half an hour after Silvio's death.

- - -

Chief Benson was walking past Mark's office when Mark waved him in. Ted stood up at attention. Gene Benson waved him back to the chair.

"So, where are we with the investigation?" Ted straightened and beamed. He was now a valued part of an investigation team. Mark handed the folder to Gene. "Ted got the red light photos from

Wednesday night. This one is from minutes after Silvio's death."

The chief opened the folder and studied the picture. "The bastard. I never liked that guy. This looks bad for him. He's coming in today, isn't he?"

"Ten O'clock. I have to talk to Professor Amos first and then Wagner. Do you want to sit in?"

Gene stood up. "No, I'll pop in around 10:15. I'll let you get what you can from him first. Feel him out about why he dropped the Enrico Fortunato case so soon."

He turned to Ted. "Good thinking on the photos. Subpoena Wagner's phone and cell records. Let's see who he's been in contact with." Benson walked out.

Ted called out a "Yes, Sir" after Chief Benson. He turned towards Mark, who smiled at Ted's enthusiasm.

"Good job, Ted. Get that subpoena but don't tell anyone. Wagner still has contacts in this department. We don't want this to leak."

- - -

Professor John Amos was shown into Mark's office by a police officer on desk duty a few minutes after nine. Mark waved him in and he half stumbled to a chair.

"How are you this morning, professor? I'm so glad you could come in."

Amos removed his coat and growled, "What choice did I have? After being patted down and later strip-searched for sitting parked outside police headquarters on Friday, I figured that I better show up. I didn't want a SWAT team descending on my apartment."

Mark smiled. "Your presence upset Mrs. Fortunato. Why were you there, exactly? That one dumb action moved you up on the suspect list. We needed to make sure you weren't armed and dangerous."

He laughed. "Armed where? Were you concerned I had a gun up my ass?"

"Believe me, I've seen weirder things. You're a person of interest in Silvio's death. You were seen talking to Silvio in The Wharf on

Wednesday night before he died. Care to fill me in?"

"Silvio and I weren't friends. We were at opposite ends of the zoning issue. Plus, he was cruel to Jessie and Rico. Professors are sometimes ears for troubled souls. I heard many stories about Silvio's cruelty."

Mark opened a notebook containing hand-written notes. "From 'Jessie,' was it?" Mark emphasized the name. "That would be Mrs. Fortunato. Did she come to you for counseling or did this all come up while you were doodling her?"

Amos turned red. "Jessie was troubled by Silvio's cruelty. She came to me about Rico's difficulties and talk turned to Silvio. She appreciated my attentiveness. We became closer, I admit. She came on to me, if you must know. She's a beautiful woman and I comforted her. This led to more intimate moments. That's what Silvio was accusing me of on Wednesday."

As Mark made notes, Amos tilted his head to see if he could make it out. Mark closed the notebook. "Why were you in The Wharf Wednesday? You don't seem The Wharf type."

"Jessie wanted me to follow Silvio and catch him in the act. She knew he was "doodling," as you call it, Carla Ciccone and wanted proof. She wanted out of the marriage."

"So you and she could sail into legitimacy unfettered by Silvio?"

"I'm no fool, Detective. Jessie was using me. I was hooked, but I could never kill someone. Not even for romance. That's only in cheap novels."

"Then where were you at eleven Wednesday night?" He again opened his notebook. "Make it good. You're on the short list."

The notebook was unsettling Amos. "I got up when Silvio left, around 10:15, dropped a twenty on the table and followed him out. He looked at his front tire and was really angry. He drove away in a huff. The back door squeaked and I saw Carla going back in. I figured Silvio wasn't planning on 'doodling' her that evening, so I left The Wharf and drove home."

"Can anyone verify that you went home?" Mark said looking up.

He thought for a minute. "I bought gas at a Riggins station about five miles out of town."

"Did you use a credit card?"

"No. Straight cash. I guess the clerk could vouch for me. Other than that, the only living thing that saw me was my cat, Mr. Whiskers."

Mark wrote MR. WHISKERS in large letters. Amos realized he was being mocked. "Did you see anything unusual on the way home?" Mark asked.

"Nothing unusual…wait a minute. I did see Detective Wagner driving ahead of me. I hadn't seen him in years. He turned down Hillside Avenue towards the docks. I was continuing out of town so I didn't give it another thought. It just seemed strange to see him after such a long time. Maybe he was at The Wharf also."

Closing his notebook, Mark said, "Ok, you're good for now. Just don't leave town." He loved saying that.

Amos stood up. "Detective, I may have "doodled" like you say, but I'm no killer. Put that in your notes." He put on his coat and started to walk out.

Mark called out. "Wait. One last question. What did you eat Wednesday night at The Wharf?"

Amos thought a moment. "I had the chili and rice. It was surprisingly good for such a dive. Why, was Silvio poisoned?"

"No, just getting all of the details. You can go." On the inside cover of his notebook Mark wrote "Buy canned chili and some rice."

He drummed his fingers on his desk and thought, so Tony Wagner keeps turning up. Tony, you're climbing the list. Looks like you may know something about two Fortunato killings.

- - -

Ted was preparing a warrant for Tony Wagner's phone records when the officer on duty summoned him to the front desk. He was to walk Tony to Detective Porfino's office and then let Chief Benson know that he had arrived. Tony was chatting up a street officer he had known when he was detective.

When he walked up, Tony turned around, smiled, and offered his hand. He was wearing a badge with Visitor in bold letters.

"Ted. You look good. What are you doing these days? Still roaming the docks and ticketing miscreants?"

Ted laughed and walked Tony down the hall towards Mark's office. Tony—seeing a few officers that he had worked with years ago—smiled and greeted each one warmly. Ted stopped and allowed Tony time for glad-handing. He watched Tony in awe; he was remarkably relaxed. It was not something you would expect of someone under investigation for murder. If Tony was guilty, Ted thought, he was one cool killer.

When they passed Gene Benson's office, Tony hesitated, but Ted pushed on. "The chief's busy, Tony. Let's go. Mark's waiting."

Mark looked up from a folder clearly marked as "Fortunato" as they came in. "Tony Wagner. Great that you could come. Thanks. We need your input on this Fortunato case."

As Tony and Ted Hanson sat, Mark offered coffee. Tony passed. "I had enough at Lucy's this morning. Might need a clear path to the Men's room, though." Mark and Ted both laughed as Tony eased into his chair. He nodded to the folder. "Silvio's?"

Mark opened the folder. "Enrico's file. There are remarkable similarities to Silvio's case, though. Except, of course, for the investigating team. Young Ted here has been very helpful."

Tony looked over to Ted, who was beaming despite himself. "Ted was a help in Enrico's case, too. He was a rookie then and, unfortunately, there wasn't much that he could contribute. It was open and shut. The man fell in and drowned. He was drunk as a skunk."

Leaning forward, Mark said, "Tony, there was always concern that maybe you wrapped up this case too soon. One week is not a typical investigation time. What convinced you that this was an accident?"

Tony seemed prepared for the question. "Believe me, Mark. I took heat for the brief investigation. Chief Benson and I had a long discussion on it. Closed door, but I'm sure everyone heard the tone." He looked over to Ted, who nodded.

"After 20 years as an investigator, you get a sense of where the evidence is leading. I kept looking for a smoking gun, something that would turn what looked like an accident into a murder. No luck there."

Mark leafed through a few pages. "And Coroner Rollins had no suspicions?"

"Frankly, Rollins wasn't much of a digger. He went through the standard autopsy steps and didn't see anything extraordinary. He concluded that Enrico fell in accidentally."

He closed the folder. "Rollins is also the doctor who confirmed that you had a bad heart and recommended that you retire. Was he your normal doctor?"

"No. But I consulted with him about chest pains I'd been having. He ran an EKG and other tests. Nothing too bad, but he sensed that I wanted out of this racket. I was only five years away from retiring anyway. He agreed to recommend that I retire for medical reasons."

Mark reopened the folder. "People considered the resignation to be pretty abrupt, especially after the investigation. Were you pressured to retire?"

Tony bristled. "No one pressures me. I can handle myself. Why the concern over this guy? He was a real prick. No one missed him. Hell, even his brother accepted the findings without question. They weren't exactly close in the later years. Who knows, maybe Silvio killed Enrico."

Entering the office just then, Gene Benson walked past Tony and pulled up a chair next to Mark. He picked up a second folder marked "Fortunato." He looked at Tony. "Well Tony, back again in the station. Must be like old times. Even another Fortunato killing."

Tony grunted. "Another Fortunato *death*. No one has said that either was killed."

Mark looked from Benson to Tony. "Tony, where were you Wednesday night between ten and midnight?"

Tony squirmed seeing that Benson, Porfino, and Ted Hanson were looking at him for an answer. "I visited my sister, Miriam, that evening. You can check with her. I left around ten and drove around for a while."

"You were seen driving towards the docks around 10:30."

"I wanted to look over the harbor at night. Nothing wrong with that."

Benson sat forward and glared at Tony. "That's around the time Silvio was killed. You have to admit that's pretty suspicious."

Tony sat back, thinking he didn't want to use his ace just yet. "Are you accusing me of killing Silvio? If so, why don't you just ask?"

"Okay, did you kill Silvio?"

"No, I did not. Maybe if you put in some effort and questioned whoever had a beef with Silvio, maybe you'll have better luck. That's what I'd do if I thought he was killed."

The Chief started to say something, but Mark held up a hand signaling him to stop. He pulled a photo from the folder and handed it to Tony. "You were caught on a red light camera leaving Long Harbor around 11:15. What was your hurry?"

The photo surprised Tony. "I guess I didn't see the light. So give me a ticket."

Benson turned red. "Did you kill Enrico Fortunato, too?"

Tony turned towards Mark. "I already said that the death was an accident. It's sad that Silvio met the same end. It's odd, I'll admit, but I didn't kill anybody. Are we done here?"

Gene stood up and walked out. Mark closed the folder. "We're done for now, Tony. Keep available for the next few days. We may want to call you back in."

Ted walked Tony out of the station. Tony thought that Ted seemed anxious around him. Maybe I can work him to see what Porfino knows, he thought. Tony patted Ted on the shoulder. Ted flinched, not expecting the contact.

"See you around, Detective."

Ted gave a half-wave and walked back into the station. Tony walked casually up the street and over to a Ford Focus. He got in on the passenger side and closed the door. He smiled at Miriam and said something brief. She started the car and drove off.

Mario was sitting in his Caddy. He started the engine, eased it into drive, and followed the Focus from a distance.

About 100 yards down the street, crossing towards the station, Jim saw Tony leave and Mario follow.

Tony Wagner and Mario Gallante, he thought to himself. "This is getting intense. I need to get myself out of this. Sorry, Jan. It's time for the truth."

– – –

When Ted returned to Mark's office, Mark handed him the toxicology results and sent him to the morgue to see if he could get anything else of interest from Coroner Wakefield. Adam was getting anxious to release the body, and Mark knew there was no reason to hold it any longer unless they found something. He put the "Enrico" folder away and reopened the "Silvio." He also opened his notebook, made notes from the Tony Wagner interview, and then started a page for Father Jim Cooper.

At 10:50, Patrolwoman Teresa McGill called Mark from the front desk. "Father Jim Cooper is here to see you." Mark closed the folder and asked her to show him to the office.

Teresa summoned Jim, who was reading an article in a months-old issue of Law Enforcement Magazine: *Effective Tasing*. It covered how to disable a perp without causing permanent nerve damage.

I hope they don't consider me a perp, he thought, as he stood and followed Teresa down the hallway. McGill kept herself in top shape, causing Jim to remember why it was difficult to keep his vows. If she was wearing a dress made of betting slips, he'd really be in trouble.

He smiled to himself at this, but then remembered he was being questioned about a murder. St. Augustine, please help me, he prayed silently as he entered Mark's office. The detective stood and motioned Jim to a seat. Teresa walked out, and Mark and Jim took a moment to watch her walk down the hall. "I don't know how you do it, Father."

This brought Jim back and he turned towards Mark. "Do what, Detective?"

"Stay away from the women, I mean. Me, I'm unlucky in love. Keeping my hands off is not an issue."

"Well, we do make vows. Keeping them is difficult though." Jim smiled. "I sometimes wish we could pick and choose our commandments."

Mark laughed, but remembering himself, frowned and grunted to project a serious demeanor. He pulled over Silvio's folder and opened it dramatically. He opened his notebook and read his note about buying chili. Without looking up he said, "So Father Jim, tell me about Wednesday night and your argument with Silvio."

"My brother Gabe and I went to The Wharf to have dinner and a few drinks. Gabe went in right away, but I was detained by a parishioner who wanted to debate about hymn selection."

Mark looked up from the notebook. "Ouch. Not good to meet the flock outside a den of iniquity. Go on."

"I went in after a few minutes. Silvio was with his men, drunk and giddy from his zoning win. I wolfed down some chili with rice and about half of my draft." Jim sighed. "Detective, it's no secret that Silvio ran a sports betting operation. Well, I was into him for two thousand dollars. I had decided to pay it off that night and end the gambling. It was ruining my life."

"For how long?"

"Off and on, for several years. I started again two years ago when I heard through one of Silvio's men that he could hook me up with NFL point-spread sheets. I did well at first, and Silvio delivered a large winning personally. He was thrilled that I had joined in. I guess he saw an easy mark. Anyway, I won some and lost some— but lost more than I won. Silvio was happy to run a tab as long as I paid a bit at a time with interest. Before I knew it, I was two thousand in the hole, and more focused on point spreads than my work. It was getting more difficult to keep up with the payments."

Jim shook his head and continued. "Then last week, Silvio met me in the confessional and told me he wanted more than money. He wanted me to talk up the zoning change. That's why I spoke at the meeting. Father Langley smelled a rat and confronted me about this. I came clean. It was his two thousand that I tried to give to Silvio that night."

Mark made a few notes. "And he took the money there? We didn't find any money on him."

"He didn't want to accept an envelope in public. He told me to mail it to Fortunato Brothers. I did later that night."

Jim didn't appear to be hiding anything. "Then you argued?"

"We had it out in the middle of The Wharf. Actually, I did the yelling. Silvio just simmered. Anyway, Gabe and I left after that."

Mark flipped through his notes. "I understand that you gave a corker of a sermon on Thursday morning, about confronting your personal demon and, what was that?" Mark moved his hand down the page. "Oh yes, 'casting your demon into the sea.'"

Thinking for a moment, Jim gasped and nodded. "That was Thursday morning, after I'd settled with Silvio. I was talking about my gambling."

"You have to realize that this makes you look like suspect number one. That was the morning after Silvio was cast into the sea."

He looked Jim in the eye. "Straight out Father, did you kill Silvio?"

"No, Sir. I may have more than my share of shortcomings, but I would never kill another person. I can't conceive of doing anything like that."

"Okay, let's continue on for now. So, you went straight home?"

Time to show my cards, Jim thought. "No, I drove to a friend's house. I was with her until around 11:30."

"I'll need a name. Had you arranged to see your friend beforehand?"

"No. It was the beer and my new sense of bravado. I was going to straighten my life out. Detective, I've been romantically involved with a parishioner for the last year. I went there to break it up."

Mark sat up. "How did that work out?"

"She didn't take it well. There was a lot of crying and arguing. Finally, around 11:30, we realized that we didn't have anything more to say, so I left."

"Her name?"

Here goes. "Jan Gillek."

Mark thought a second. "From the zoning board meeting?"

Jim nodded. "Detective, she'll back me up about Wednesday night. As you can guess, this isn't something we want to turn into a scandal. I know you're conducting an investigation, but if you can be discreet, I'd be grateful. This can ruin both of our lives and hurt the good that we've both done in the community."

"I'll do what I can, Father. But I can't make any promises." He closed the folder. "You can go now. Do you know your way out or shall we call Teresa again?"

Jim stood up. "No thanks. Enough memories for one day." He left the office and walked down the hall, responding cheerfully to a few "Good Morning, Father" salutations from officers. He looked back at Mark, who nodded in understanding.

- - -

Calling from the morgue, Ted told Mark that he and Wakefield had gone over the autopsy and toxicology notes and nothing seemed out of place. “As you know, there was the odd circular bruise in the middle of his chest. Why? No clear explanation. Could have happened falling in, or while he was already in the water. Other that that, there was nothing to indicate foul play. Wakefield wants to release the body to the Danzetti funeral home. What should I say?”

Mark knew that the bruise was the only thread they had.

“Measure the bruise and take photos. Ask Wakefield to estimate the depth. Let’s see what we can figure out. In the meantime, tell Wakefield he can release the body but to not record the cause of death until I speak to him.”

Mark looked at his watch. 11:45. He picked up his phone and called Jessie Fortunato, but he got the voicemail. “Mrs. Fortunato, this is Detective Porfino. The toxicology on Silvio came back. He had a high alcohol content but no other substances in his system. Coroner Wakefield is releasing the body to Danzetti’s. Please be assured that this investigation is not over. We are looking into every possibility. Please call me when you get this.”

Putting down the phone, he made notes about Wakefield’s findings in the Silvio folder. He wondered what could cause a large symmetric bruise in the middle of his chest. That had to be key to Silvio’s death. He looked at his watch, high noon. He was interviewing Gabe Cooper at one. Time to make a run to Taco Bell.

– – –

There wasn’t a lot of work in winter for Cooper Renovations, especially just before Christmas. Gabe sat at his desk going over invoices, while Lou was supervising the few projects they had this morning. He kept looking at his watch anticipating the one o’clock interview with Detective Porfino. He still had his alibi. The alternative was to confess.

At noon, he opened his bag lunch of a hastily assembled ham sandwich, chips, and a sad-looking pear. He switched on the TV in time for the news. Gail Walters, the noon anchor, was reporting on Silvio’s death and the ongoing investigation. Tony Wagner had been interviewed and was shown afterwards departing in Miriam's car.

Father Jim was shown entering and leaving about forty-five minutes later. He had not answered the reporter's questions and drove off.

Professor Amos had been interviewed earlier, and next on the agenda was Gabe Cooper, well-known businessman known to be at odds with Silvio. Gabe's picture appeared on the screen.

Putting down the sandwich, he dialed Jim's cell; voice mail. He left a message asking how the interview had gone. He wrote out a note for Lou that he would be out for the remainder of the day, and left the office. He slid into his car and drove to town.

- - -

Claire Woodward put down her macramé and turned on the noon news. Gail Walters was reporting on the death of Silvio and the resulting investigation. She watched Tony Wagner leaving the police station. I never liked that man, she thought.

Then Jim left the station. She pulled down her reading glasses. Why that looks like the young man who flipped me off the other night and just missed hitting me yesterday, she thought. She saw Jim get into his car and drive away. But there's that blue car again. Does he have two cars? These priests must make a lot of money.

She walked over to her roses. Walters was announcing that Professor Amos had also been interviewed and that Gabe Cooper would be interviewed next. Gabe's picture appeared, but Clair was busy pulling dead leaves off the roses. They were still blooming.

He does have nice taste in flowers though, she thought as she looked again at the card. She read "Sorry for my behavior last night." Claire mused. "No signature. I guess this young man wasn't proud of what he did Wednesday night."

- - -

Walking into the Long Harbor police station at 12:45, Gabe told the pretty desk officer that he had a one o'clock interview with Detective Porfino. She picked up the phone and dialed a three-digit extension.

"Gabe Cooper is here to see you." There was a pause. She put down the phone. "I'm to take you back. Follow me."

He staggered. The officer came over. "Are you okay?"

"I'm okay. Just got a little light headed."

Teresa smiled. "I guess this place will do it to you. Follow me."

As they walked down the hallway, Gabe saw that the officers working at their desks looked up as she passed, which was okay with Gabe. He was nervous enough without feeling like he was being scrutinized.

Teresa slowed and turned towards a glassed-in office. The blinds were open, revealing a man hurriedly finishing lunch.

Knocking twice on the metal frame, she went in, alone. She nodded towards Gabe and then spoke with Porfino for a minute. Gabe heard an "I understand, Officer. Thanks. Please have him come in."

Motioning to Gabe, she announced, "The detective will see you now."

Gabe walked in as Teresa left. Mark stood. "Gabe Cooper. I'm glad that you agreed to come in. Have a seat."

He walked over and closed the door after a last quick look in McGill's direction. He walked back to his desk, crumbled up a few wrappers and tossed them towards the wastebasket with the confidence of Lebron James burying a three. The shot bounced off the rim and landed on the floor.

Mark considered retrieving the wrappers but shrugged and returned to his chair.

"Teresa is a fine young officer, Gabe. I must say she's a darn good sport too. Her two days a week on front desk duty must be uncomfortable for her since these goofballs can't keep their eyes off her, and I'm no better. She handles it quite maturely, especially when you consider that she could beat the snot out of anyone out there. She takes intense martial arts training five days a week."

Moving aside his Cinnamon Twists and 40-oz. Pepsi, he glanced up to see Gabe staring at his desert. Mark smiled. "I guess I can't claim to eat right, or for that matter, exercise regularly."

Mark pulled over a notebook page marked *Gabriel Cooper*. "So, what's your regimen Gabe? I understand you lift a few several times a week at The Wharf. Tell me about that. Start with Wednesday night. Did you kill any?"

Gabe was startled by the directness. He expected a gradual lead-in to Wednesday. He had been drumming his fingers, but stopped and sat up.

"I went to The Wharf Wednesday with my brother Jim. We were there to kill a few, as you say."

Mark took a long pull on the Pepsi, the sound of air traveling through a straw indicating that the cup had surrendered its last. "I understand that Silvio came over and that you two had words."

"Silvio was angry about my relationship with Jessie and Rico. He said I was too close. He wanted me to back off and he threatened me. He said he could make me disappear. He could throw me into the Harbor and I'd never be seen again."

Mark wrote this down. "What did you say to that?"

"What could I say? He probably could have had me killed. I let him have his say and leave."

"I heard that he sampled Father Jim's chili and rice."

Gabe snorted. "Yeah. I guess he wanted to show me that he could do anything he wanted. Typical playground bully. That was Silvio."

Mark sat back to think: Gabe had as much reason to kill Silvio as Father Jim or Tony. If he didn't have an airtight alibi, I'd really lay into him.

Grabbing the half-empty Cinnamon Twists container, he went to put one in his mouth and saw Gabe staring. He waved the container towards Gabe in a "want one?" manner. Gabe shook his head.

"So, what happened when your brother Jim came in?"

"We talked for a few minutes as he ate some of the chili. I had ordered a new bowl for him. He emptied his draft and then he got up to talk to Silvio. They talked for a few minutes and really argued. Jim wanted to leave after that."

"Then what?"

Gabe hesitated. "We left and talked outside for a while. You know...brother talk. We were both pretty wired after dealing with Silvio. We decided to call it an evening. I started to walk home to sober myself up."

"You didn't drive after you left?"

Realizing he had just called his alibi into question, he said. "After a few minutes, I realized I'd have to retrieve my car the next day. I went back."

"Did anyone see you drive off?"

"I saw no one when I drove off. Why?"

Mark wrote a few notes. He looked up but didn't say anything. "Go on."

Gabe was sweating. What had Detective Porfino written down? What did he know?

"Anyway, I needed some time to clear my head. I decided to take a drive. I needed to go anywhere at all, just away from The Wharf."

"What time was this?"

"10:30 or so?" He wondered if he was the main suspect after all.

Mark held the Pepsi cup to the light. Nothing remained. No last sip.

"Continue."

Have to keep this plausible, Gabe thought. "I drove around, away from the city. I got to the slower two lane roads. I ended up behind a woman who was creeping along ten miles under the limit. I got impatient and gave her the finger. Not my finest moment."

"Mrs. Woodward. She called it in immediately. She is your alibi." He paused to let that take effect.

"Go on."

Gabe now knew that Porfino suspected him.

"Not much more detective. I realized I was being an idiot and decided to drive home. I got there around 11:30."

"And no one saw you after you flipped off Mrs. Woodward?"

"Not that I know of. I went home and slept it off."

Mark made a few more notes. He also flipped through a few pages after briefly studying each, and started to drum his fingers. Is he imitating me? Gabe wondered. For a moment, it seemed like he had forgotten that Gabe was even there. Finally, he closed the folder and looked up. "Ok. You're free to go...For now."

Gabe swayed before steadying himself.

"Anything else you want to say, Cooper?" This question and the use of his last name seemed mocking.

"Nothing else, Detective. Goodbye." He turned and walked out of the office and down the hall.

The detective stood in his doorway as he watched Gabe pass the officers at their desks. No stopping to chitchat, no waves. Just head down and pointed towards the exit. Mark thought that Gabe was the guiltiest man with an airtight alibi he'd ever seen.

He called Ted Hanson. "Ted, get me Gabe Cooper's cell records also." He thought a moment. "And call Claire Woodward. She lives in Glen Heights. Ask her if we can come over this afternoon for a visit."

The phone rang. "Detective Porfino. This is Jessie Fortunato. I got your message. Silvio's on his way to Danzetti's. We're setting the funeral for Thursday."

"Thank you, Mrs. Fortunato. Please know that we are not even close to finishing our investigation."

There was a pause. Jessie spoke with a broken voice. "So you agree with me that Silvio was murdered?"

He examined his cup one last time. "I have no doubt now. We'll get the guy, Mrs. Fortunato. I assure you."

- - -

Mario went straight to Fortunato Brothers from Lucy's. He spoke to Sal and they commiserated over Silvio. The foreman had taken it on himself to function for Silvio for both the plumbing calls and the sports book, and he briefed Mario on both ends. He was a good man, dedicated to each line of business.

Mario thanked him for covering, and told him he'd be here for this week to review the books and look into Silvio's death. Sal was to continue leading the day-to-day operations until Mario named a replacement.

Picking up the mail from the "In" basket, he strolled to Silvio's private office. He switched on the TV and swung into Silvio's rolling easy chair. The last few minutes of The Price is Right was on. He was sorting through the mail, mostly advertising flyers and a few bills, when he noticed an envelope addressed to Silvio. What stood out was that "Silvio" was in the middle in large letters.

It contained two thousand dollars in $100 denominations; no note inside, no return address. The postmark was Long Harbor.

"So who owes Silvio two grand?" he wondered. He put the envelope into his coat pocket. On TV, a woman with large flopping breasts and a loose t-shirt that read "Drew Carey Rocks" jumped up and down as she was named to the bonus round. She ran on stage and gave Carey a big kiss on the cheek. Carey looked more closely at her shirt and complimented her on her wardrobe.

Mario smiled. Not a bad job, he thought. He watched the bonus round focusing his attention on the ebullient woman. Her breasts fought to escape their Lycra prison as she spun the giant wheel. Fabric and fortune were with her that day and she won the grand prize.

Her "prisoners" jumped for joy as the credits rolled. Mario stood up to switch off the TV, but as he reached for the power button, a promo for the noon news promised an update on the investigation of Silvio's death.

He turned up the volume and sat back down. After the catchy opening tune with shots of Cambria and Long Harbor, the anchor came on with a report on the investigation. Tony Wagner, identified as a former detective and lead investigator of Enrico's death, was shown exiting the police station and driving away with Miriam. The reporter mentioned Jim Cooper and then Professor Amos. The creep who was trying to kiss Jessie Fortunato, Mario thought to himself. Well, well.

Then Gabe Cooper's picture appeared on the screen. So, both Coopers are in on this. I have my work to do.

He went over Silvio's books. Soon, Mario had a clear picture of where the two thousand came from.

His cell rang. He looked at the incoming number. It was his contact in the Long Harbor police. "Speak."

A young voice: "Uncle Mario...," He interrupted. "No 'uncle' here. In fact, no names. Speak."

"Sorry, Unc..., Sorry. Detective Porfino has requested cell records for Tony Wagner and Gabe Cooper. Wagner seems more promising but Cooper was the most nervous. Mark, er Detective Porfino, also set up an interview this afternoon with a Claire Woodward in Glen Heights. Not sure what that's about."

He jotted down 'Claire Woodward, Glen Heights.' "What about Professor Amos?" He heard a quiet laugh on the other end. "Stupid but harmless is the appraisal. Infatuated by Jessie Fortunato but no real suspicion there."

Mario was saddened by this. He would have liked to cause Amos some pain.

"What about Father Jim?" There was a pause. "His alibi is being investigated. Apparently, Father has been catting around. I'll know more tomorrow."

"Thanks. This was helpful. Say hello to our mutual friend."

A short laugh. "I will. Over and out."

He hung up and laughed to himself. "Over and out. She kills me. Still, it helps to have a niece in the police department."

- - -

Gabe returned to Cooper Renovations, ignored a hello from Lou, walked to his back office and closed the door. He flopped into his swivel chair and almost rolled into a file cabinet before lunging to grab a hold of the corner of his desk. He rolled back into his normal carpet groove and thought over what just happened.

I was a mess. Now Porfino suspects me. Maybe it's time to get it off my chest. It was self-defense. Why am I so afraid?

He picked up the phone and dialed Detective Porfino. After a few rings, Officer McGill came on. "Hello. This is Detective Porfino's office. He is not in the office, how can I help you?" Gabe was silent for a moment.

"Is this an emergency? Who is calling, please?" Gabe was shaking. He had to hold the phone with both hands. "No emergency." He hung up.

She had recorded the incoming number and made a note for Mark. Before she delivered it, she opened the department search app and entered in the caller id. "So, Gabe Cooper called back. He sounded nervous, too. This is getting better and better."

Wondering what to do next, Gabe looked at the stack of invoices on his desk. I guess I need to jump into this for a while. I'll call Jim and invite him to meet me at Lucy's for dinner. It's bean soup night.

- - -

Jim returned to the rectory after his interview. He raided Ray's refreshed stock of Flying Dog, walked to his office, kicked off his shoes and removed his collar. He fell into his chair and almost fell backwards.

Staring at the crucifix on the opposite wall, he took a few swigs and pulled out his cell, dialing Jan. Her voice mail came on. "Jan, this is Jim. I just interviewed with Detective Porfino."

He needed to speak to her in person. "We need to talk. Please get back to me. Detective Porfino will be calling or stopping by to speak with you. I'd really like to talk about this. Anywhere you want."

He hung up as Father Ray returned from visiting hospital patients. Jim stood and started to walk out of his office to meet Ray. It was time to give all the details about himself and Jan. He thought about taking his cell, but decided to leave it on his desk.

When she received Jim's call, Jan recognized the incoming number and let it go to voice mail. After a few minutes, she stepped away from her desk, went to the break room and retrieved the message. It must be out in the open, she thought, if he wants to meet anywhere. She dialed Jim's number. There was no answer and she hung up instead of leaving a voice mail.

Noticing another message, she selected it. Detective Porfino asked for an interview. He had an appointment in Glen Hills but would be in her area around four-thirty or five. Could he speak with her if she was available? She saved the message but didn't return the call. She considered what to do and concluded that she needed to see Jim first, and since it's all out in the open now, she may as well do it in St. Augustine's rectory. She'd go straight from work.

– – –

Tony sat quietly on the drive back to Miriam's, but loosened his tie and sank deeper into the seat. "They think I killed Silvio. And they also seem to suspect that I killed Enrico."

Miriam turned at Tony. "What? I thought the investigation was over and-"

"Red light!"

She turned her eyes back to the road and jammed on the breaks, but it was too late. They skidded through the intersection. There were no cars crossing, so at least no accident. There was, however, the bright flash from the red light camera.

"Great," sighed Tony. "I must be the most photographed man in town."

She regained her composure and continued driving. "What do we do now?"

"I'm not sure. I do have an ace up my sleeve with respect to Silvio's death. I'll play it if I need to. For now, it's more valuable to keep it to myself."

They arrived at Miriam's and sat in the driveway. "No matter what happens here, you won't be brought into it," he said. "Enrico was a real prick and he abused you and he wasn't going to stop. A lot of us wanted him dead. I just got the short straw, so to speak."

His sister started sobbing. "I thought this all went away. It wasn't easy knowing that you killed someone, even if it was for my safety. Be careful, Tony. You're the only one I have left."

"Let's go inside and get a stiff drink," Tony said calmly. "I want to check my contacts in the department and see what the sentiment is."

"I'll see what I can cook up," Miriam whispered as she dabbed her eyes.

Tony smiled. "Tell you what. Let me take care of a few things and then we'll go to Lucy's later. I think its bean soup night."

- - -

Mrs. Woodward returned Mark's call and said she would be delighted to talk. They agreed to meet in half an hour or so. He told Ted to grab his coat and meet him out front in a cruiser in five minutes. They were going for a ride to Glen Hills.

Putting the notes for Gabe Cooper, Jim Cooper, Tony Wagner, and John Amos into his satchel, he told Teresa that he'd be out the rest of the afternoon. She was to take his messages.

Ted was in his cruiser with the motor running. Mark climbed into the passenger side. This was an experience. He rarely sat in a fully loaded police car: there was a video recorder, speed gun, two-way speaker connection to the dispatcher, and what looked like a video monitor. "To check on drivers I pull over, real time identification," explained Ted as he switched on the siren. A series of "whoop whoops" told all present they were ready to go. Ted also pulled out his taser and patted it. "Ready, Detective."

Mark shook his head and laughed, pointing to the roof. "You can turn that off." Ted was disappointed, but complied. "There's also no need for the taser. "We're going after a nice old lady."

- - -

Claire was thrilled to receive the call from Detective Porfino. She invited him to come over right away and proceeded to clean her already-immaculate house. She put coffee on and opened a new tin of Danish cookies. "Imagine coming all this way to interview me about a rude driver." She straightened up the roses and removed a dying leaf that she'd missed when she'd fed them earlier in the day.

Propping up the card from her mysterious yet contrite rose patron, she thought, "I guess this poor young man will soon be meeting with Lady Justice. I hope she looks kindly on him."

She looked around her living room, closed an open magazine, wiped imaginary dust from the coffee table, fluffed up both couch end pillows, sat in her easy chair, and waited.

Mark and Ted arrived thirty minutes later. Ted started to knock but Mark stopped him and rang the doorbell instead. *Fly me to the Moon* it chimed. They both laughed and straightened themselves as they heard footsteps approach the door. "Coming, Officers."

The door opened revealing a thin four-foot smiling senior in a floral print dress, wiry and alert. She uttered a rousing "Please come in," directed them to hang their coats on the hallway stand, and gestured for them to have a seat on her couch. Mark introduced himself as lead detective for the Long Harbor police department and the man who took her 911 call. He introduced Ted Hanson as his investigator, causing Ted to beam.

She offered coffee and walked into the kitchen to prepare a tray. The men sat on the plush couch, sinking in as the cushions welcomed and embraced them.

Mark looked around the room. "Very clean and bright," he said. It was sparsely furnished with a rocking easy chair, some knitting supplies sitting on an adjacent tray table, the comfortable couch, a few end tables with tiffany lamps, and, in the corner, a small TV. Next to the TV was a round accent table with a vase filled with red roses, with a card displayed next to them. He attempted to stand and almost fell back onto the couch as the cushion refused to yield. He steadied himself and walked over to the roses. He picked up the card. "Sorry for my bad behavior last night."

Claire walked in and put the tray on the coffee table in front of Ted, who poured a cup and added some cream from a metal cow. He picked up the cup and started to drink. Claire looked up and saw Mark reading the card. "That's from the nice young man who flipped me the bird Wednesday night."

Ted did a spit take worthy of any sitcom. The coffee sprayed about a foot, landing on the coffee table and splattering Claire's dress. He coughed and spat out a sincere "Very sorry. Please excuse me," as he caught his breath.

Grabbing a napkin and dabbing at the coffee on her dress, she calmly said, "No need to apologize. These things happen. No harm done. It will wash out."

He took another napkin and hurriedly cleaned the coffee from the table.

She turned again towards Mark. "Those *are* beautiful roses, aren't they? The young man has good taste despite his lack of civility. I understand that you are here to discuss his behavior."

Mark smiled. "Yes, please." He walked back to the couch, sitting gingerly. He smiled at Ted, who looked like a schoolchild just caught picking his nose. Pouring a cup of coffee and adding two spoonfuls of sugar with what had to be the world's smallest spoon, he also picked a few butter cookies from the plate. After a bite, Claire received a sincere "Ummmmm."

Ted reached over and picked up a few cookies with both hands, looking to avoid a second faux pas. He took a bite and joined Mark in his verbal appraisal.

This little get together was going well, she thought. She poured herself a cup of coffee, selected some butter cookies and sank into her chair. "So, how can I help you gentlemen? I hope you aren't going to be too severe on the young man. It's not like he killed someone after all."

Ted coughed but caught himself before butter cookie crumbs went flying. Mark handed Ted a napkin and smiled at Mrs. Woodward. "Mrs. Woodward..." She stopped him. "Please, call me Claire, Detective, and you too young man. No need for formality here."

Mark nodded and continued, "We just want to make sure that you can clearly identify the man who made this gesture. I want to give him a talking to."

"Okay. Please don't be too stern. We all do things that we regret later."

He opened the folder and pulled out an old picture of Gabe, wearing a Cooper Renovations golf shirt and standing near a completed landscaping.

"Is this the man?"

Claire put on her bifocals and looked it over carefully. "We'll, it could be. I only really saw the back of his head and his eyes in his rear view mirror. I don't suppose you have a picture of the back of his head?"

Mark smiled and looked at Ted, who shrugged. Ted picked up the Jim Cooper picture. Jim was in his vestments after a community mass. "How about this man?"

Putting Gabe's picture down, she took Jim's photo. "He's a priest, well, well. I've seen this man around town a lot lately. In fact, he almost hit me after nearly running a red light the other day. It's funny. When I saw him, I thought it was the same man as from Wednesday. Except, he was driving a blue car. The car Wednesday was yellow."

Mark looked at Ted and then back at Claire. "Can you definitely identify Wednesday's driver as this man, Father Jim Cooper?"

Confused and getting upset, she shook her head. "They both look so much alike. It was only for a minute while we were at the red light."

Mark picked out the pictures of Tony Wagner and John Amos. "I don't suppose that you recognize either of these men, do you?"

"Well, neither of these gentlemen flipped me off, if that's what you're asking."

She looked closer at the picture of Tony Wagner. "That's Detective Wagner, isn't it?"

"Yes, it is. He retired three years ago. We have been speaking to him about Silvio's death."

She frowned and was clearly angry. "I never liked that man. I always thought he was dirty. Don't believe a word that man says, Detective. He's got criminal written all over him. I may be old, but I know people. He's dirty."

Mark put the pictures back into the folder, grabbed a few cookies, and put them into a napkin, which he then deposited into his pocket. He stood while waving Ted up also.

"Thanks for your time and hospitality, Mrs. Woodward. You've been a big help."

"You're welcome, Detective, and you, also, young man. It was my pleasure to help."

The men retrieved their coats and walked into the late winter afternoon air. They turned and waved to Claire, who smiled and waved back.

Ted spoke up. "I guess we need to talk to the Coopers again. Get this alibi situation straightened out."

Mark nodded. "But I still like Tony Wagner for this. Old ladies are like weather vanes. They always point in the right direction."

Dialing Jan's cell after returning to the patrol car, Mark hoped for an answer. None. He left a message: "Miss Gillek, this is Detective Porfino. I was in the area and hoped to speak to you about your activities Wednesday night. This is my second call to you. I know about your relationship with Jim Cooper. I don't want to have to subpoena you. Please call me back."

Ted looked over. "Should we drive to her house and wait?"

"No. That's enough crime fighting for one day. I'm hungry. Let's go to Lucy's and grab some dinner, my treat. It's bean soup night."

- - -

Jan pulled into the St. Augustine's parking lot and saw the new message on her cell. She listened to Detective Porfino's message, sighed, and walked to the rectory. Before she could ring the bell,

Father Ray opened the door.

"Hello, Father."

"Hello, Miss Gillek. Father Jim and I were just discussing you. Please, come in."

Jan gave a weak smile and walked in. Father Ray led her into the dining room where Jim was sitting in front of a couple of empty Flying Dogs.

Jan felt outnumbered. "I have an idea. Let's all go to Lucy's. It's bean soup night."

– – –

Chapter 10

They Shall be Known in the Breaking of the Bread

Lucy's was famous for its Monday night bean soup. It was rumored that Lucy Morgan, proprietor, had attained the recipe though an exchange of services with a TV chef in town for the night waiting for his Maserati to be repaired after breaking down on the interstate. While not likely true—the Maserati part at least, not Lucy's loose interpretation of hospitality—it enlivened the mystique already surrounding this otherwise typical northeast diner.

Tonight's crowd was like any other Monday: blue-collar men with their wives and kids in tow; and singles looking for a quick meal.

Mario sat by himself at a corner booth as the diner filled. He had nursed a Flying Dog and now plunged spoon first into a bowl of the bean soup, which was quite an act of faith after his misadventure with the creamed chipped beef. He was waited on by his favorite waitress, Sheila, who must have been a looker years ago, he thought.

The bean soup was quite good, with chunks of ham, beans not too soggy, and just right with the onions. Lucy must have driven a hard bargain. Mario had just ordered a second bowl along with more cheesy bread and a Flying Dog, when he saw Gabe Cooper enter.

Gabe looked like someone had just run over his dog. Mario was going to call over to him, when he heard a "Yo, Gabe," and Gabe turn to the caller and smiled. He walked over to the table where Jessie and Rico were seated. Rico slid over to allow Gabe to join them in the booth.

Jessie, the grieving widow, was all smiles. She looked at Gabe, exchanged pleasantries and seemed almost giddy that Gabe had joined them. Mario wondered about this effect Gabe had on the Fortunatos. Rico looked at him with what might be described as hero worship. Jessie looked more interested in ripping his clothes off.

I guess grief takes many forms, Mario thought. Still, I wonder if anything is going on. Silvio had hinted that Jessie might be having an affair.

The front door opened again and the bells attached to a rod over the door announced a new entrant. In walked Tony Wagner, and his sister Miriam. Tony looked like he had just run over someone's dog. Miriam was somber. The hostess showed Tony and Miriam to a small table.

Mario slid down to avoid being spotted. Sheila walked over with the Flying Dog and a piping hot bowl of soup and noticed his act of concealment. "Hiding from an ex-girlfriend are we? I don't see you with Miriam Wagner. Good to get out while you can. She and Enrico had quite a thing going before he died. She may look like a schoolmarm, but she's a wildcat. And her brother is protective of her."

Playing along, Mario already knew this. "I thought Enrico slept around."

"He sure did, Honey. He couldn't keep it in his pants. But he was smitten with Miriam and very controlling. I wasn't surprised when he showed up dead. I just couldn't figure out why they let Tony Wagner run the investigation into his murder." She paused for effect. "I mean his untimely, accidental death."

Mario raised his beer in a toast to Sheila. "Sheila, you are a wealth of information. There's an extra $20 in your tip if you come up with anything else tonight." Sheila smiled. This guy is gold, she thought as she walked away. It pays to know everyone's business.

Mario looked around and wondered if he was dining with Silvio's murderer. Maybe two murderers, if you count Enrico. He took another swig of beer and attacked the bean soup with new vigor. Damn, better than the first, he thought.

As he was opening a pack of oyster crackers, the front door bells rang again. In walked Father Jim and Father Ray from St. Augustine's. With them was a wholesome yet hot late-thirtyish woman who seemed to be leading the threesome in their quest for bean soup. She smiled like she had just stolen Fr. Ray's dog.

The hostess sat them near Gabe, Jessie, and Rico. There were awkward hellos. The brothers Cooper regarded each other with "what the fuck" stares. Then, the reverends and their femme fatale sat down and opened their menus.

What's going on there? Mario looked around for Sheila, his mole, as he pondered the cast of characters chatting, slurping, and stealing looks at the other diners.

He grabbed a roll, still warm, broke it open, slathered enough butter on it to assure future arterial blockage, and took a slow bite with eyes closed. It was heaven on earth. I'm going to marry this Lucy; that is, if Sheila doesn't steal my heart first, he thought.

Another jingle of the front door caused him to open his eyes and look over. In walked Detective Mark Porfino and a patrolman he didn't know. The hostess looked around for an empty table and found one next to Mario.

She placed menus on the table as Mark and Ted noticed Mario. He raised his beer in salute. Mark smiled as he sat down. Ted nodded uncomfortably and settled with his back to Mario. In the adjacent wall-length mirror, Mario could see Ted mouthing to Mark, "That's Silvio's boss." Mark returned an "I know."

Ted looked over the menu. Mark had no need to look. Bean soup, meatloaf, and a Flying Dog. Why complicate things with a menu?

Mark looked around and saw Gabe sitting with Jessie and her son. He tapped Ted's arm, tilted his head and said "Ted, we're dining with friends."

"Well I'll be dipped," he said.

They both looked around and saw Father Jim, Father Ray, and a woman who had to be Jan Gillek.

"This is unreal. Who else is here?" Mark said. Glancing another forty-five degrees, he saw Tony Wagner, fully engaged in a bowl of bean soup while his sister sat stirring her bowl listlessly, lost in thought.

"I couldn't get this group together with a subpoena," Mark said, as he completed his loop and saw Mario, smiling. He called over to Mark, "You couldn't write this, no one would believe it."

Just then another chime: Professor Amos with a young blond, no doubt a coed infatuated with environmental science. Amos looked like he had just gotten a puppy from the kennel and wanted to show it off. He stopped smiling when he realized that half of the restaurant had stopped eating and was looking at him. He collected himself and followed the hostess towards the back, his blond student in tow.

The path to the table took Amos past Gabe, Jessie, and Rico. He stopped and said, "Jessie and Rico, it's good to see you out and about. This is much better than sitting in your house mourning. Life must go on."

He looked at Gabe. "And Mr. Cooper, providing aid and comfort in this time of need. How are things?"

Gabe shrugged his shoulders. "Fine, professor. Out on a student trip, I see."

Amos looked towards his ingénue, who appeared somewhat embarrassed. "This is Amy. She's in my environmental science class. We're taking a break from the rigors of study. Rico, I believe that you already know Amy."

Rico looked stunned. He and Amy had dated briefly. "Hello, Amy, you look lovely."

Amy smiled. "Thanks, Rico."

After a pause, Amos shrugged. "Awkward."

The hostess stood at the empty table. Amos waved at her. "We must be going. We mustn't keep our hostess from her appointed duties."

Rico watched as Amos and Amy sat down. He turned back to see Gabe staring at Jessie, who was seething. "Who thought he'd turn out to be a prick?"

Jessie broke out of her trance and looked at her son. "You don't know the half of it."

Mario, Mark, and Ted had watched the exchange. "I think we have to start taking notes," Mario said. "I'm getting confused."

Mark shook his head. "That's why I love this job."

The policemen ordered in the time gap when no one else of interest entered. Ted opted for the vegetable soup.

Mark looked at him. "Ted, when in Rome."

"Make that a big bowl of your bean soup."

He looked at Mark, who gave a nodding approval. "And

meatloaf?" Mark smiled and nodded.

"Do you have Chablis?" he asked. Mark stared again. "Make that a Flying Dog."

The detectives started talking about the day's events. Mario ordered another bowl of soup and more of the rolls.

The doorbells rang as if bored at the inactivity. In walked Mr. Richardson holding Reggie in his arms. Reggie looked remarkably calm. Lucy's didn't normally allow animals, but Reggie had won the hearts of the staff and was now considered an honorary person. The hostess smiled, exchanged greetings with Mr. Richardson, then went behind the counter and brought out a bowl marked *Reggie* in Sharpie blue. They started to walk towards an empty table in the back.

Mr. Richardson stopped when he saw Gabe, Jessie, and Rico. Reggie started squirming, clearly agitated. "Mrs. Fortunato and young Rico, I am so sorry to hear of your loss. I can picture talking to your father like it was yesterday."

He turned towards Gabe who was drained of color and eyeing Reggie. "And my neighbor, Gabe. Here, no doubt, for the bean soup, and to console the saddened family. I'm sure Silvio is watching over this moment now and smiling."

Barking loudly and squirming, Reggie started to get loose. Mr. Richardson steadied his grip on Reggie. "Reggie, please. Don't be rude to our friends, especially in this public place."

He looked at Jessie again. "Sorry. Reggie was very fond of Silvio. He would give Reggie a treat whenever he saw us walking through town and the few times I needed to conduct *business* with him." He gave a wink on business.

He looked over at Gabe and then at Jessie. "I always thought Silvio and Reggie were kindred spirits. Maybe because they could smell a rat a mile away." He looked towards the hostess. "Ah, our table awaits. They give Reggie a treat each time he's here. The bean soup doesn't agree with him, though." Mr. Richardson laughed. "I found that out the hard way."

He walked towards the table with a firm grip on Reggie. They passed Tony Wagner and Miriam's table as Tony was returning from the Men's room. Reggie again started to bark and growl. Tony jumped, startled at the high-pitched noise. Recognizing Reggie as his annoying intruder from Wednesday night, he shouted, "That fucking dog again."

Everyone's attention was drawn to the scene. The f-bomb will do that. He noticed Mark Porfino and Ted Hanson watching intently. "Look mister, sorry for the language. Just keep your dog under control. People are trying to have a quiet meal here."

Mr. Richardson stroked Reggie's head. "There, there Reggie. We mustn't disturb the diners. I am sorry, Sir. I don't know what's gotten into Reggie. He hasn't been the same since he ran away Wednesday night. Is that when you met him?"

Tony had Mark and Mario's complete attention. "I guess it was. I stopped on the harbor lookout to smoke a cig and take in the night air. You're filthy mud-caked mongrel ran right into me. I'll admit, I gave him a swift kick. Maybe that's why he's angry. Keep him on a leash from now on."

"Young man, I'd rather keep him chained than have him deal with the likes of you and your temper." Mr. Richardson looked towards his table. "Now, if you'll excuse me, we are preparing to dine. Good evening to you, Sir and your lady friend." With that, Mr. Richardson walked away.

Ted looked at Mark. "So Wagner admits to being at the harbor around the time of Silvio's death. Maybe he's good for the killing."

"Or maybe he saw who did it," Mark said.

Mario appeared deep in thought. Seeing Mark staring, he said, "You have your work cut out for you, Detective. Who's your money on?"

Mark smiled. "I'm not a betting man."

"That's a pity. Maybe we could work out the line on who's the killer."

The waitress arrived at Mark and Ted's table with the bean soup and Flying Dogs. Mark signaled to the food and Mario nodded. "Enjoy," he said and stood up.

"Detective, I need to recycle the beer and some of the soup. If Sheila comes over, please tell her to leave more of the cheesy bread. Oh, and tell her to bring a Bread Pudding with plenty of whipped cream." Mark waved his spoon to signal compliance.

Mario sauntered to the Men's Room, pushed open the door,

positioned himself at a urinal, unzipped and emptied as he whistled an Italian opera favorite. He finished, shook the required two times, and headed for the sink.

He washed his hands and as he dried, bent over and looked to see if the stalls were occupied. Taking out his cell, he called a Cambria number. "This is Mario. I'm going to need you for a few days. Come into Long Harbor tomorrow and we'll talk in the office. I'll tell them you came in to help with the books."

Mario listened to the response. "No. I'm not sure who yet, but I'll know soon."

Starting for the door, he realized that his bending to check the stalls had started a reaction. He did a 180 and headed from the first stall. He had barely lowered his pants and positioned himself on the throne when the gastronomic excesses of the evening manifested themselves in a dark liquid thunderstorm. He flushed and prepared to clean himself when a second front moved in, as telling as the first. Mario realized that he had to wait out the storm.

In the meantime, Mark had wolfed down his soup and decided to spend the time until the meatloaf arrived by greeting the assembled guests. He told Ted to enjoy his soup and that he'd be back in a minute. Ted decided to visit the Men's room while Mark socialized.

As Ted approached the door, he saw Mario walking out. Mario smiled and said, "I wouldn't go in there for a few minutes, Officer. It's not for the feint of heart."

"I am an officer of the law, Mr. Gallante. I am ready for anything."

"As you say. Good luck and Godspeed."

As Mario headed back to his table, he heard a distressed "Oh, my God!" He shook his head and walked calmly away.

\- - -

Mark walked towards Gabe, Jessie, and Rico's booth, but stopped first at Mr. Richardson's table to introduce himself. He patted Reggie, who was calmly gnawing on cheesy bread. Mr. Richardson smiled. "I've heard of you, Detective. You have a reputation for being thorough and forthright. Sorry about Reggie's outbursts. I hope you're not planning to take him away."

"No sir. Dogs will be dogs. However, I'd like to hear more about Reggie's disappearance Wednesday. I'd like to invite you to my office tomorrow. You appear to be a wealth of knowledge on Long Harbor and its inhabitants. How about ten?"

Baring a toothy grin, the man replied, "I'd be delighted, Detective. Reggie and I would be glad to help."

"Tomorrow, then. Enjoy your soup. And try the cheesy bread, if you can get it away from Reggie."

He walked on and nodded to Professor Amos and his coed. Amos gave an embarrassed smile. "He's stupid, but probably innocent," Mark thought.

Passing Tony and Miriam's table, Mark stopped and smiled. "Good evening. I'm just doing my rounds while waiting for my meatloaf."

Tony sat back, put down his knife, which he had been using to slathering butter on a slice of cheesy bread, and said, "Hello again detective. You know my sister, Miriam?"

"I do. Hello, Miriam."

"That was quite a commotion with Mr. Richardson's dog. Maybe we can talk more tomorrow about your rest stop. How does eleven sound?"

He turned towards Miriam. "You are welcome also if you're not otherwise engaged."

Tony bristled. "I'll come in again Mark, but there's no need for Miriam to disrupt her day. Now if you don't mind our dinner is coming." He saw the waitress arrive with a prime rib completely covering the plate, and an order of fries that could single handedly cause a heart attack. There was also a chef's salad. No difficulty telling whose meal was whose.

Mark continued his journey until he reached Jan, Father Ray and Father Jim. Jan was nibbling on a piece of bread, Jim was poking at the bean soup seemingly lost in thought, and Father Ray was chowing down like Lent was just hours away.

Mark uttered a rousing, "Hello."

"Detective. How are you? Just three friends here having a quick dinner after a long day."

"I'm sure this has been quite a day for all three of you, Father Ray.

I won't be long."

He turned towards Jan. "Miss Gillek. I keep leaving messages but we can't seem to connect. Let's make this a command performance. Please come down to the station tomorrow afternoon. Does one-ish sound okay? Assuming, of course, Father Jim doesn't have you tied up."

Jim had been drinking a Diet Coke trying to appear nonchalant. This remark, however, caused the second spit take of the day. Father Ray looked at his sleeve and calmly brushed the liquid from his coat.

Picking up his napkin, Jim started wiping Ray's sleeve. Ray waved him off. "It's okay, Jim."

Jan spoke up. "I'll be there, Detective."

"I appreciate the cooperation. One tomorrow, then?"

Jan nodded. Mark waved, uttered a "bon appetite" and started towards Gabe, Jessie, and Rico.

- - -

Mark was thinking how productive this dinner had been. He hadn't even attacked his meatloaf yet, and the suspect list was narrowing. He hoped the winner would be Tony Wagner, although he sort of liked Gabe. He looked over at his own table. The waitress was bringing the meatloaf. He looked at Ted, who looked pale. He then glanced at Mario who was laughing and apparently saying something to him. I need to save Ted. Just a few more minutes here, he thought.

Mark stopped at Gabe's table and waited respectfully until he caught Jessie's attention. She put down her soupspoon.

"Detective Porfino. It's nice of you to stop over. I left a message. Silvio's funeral will be Wednesday instead of Thursday. I think there's no reason to prolong the waiting."

Mark nodded. "I understand. Please know that we are investigating Silvio's death as a murder. Of course, you already suspected that. We'll get the guy, Mrs. Fortunato. The chips will fall where they will."

Turning towards Rico, he said, "Take care of your mother. Don't let her be influenced by those wishing to capitalize on this."

Rico seemed confused by this statement and looked at Gabe.

That was too easy, Mark thought. "Not that people won't sincerely try to comfort your Mother and yourself. Just proceed with caution."

"Detective, I'll protect my Mother."

Rico then turned completely towards Mark. "We may not have seen eye to eye on many matters, but I owe it to my dad to protect my mom and make sure the killer gets what's coming to him."

This comment and tone unsettled Jessie. Mark was also surprised by this sudden change in Rico. He looked at Gabe, who seemed somewhat unnerved.

Mark bent down, put his palms on the table, and faced the young man.

"I understand, but let the police get down to matters on this. We'll find your father's killer."

Turning to Gabe, he smiled. "Gabe, it's good to see that you're comforting the Fortunatos. A friend in need, I guess. Let's talk again tomorrow. There are a few things I need to clear up about your whereabouts on Wednesday night. Let's say two?" Jessie and Rico looked at Gabe inquiringly.

"Now, I have meatloaf and mashed potatoes waiting for me." He looked towards his table. "I also appear to have an associate who looks like he's somewhat in shock. I hope it's not the meatloaf. I'm starving. Enjoy the rest of your evening."

On the way back to his table, he passed Ray, Jim, Jan, Tony Wagner, Miriam, and Professor Amos. Ray looked unphased by the recent interaction with Mark. He was busy swigging a Flying Dog and stuffing himself with bread. I guess nothing surprises him anymore. Must a good trait to have, he thought.

Jim was stirring his soup and squeezing his bread like a baseball pitcher adjusting his grip from fastball to slider.

Jan had broken off half of a bread and put the other half back. Must be saving a few calories, he thought. Jim and Jan had looked down, hoping not to make eye contact.

Tony stared at his soup and appeared lost in thought. He picked up a new slice of bread and stared to eat it slowly without slathering on butter. Pure heresy for Lucy's. Clearly, his mind was elsewhere.

Miriam munched on a slice of bread coated heavily with butter. She seemed lost in thought also but it wasn't affecting her appetite. No half slice for her, Mark thought. I wonder where she fits in this puzzle.

Amos attacked the bread and had butter lodged in his beard; he was in deep conversation when not chewing. The coed had ordered a salad and skipped the soup and bread. She looked uncomfortable, maybe thinking that there must be an easier way to get an A.

Continuing toward his table, he spotted Mario grinning like a fool, and digging into an enormous bread pudding. Mark smiled at Mario and sat down. Ted was on his cell; he whispered, "See you later," and disconnected.

Mark nodded towards Mario. Ted looked over and saw him raise his spoon to the men in salute. "I wonder where he puts it."

"Walk into the Men's room and you'll find out. They may need a hazmat unit."

Mark laughed loud enough for most of the restaurant to hear. His persons of interest all looked over. This night had not been hilarious for most of them.

"Care to join me, gentlemen?" Mario called over.

They declined. "We have some things to discuss between ourselves," Mark replied.

Mario dabbed at his mouth, saw a gob of whipped cream on his napkin and licked it off. "Maybe we can talk some other time. Tonight has been interesting."

Mark raised his Flying Dog in salute, and started catching Ted up on the conversations as he attacked his meatloaf and mashed potatoes.

A few minutes later, Mario stood, peeled off a twenty as a tip, laid it on the table and said goodbye to Mark and Ted. He also made sure to greet the assembled persons of interest as he walked by. Everyone knew who he was. If they weren't nervous before, they were now.

Ted stood. "I have to go. I'm meeting someone." He pulled out his wallet but Mark waved him off. "It's on me. We'll do this again when we nail Silvio's killer."

The young officer strolled out of Lucy's and headed down the street. After a few minutes, he climbed the front steps of an apartment building, entered an apartment number on the security key pad and buzzed. The voice of Teresa McGill came over. "Come on up."

- - -

Chapter 11

Give Us Barabbas

Tuesday morning. The headline in the Long Harbor Press read, "FORTUNATO TO BE BURIED WEDNESDAY." The subheading read, "Persons of Interest Grilled at Lucy's". Mark laughed and shook his head. I guess everything that happens at Lucy's is public domain, he thought.

He read the story by beat reporter Lisa Channing. She had the details right. Either she was there also or she knew someone who was. I wouldn't put it past Sheila, he thought.

The article took him to page four. When he finished, he noticed an adjacent article titled "The Death of a Mobster. Is the Killer a Hero or Villain?"

The article was by John Gibson, senior contributor. Great, the town hothead. I wonder which way *he* sees it.

The article was an indictment of organized crime activity in Long Harbor, especially illegal sports betting and the inability of the police to rid the town of its influence. "Now someone has drowned the serpent," the article stated. "Bully for him. May it happen to his cohorts and to his masters in Cambria."

In italics at the end of each article was a note indicating these articles were also posted on the Long Harbor Press web page and comment was welcomed. Mark closed the door to his office and opened the web site on his monitor. He chose the Newsroom link.

After each article was a comment section. Channing was praised for her thorough reporting. Most readers were amused by the happenstance of all parties being present at the same time.

The comments were almost unanimously supportive of Gibson's "hang 'em high" approach and agreed the perpetrator should be awarded a medal. One reader concluded that Silvio got just what his brother Enrico before him got and that it was well deserved.

Only a few respondents called for calm to allow the police to conduct an investigation. The responders to this opinion scoffed and cited the hasty conclusion that Enrico died accidentally. "So much for justice," one concluded.

That's not happening on my watch, Mark thought. I intend to get the killer of both brothers.

His ringing cell interrupted his musing. It was Adam Wakefield. "Mark, about the bruise on Silvio's chest."

"Yeah?"

"I think it's a head butt. It's the right shape and the depth would indicate that the killer hit him with some force. Maybe ran at him. Looks like a men's large hat size but that's a guess."

"Not sure if that narrows it down, Adam. Do me a favor, look over Enrico's records and see if there's a similar bruise."

"I took the liberty. No similar bruise. The first killing, if it was murder, was more cleverly carried out. I'm not even sure how the killer got him into in the water. Silvio's death was more brute force. It was possibly an act out of a moment of passion or, maybe, even self-defense."

"Adam, you'll be a detective yet. Call me if you ever get tired of slicing people open."

Adam laughed. "Will do."

- - -

Ted walked into Mark's office carrying a copy of the Long Harbor Press opened to the John Gibson article. Mark waved him to a chair.

"We have a full round of interviews today, Ted. Maybe I was impulsive to bring everyone back one day later, but I want to keep the pressure on. One of these people killed Silvio. I need to bring the guy in before they erect a statue to him."

Mark pulled his Jim Cooper notes; the womanizing priest. "What do you think about Father Jim, Ted?"

"He's not likely to be a killer. Also, if Miss Gillek vouches for him, there's not much else to go on. I think his brother is more interesting.

If we could just shake his alibi."

Mark nodded as he took the picture of Gabe. "Model citizen. He's a pillar of the community, yet, he's pretty chummy with Jessie. I know they used to date in high school. Then apparently it fizzled out."

"I hear it was Gabe who cooled things off. Mrs. Fortunato is pretty hot. Maybe he's gay."

This bothered Mark. "Ted, people are complicated. Gabe must have had his reasons for ending it with Jessie." He studied Gabe's picture. "Maybe Gabe felt protective of Jessie. Silvio was known to be pretty rough on her and Rico. Maybe Gabe had enough and did him in."

Ted shrugged. "Still, it could only have been a crime of opportunity. Gabe doesn't appear cunning enough or to have the mettle to have planned this."

Mark agreed. "Ted, you have a good intuition and sense of reasoning. You'll be a detective yet."

"Thanks, Mark. This is fun," he said, then added, "If it wasn't for all the killing."

"Got ya."

Ted craned his neck to see the next page of notes. "What about Professor Amos?"

Mark searched for his picture and examined it. "No," he said, "he's a bit of a hot head, I hear, and I think his dick got the better of him over Jessie Fortunato. I just don't see him killing Silvio over her. If he had, he wouldn't have flaunted the coed in front of her."

Tony's picture came next. "And now for the man I love to hate: Tony Wagner. He whitewashed Enrico's investigation and left town. I think he killed the man. So does Chief Benson."

Ted sat up. "Do you think he left to remove suspicion?"

"What do you think, Ted? Did Wagner run a thorough investigation on Enrico's death?"

Ted frowned. "It was my first case. I didn't want to question the approach of a seasoned detective. I think he left some things dangling, but I felt uncomfortable asking."

"Like what?"

He appeared to be trying to put his thoughts into words.

"Tony didn't seem willing to look into possible suspects. Enrico had been seen arguing with both Silvio and Mario the night before. I believe it was over Miriam. He wasn't very discrete and his abuse of Miriam was becoming well known in town. Also, Tony himself couldn't stand the man. Chief was insisting that Tony pass the case on to someone else, but Tony insisted he could do the job."

Staring at the ceiling, Mark thought this over. "Do you think Mario or Silvio, his own brother, could have killed Enrico?"

Ted shook his head. "Silvio, no. Brothers work things out differently. There was no Cain and Abel there. But Mario is a practical man. If it was hurting the business, Mario wouldn't be above having him killed. He wouldn't even be above having Tony do it."

"You've thought this over, Ted."

Ted nodded. "But there's a long way between conjecture and proving it. You also don't advance in a police department by accusing superiors of murder."

"No, you don't. So let's see if Tony is good for Silvio's killing. He was spotted in the vicinity and he seems to be holding something back."

"Yeah. Like he thinks he'll get away with it again."

Mark closed the folder. "Or if he didn't do it, he knows who did."

- - -

Jim walked through the rectory, his coat on and head down. Father Ray was preparing to leave for morning mass when he spotted Jim. "Jim, come in here please."

He looked at his watch. "I was going out to see Jan. I wanted to speak with her before she was interviewed by Detective Porfino."

"That's not 'til one. How's it going with your sermon for Silvio's funeral mass?"

Putting his gloves on the desk, Jim unbuttoned his coat and sat down. "Well, I started it Saturday between confessions. Then I put it on hold with everything else happening. It's not going to be easy to write. I don't want to present him as a saint."

"Regardless, I need you to get cracking on the sermon. It's tomorrow and we need to be ready. This is the closest thing Long Harbor will have to a high-profile funeral and there will be press coverage. I want the service to be respectful even if Silvio was a slug. Have you read the papers? His killer is being hailed as a hero."

Ray continued. "Yet others, such as Mario, are waiting to find out who did it. Mario's not going to pin a medal on whoever did it, that's for sure. We can't have people thinking that law and order can be ignored. Your sermons are improving, Jim. Crank out a good one for Silvio. Don't kiss his ass, but explain how it affects us all. Murder in a small town, tight community, all of that. But vengeance is never the answer. You get the idea. Let's restore sanity before this gets out of hand."

Jim stared at the ceiling, then looked back at his boss. "Maybe this will be a penance for screwing up my life by getting involved with Silvio in the first place. I'll work on it now. Let me just call Jan and arrange to meet her later."

"Knock 'em dead Jim. Just nothing about drowning your demon, okay?"

\- - -

Mr. Stanley Richardson, 80ish retired high school civics teacher and oracle of human nature, accompanied by his faithful companion Reggie, was shown to Mark's office promptly at ten a.m. Teresa announced the presence of man and dog to the detectives. On making eye contact with Ted, Teresa blushed, a change of color noticed both by Mark and Richardson. Reggie seemed oblivious.

She turned and walked down the hall, to the admiring gaze of Richardson, Mark, and half of the officers in adjoining cubes. Ted seemed agitated that Teresa was on the receiving end of lustful stares. Stanley sighed. "If only I was only 50 years younger and a stud like young Hanson," he sighed. "Oh well. Life goes on."

Mark regained his focus and waved Stanley to a seat. "Would you like something to drink?"

"Perhaps something for Reggie. I carry my own."

With that, he pulled out a flask of Jim Beam and unscrewed the cap. He took a whiff and then, satisfied that the contents were fresh, downed a healthy swig. Mark and Ted were staring. "Oh, where are my manners?" He waved the flask around. "Gentlemen, care to partake?"

Ted shook his head. Mark smiled. "No thanks, Mr. Richardson. It's a little too early for me. It's ten a.m."

Stanley looked at the clock. "I don't have many ten a-ems left. Might as well enjoy."

Ted walked to the credenza and picked up a coffee cup. He drew some water from a bottle on the table, poured it into the cup and placed it in front of Reggie. The dog stared at the bowl, waiting for the next ingredient. Mr. Richardson unscrewed the cap on the Jim Beam, leaned over and added a small dose. "Mustn't over do it. Reggie is a mean drunk."

The three men watched Reggie lap the fluid, almost burying his face in it. After a minute, Reggie raised his face, licked a few wayward drops with his tongue, emitted a canine "ahhhh" and gracefully settled into a comfortable reclining position.

Stanley smiled. "Man's best friend." He looked at Mark and Ted. "So, how can I help the investigative arm of the fine Long Harbor police department?"

"Mr. Richardson, you have your ear to the ground. Who do you think killed Silvio?"

"Detective, if we're going to apprehend this scoundrel, feel free to call me Stanley."

He then looked over to Ted. "And that goes for you too, no formality needed."

"Ok, Stanley. Good to have you on board. Call me Mark, and I am sure Officer Hanson is ok with Ted." Ted nodded.

Stanley reached for the folder. He stopped and looked at Mark. "May I?"

"I can't show you everything, but I want you to review the persons of interest and a brief summary," Mark replied handing over the first photo.

Stanley examined Father Jim in priestly garb, and read a summary of his alibi. "Well, our young reverend has been dipping into the fleshpot. I can't say it surprises me. A young and handsome man must be sorely tempted, no matter what vows he takes. I don't see him as a killer though. How about you, Reggie?" Stanley held the picture of Jim in front of him. Reggie opened his eyes, squealed disinterest and closed his eyes again. "Well, I guess that clears him."

Mark laughed as he studied the terrier. "Actually, I don't think dogs can distinguish pictures, but who knows with Reggie, the wonder dog." He turned towards Mr. Richardson. "Tell me, Stanley; is Father Jim capable of flipping off an elderly lady in a road rage incident?"

"What an odd question. I guess we all are, if stressed enough. I myself stopped driving when the ratio of loony to rational was even-steven. Also, I was driving slow enough to warrant my own share of single digit salutes. So, could he have done something like that? Yes."

Next picture. "How about his brother?" Stanley studied Gabe's picture and his summary.

"Hmm. I would think Gabe even less likely than his brother of flipping off an elderly lady. Yet, in the back of my mind, I can see him killing Silvio. Not premeditated, mind you, but maybe out of passion."

Stanley took another swig. "Especially if he was drunk, which is poor Gabe's demon. I have to say, I've had this indescribable feeling about Gabe in the last few days."

He laughed. "As Obi-Wan Kenobi once said, 'I sense a disturbance in the force.' Gabe looks preoccupied and lethargic, like he's carrying around a burden."

Stanley took Gabe's picture and place it in front of Reggie. "What do you think Reggie?" Reggie opened his eyes and immediately started to bark. It was an odd bark given that Reggie was clearly inebriated, but a bark followed by a growl nonetheless.

"Reggie and Gabe had an uneasy tolerance until a few days ago. Now Reggie does this at the sight of him. Gabe seems sheepish towards Reggie. It's as if they share some uneasy secret."

Ted looked at Reggie with new admiration. Mark handed over Tony Wagner's information. "And suspect number three."

Stanley took the picture and studied the summary.

"Sisters make good alibis, maybe even better than girlfriends. I heard he was spotted in the area around the time of the killing. I never liked the man. I think he whitewashed the Enrico investigation. He may have even killed him. He was certainly capable."

Stanley enjoyed bring consulted. He studied the ceiling to project deep thought. "Now the question seems to be if he killed Silvio. If he did, it would be premeditated, I am sure. I mean no offense, Detectives, but I'm sure if a cop really wanted to kill someone, he could do it quite easily and make it look like an unfortunate accident."

Stanley held Tony's picture in front of Reggie. "What do you think my friend?"

Reggie's head went up and a louder bark and growl came out. It looked like Reggie thought even less of Tony than of Gabe.

"Reggie reacted this way last night in the diner. Whatever happened Wednesday night between them left an impression. Wagner didn't seem too fond of Reggie either."

Stanley handed back the pictures.

The men looked at Stanley in quiet admiration. Stanley misunderstood. "Me? I'd never kill anyone. People may get under my skin occasionally but I'm not one for violence. Besides, I have an alibi. I was wandering around my apartment complex looking for Reggie. He had gotten loose earlier. I must have banged on every door and stopped everyone passing by. When he came back he was covered in mud and what looked like his own crap. He was also limping and squealing. No doubt from Wagner's kick."

Mark sat up. "Do you think Reggie saw the killing?"

"Who knows? His favorite place to run and crap is around the waterfront near where Silvio fell in."

Stanley picked up Reggie and looked him in the eye. "Who killed Silvio, Boy? What do you know?"

– – –

Tony Wagner arrived at the Long Harbor police department at 10:30. He was early for his 11 o'clock appointment with Mark, but decided that enough was enough. He would tell Mark that he saw Gabe kill Silvio. It was self-defense in his mind, but he had intended to hold onto this information until he found a way to hang this over Gabe.

It was too late for that now; suddenly, he was a suspect in Silvio's killing and the department was asking questions about Enrico. He had to stop that before the noose went around his neck.

He checked in with Teresa who dialed Mark. "Sorry to interrupt you Detective, but former Detective Wagner is here. He has an 11 with you. Should I have him wait?"

There was silence on Mark's end for a moment. "No, please bring him back now."

Mark looked at Ted and smiled, and then looked at Stanley and Reggie. "Tony Wagner is being brought back now. I'll give you a chance to say your hellos."

Stanley grinned. "You have an edge, Detective. I like that. We would be glad to meet Detective Wagner once more. Wouldn't we, Reggie?" Reggie did not appear to understand why everyone was staring at him.

Teresa approached Mark's partially closed door. Tony was chatting up Teresa and, from the sound of it, appeared to be hitting on her despite their ages. Tired of hearing this banter, she turned as Tony was in mid-proposition and knocked on Mark's door. A firm "Show him in, Officer," came from the room.

She opened the door and entered. "Former Detective Wagner is here to see you detective." She then turned, smiled, and motioned Tony in.

He walked in to see Mark seated at his desk, Officer Hanson, who was staring angrily at him, and a man holding a squirming dog in his lap. Reggie barked and then appeared to hiccup, causing Tony to take a step back.

"It's that mutt again. Get him out of here. What are you running Mark, a kennel for crazed dogs?"

Standing, Mark smiled at the pair. "Mr. Richardson, Stanley, I appreciate both you and Reggie coming in. You added a great deal of clarity to the investigation."

"Please show Mr. Richardson and Reggie out. See if you can find a treat for Reggie," he instructed Teresa.

Stanley stood and offered Reggie to Teresa. Reggie gave a contented squeal. "See, Officer, Reggie is a model citizen when not provoked. Be careful though, he's something of a charmer."

Teresa pulled in Reggie, kissed him on the nose and said "He's a sweetie." She then turned towards Tony. "Some people could learn from him."

- - -

Mario was having a late breakfast in Lucy's. Sitting across was Vincent Ferrante, valued employee of Mario and his favorite hit man. Vincent had arrived in town this morning and was awaiting instructions from Mario on whom to kill in retribution for Silvio's death.

Sheila took their orders: a ham and cheese omelet for Mario, with plenty of home fries. It was bacon and eggs for Vincent; Vincent had bacon and eggs every day of his life.

Mario marveled at how the man was pencil thin and yet he consumed enough cholesterol and grease to fatten even the fatted calf.

He laid out the developments he'd learned. It boiled down to: Father Jim Cooper, not likely; his brother Gabe, a man unlikely to kill, but whose nervous demeanor over the last six days had police trying to shake his alibi; and lastly, Tony Wagner, former detective in Long Harbor, who had come up empty in Enrico's killing, and was spotted in the vicinity of Silvio's death.

"Just be ready. I want this completed before Silvio is buried tomorrow. Let's show whoever killed him that he fucked with the wrong people."

The men looked up as Sheila approached with the food. She placed the dishes in front of the hungry men and filled their cups. She stood there until both men took a bite. "How is it, Gentlemen?"

Vincent nodded his approval. Mario swallowed a bite laden with perfectly cooked eggs, sweet ham, and a cheddar sent from heaven. "Perfect, Sheila. Marry me."

She laughed. "I can't. So many men would be disappointed. I must spread the love."

This caused Mario and even Vincent to laugh. "Tell me Sheila, what do you hear today about the killing?" Sheila looked around to make sure she wasn't being overheard.

"I hear that they are grilling Tony Wagner now. He was identified by the only known witness to the crime, Reggie, Mr. Richardson's terrier. Apparently, Reggie was doing his business as the killing occurred. Tony was there and admits to giving Reggie a swift kick. He still denies killing Silvio, but Reggie goes crazy at the sight of Tony, a man Mr. Richardson swears Reggie has never seen before."

Mario's jaw dropped. Is she clairvoyant? Does she have even better moles than I do?

He looked at his plate, studied the home fries, took a bite and closed his eyes as he experienced gastronomic nirvana. "Perfection," he exclaimed as he reopened his eyes. "Reggie is the best Porfino has? Not exactly something you can arrest on."

Sheila looked around again. "Actually, they like Tony for Enrico's killing. They are apparently trying to draw lines from his death to Silvio's."

He put down his fork, patted his mouth with his napkin, and studied Sheila in admiration. "What about Gabe Cooper?"

Sheila looked around again.

"Please, Sheila, we're out of earshot. There's a reason I asked for this back table and had the hostess steer people away from this area. Go ahead."

"Well, he's coming back in at two. He has an airtight alibi. He was actually seen all the way across town at the time of the killing. Mark Porfino hasn't been able to disprove the alibi yet. Frankly, if Gabe hadn't been such a nervous wreck, they wouldn't be considering him. On the minus side for Gabe, Reggie hates him also."

"Thanks, Sheila. My associate and I need to talk." Sheila seemed miffed by this but walked away. The men stared at their mystic.

Vincent spoke up. "Well?"

Mario thought for a second. "Stay ready. I'd like to shoot Tony Wagner on general principle, but let's see what plays out."

- - -

Jim was sitting in his small office laboring over the sermon for Silvio's funeral. He shuffled through his notes from his Saturday confessional musings. "Now let's see, where did I leave off?"

...One man dying for the many. Silvio died so that others may live. He wasn't our Christ, but he sure was our Barabbas. He was an insurrectionist and probably a murderer. Pilate let the wrong man go. Maybe this time they

got it right.

He frowned. Scratch that, he thought. Wouldn't exactly be breaking new ground. Also, not good to trash the deceased before sending him off to his judgment. Not to mention that there will be too many other guilty parties at this funeral, present company included.

We should always be ready to meet God and account for our actions. We reap what we sow.

Crap. True, but then again I could be speaking for the mourners, not for the deceased.

However, the quality of God's mercy is not strained. We are all sinners who must trust in God's mercy and love.

That's more like it.

Jim took out his lead pencil, Ticonderoga No. 2, worn down to half its original size. Someday, I have to put these on a laptop, he thought. Yet, there's something forgiving about a Ticonderoga. If I make a mistake, I can erase it and it never happened. Just turn the pencil over and apply the eraser liberally. He laughed to himself. If only we could do that with our sins.

– – –

While Jim was working on the sermon, Jan was preparing for her interview with Mark. She dressed in a conservative grey skirt and white blouse. This was not a seduce-your-local-priest occasion. Speak of the devil; Jan was meeting Jim at Lucy's at noon to discuss what to say. She looked at the clock, 11:30. Now or never, she thought.

Locking her front door, she tripped over then kicked aside a local advertising newspaper, and slid into her Camry. Her car was her oasis from the world. No dalliances with the local clergy took place here, although Jim tried for second base once. The Camry didn't judge her. They had a symbiotic relationship. Cammy, her pet name for the Toyota, took her where she wanted to go, and Jan fed her a steady supply of gas, washed her, and on her birthday, got her detailed. "Oh Cammy, let's run away and forget we ever heard of Long Harbor," Jan said aloud. The car was non-committal. Maybe she has a boyfriend, Jan thought. Don't bother, Cammy. They're just trouble.

She backed out of the driveway, started towards town and was almost sideswiped by an elderly woman who ran through a stop sign in a cross street.

Jan jammed on the brakes, skidded to the shoulder, threw the engine into Park and sat, stunned. The other driver applied the brakes herself and veered to the opposite shoulder, away from Jan. It was Mrs. Woodward. She sat for a minute to collect herself and then left her car and hurried over to Jan.

Mrs. Woodward tapped on Jan's driver side window and appeared to startle her. She rolled down the window. "Are you okay, Dearie? I don't know what happened."

Jan turned crimson. "What were you thinking, you old bat? You ran a stop sign and almost killed me."

Mrs. Woodward stepped back. "There's no reason to get snippy, young lady. Neither of us is hurt." She looked at Cammy. "And it looks like both cars came out all right. Do you want to call your insurance company?"

Jan took a second to collect herself. "I'm sorry I snapped, Ma'am. I've been under a lot of stress. There's no reason to call the insurance company."

Jan looked at her dashboard clock. "Now I must be going. I'm meeting my boyfriend for lunch."

Mrs. Woodward smiled. "Young lady, you are so kind to forgive an old lady her lapses." She took a few moments to study Jan. "You're also so pretty. You should let your hair down and open your blouse a bit. Let the men out there know what they're missing."

She offered her hand. "My name is Mrs. Claire Woodward. It would be my pleasure to have you over and chat with you some time when you are free and not in a rush."

Taking out a pencil, she continued, "Here's my name and number. I'll look forward to talking whenever you feel up to it. It's better to go through this world with friends you can talk to."

Jan studied the woman and smiled. "My name is Jan Gillek." She pulled a business card from her purse, wrote her cell number, and handed the card to her new friend.

"It would be a pleasure to speak with you, Mrs. Woodward. I must go now." Jan started her car, smiled again at Claire, and drove off once more.

What a nice young lady, thought Claire. I hope her young man appreciates her.

- - -

Mark and Ted walked into Taco Bell. Mark was royalty, having eaten lunch there frequently. Ted was a neophyte but accepted as Mark's friend. Mark ordered a Cheesy Gordita, beans and rice, and a 20-ounce Mountain Dew. He finished off with an order of Cinnamon Twists.

Ted ordered the Cantina Bowl and a Diet Coke. Mark paid the cashier for both and directed Ted to a side table which was known to the crew as "Mark's lunch booth."

Bringing back enough napkins to wash a mid-sized car, Mark dropped a few in front of Ted, also depositing a spork and knife. He had none for himself. "I eat mine with the hands God gave me," Mark said.

Mark took a few bites, closed his eyes and savored the experience.

"So what—," started Ted.

Mark raised his hand, grabbed his Mountain Dew, took a long slurp to wash away the remaining lettuce, sauce, and ground beef, and looked at Ted. "So, what do I think?" Ted nodded.

"Tony Wagner says that he saw Gabe kill Silvio. Says that Silvio instigated the exchange and was kicking Gabe's ass. Gabe got up and charged Silvio, head butting him and making Silvio fall into the water where he hit his head on a pylon going in. That's consistent with our head-butt theory. Then again, Tony probably has moles in the department and could have been told the head-butt theory."

Ted put down his spork after playing with the salad. The salad was healthier for him but Mark's Gordita looked pretty darn good. "I don't care for Tony but I believe him. If Gabe did kill Silvio in self defense, why didn't he come clean when he had a chance?"

"Maybe he did at first. Remember, there was a call from Silvio's phone? Maybe he got cold feet. Maybe he feared retribution from Mario."

Dabbing at a baked chicken strip, Ted mulled this over. "Then again, Gabe does have a pretty firm alibi."

"Ah, there's the rub. Mrs. Woodward can't tell Gabe from Father Jim. We'll need to see what Jan says when she's in at one. We also have Gabe at two. We'll put the screws to him. If no progress, we'll have to decide who we believe. Either Gabe or Tony killed Silvio. I'm sure of that."

- - -

Lucy's at noon was hopping. Jan saw Jim sitting in a booth writing on a steno pad, walked down the long aisle and stood before him. He was lost in his writing. "Ahem." He looked up, put down his pencil, and stood. "Hi Jan." They embraced in an awkward hug.

Jim looked around to see if they were being observed. "Jim, we're old news by now. No need for the cloak and dagger," Jan said. sliding into the booth.

They ordered turkey clubs and Diet Cokes and Jim asked if she was nervous about the interview.

"I admit that I was, but then I ran into this kind old lady; actually, she almost ran into *me,* and after talking to her, I realized that I shouldn't hide my feelings. I'm my own person and shouldn't stress out over pressure from others. I'm going to go in there, tell my story that I'm in love with the parish priest and that he was with me on the night of the killing. If Mr. Detective doesn't like it, he can kiss my ass."

Jim was surprised by the new Jan—but liked it. He smiled that smile that he knew would melt Jan. "What are you doing after the interview?"

Jan thought for a second. "Fucking my boyfriend, I hope."

- - -

After lunch, Jim offered to walk Jan to the police station, but she declined. "I need to freshen up. I'll call you when my interview is over."

He gave Jan a full kiss, different from his awkward embrace on their meeting, and then went to the counter to pay while Jan went to the Ladies Room. After she left the stall and washed her hands, she looked at herself in the mirror. She undid the ribbon holding her ponytail and shook her head to let her hair fall fully into place.

Undoing the top two buttons on her blouse, she looked at herself. Well, well, I am pretty hot, if I say so myself. She then undid a third button and liked the effect even more. She pulled out a small perfume from her purse and sprayed just enough for a hint of sexiness.

Walking down the aisle to the front door, she practiced a new strut, which caused a few male heads to turn. It was "so far, so good" for the new Jan.

She walked into the police station continuing her new swagger. Normally, Teresa would evoke the stares from the distributed male officers, but today Teresa was old news as eyes focused on Jan. She smiled and continued her walk down the runway.

The officer noticed the attention that Jan had drawn. "Don't worry about these characters, Miss Gillek, they're harmless. They just appreciate a good-looking woman." Jan beamed. Christmas had come early.

On knocking, "Enter" came from within. When Teresa walked in with Jan, both detectives looked up, froze for a second and then subconsciously straightened up their appearances.

They stood; Ted was clearly in awe. Teresa noticed and was not pleased.

"Gentlemen, Miss Gillek for her one o'clock. Perhaps Officer Hanson can stop examining Miss Gillek long enough to pull out a chair for her."

Ted looked at Teresa, embarrassed. "Of course, Miss Gillek, please have a seat."

He clumsily pulled out a chair. Teresa smiled briefly and turned to Jan. "I'll leave you here. They're harmless, too."

Jan sat in the guest chair. At eye level to Mark and Ted, her blouse did little to hide her cleavage, which appeared to be fighting to escape her bra. After a second or two, enough blood returned to Mark's brain to restore his concentration. He pulled the folder marked *Silvio Fortunato.*

"Miss Gillek, as you are aware, we are investigating the death of Silvio Fortunato on the evening of Wednesday the twelfth. How did you spend that evening?"

As she crossed her legs, Mark and Ted thought of the interrogation scene from *Basic Instinct.* Long Harbor's surprise own Sharon Stone was distracting a murder investigation. "Well, actually I was home all night. It was just a normal Wednesday evening."

"And you were alone all evening?"

"I had a gentlemen friend over: Jim Cooper."

"When did he arrive?"

Jan pretended to think for a moment to add to the suspense. "Around ten-thirty or eleven."

Ted revived enough to ask, "And how long did he stay?"

Jan looked over at Ted and smiled. Ted started to melt just a little.

"Until about twelve-thirty. We had a lot to talk about."

Mark reached for his soda, which was now just a few ice cubes, and almost knocked it over. He caught it in time. Jan giggled. She didn't laugh, she giggled. She was picking this up quickly.

Mark looked Jan in the eyes to avoid further distraction. "His late arrival didn't surprise you?"

She shook her head, making sure the hair brushed her breasts. "No. My boyfriend has odd hours. He comes when he can."

Mark understood the double meaning. "Did Jim discuss his trip over to see you? Did he mention anything out of the ordinary?"

Jan was puzzled by this. "No. Why?"

"Did he mention the traffic coming over that time of night? Maybe talk about any slow drivers getting him angry?"

"No. He was intent on talking to me. Why, is that important?"

He decided to play the advantage he was gaining. "We have a report from a Mrs. Claire Woodward that around ten-twenty that night a young man matching Jim's description made an obscene gesture at her as they were waiting at a traffic light. Did Jim mention this to you?"

Jan sat up causing exhibits A and B to shift. "Mrs. Woodward?

That sweet lady? I can't imagine Jim doing such a thing."

"And he would have mentioned it to you if he had?"

Jan didn't know how to answer this. "Is Jim being charged with lewd conduct?"

"No. We are just trying to establish whereabouts and time frames. Tell me, what car was Jim driving that night?"

She shook her head. "I couldn't tell you. Jim always parks about a block away. He's still shy about our relationship."

Mark closed the folder. "How about his brother, Gabe? Could he have done such a thing?"

She thought for a second. "I really only know Gabe in passing. I know Jim thinks the world of Gabe. It would surprise Jim if Gabe did such a thing."

Ted sat forward. "Maybe you can ask Jim. See what he thinks."

Jan sat back. "I just might."

– – –

Gabe closed the work log he was reviewing in the work trailer. He looked at his watch. It was 1:30, thirty minutes to his appointment with Porfino. He had to play this cool; he couldn't be the sniveling wreck he was last time.

He thought over what had taken place during this last week, and was tired of living with the crushing truth. Maybe he should just come clean to Porfino.

He immediately felt a sense of relief and the weight lifted. He smiled, put on his coat and left the trailer. He saw Lou walking up.

"Lou, I'll be out for the rest of the afternoon. I have important personal business to take care of."

His foreman took off his cap. "Gabe. Are you talking to Detective Porfino? The men are wondering if you're involved in Silvio's death. You've been acting awful strange lately, not at all like yourself."

Gabe zipped his coat and sighed. "This whole mess will be over soon, Lou. I'll talk to you when things settle down. In the meantime, keep everything running. I appreciate your covering for me."

"Anything, Gabe. You've always been straight with me and the men. We'll stick with you."

Gabe mumbled a "Thanks," trying to stay composed.

"I'll see you soon." Gabe slid into his car and started the engine. He waved to Lou who was studying Gabe.

I wonder if he's coming back, thought Lou.

It was only a five-minute drive. He found a parking spot adjacent to Lucy's. As he got out of his car, he saw Mario Gallante talking to a stranger. Mario had his arm around the man who was nodding and both saw Gabe at the same time. Mario spoke to the man, saying what looked like "That's Gabe Cooper."

Gabe pretended not to notice and walked across the street. He headed south to Police Headquarters. He remembered why he was reluctant to admit to killing Silvio; Mario would certainly seek vengeance. He was not a man to wait out the Law and Order process.

Sitting on a bench outside headquarters, he looked at his watch and tilted it to read the dial over the glare of the warm sun. One-forty-five. Just a few minutes to think this over. He peeked up at the sun, then looked around at the men and women walking about the town square. Everyone seemed happy, with their coats open or no coats at all. One had to enjoy a warm winter's day when it came.

He closed his eyes and thought about what he needed to do. The terrible crush of knowing that he'd killed a man and that the man's family and community had no closure, weighed on him. On the other hand, Mario would not be sympathetic. Bad business to kill an employee.

He decided he was going to continue his charade until circumstances forced his hand. He stood, brushed his shirt and pants—more from anxiety than fashion awareness—and walked towards the entrance to the station.

Midway up the steps, he saw a striking woman with flowing hair push open the door and walk into the sunshine. After a second, he realized it was Jan. He remembered that she was interviewing at one. Wow, she really dressed up for her interview, he thought. Now I understand what Jim sees in her.

She noticed Gabe and stopped. He hesitated, unsure of what to do with his hands. He shoved them into his pockets. "Hi, Jan. You're looking well today. How did the interview go?"

Jan turned serious, almost angry. "Hi, Gabe. It went well. Everyone was so nice."

She thought a second. "Gabe, I heard that you flipped off dear Mrs. Woodward the other night. Is that true?"

Turning pale, he smiled weakly. "Not my finest moment. I was driving around last Wednesday night and got stuck behind her. I guess the beer and the night caught up with me. I let fly with a quick one-fingered salute."

Gabe didn't think Jan believed him, so continued. "Porfino confronted me the next day and demanded that I apologize. I sent Mrs. Woodward a dozen roses with a note."

She pressed the advantage she had over him. "Funny. Porfino thinks it was Jim who flipped her off. And all the time it was you. I guess the two of you are pretty hard to tell apart, especially at night."

Before he could answer, she continued. "I wouldn't worry about it, Gabe. It's not like you killed someone." With that, she continued down the steps. Gabe turned around to watch her descend. She stopped and turned around. "Have a nice interview, Gabe," she said and continued to sashay down the steps to the admiring glances of officers and civilians alike.

– – –

As Gabe followed Teresa down the aisle towards Mark's office, male faces peeked out of cubicles, frowned, and as disappeared. Teresa turned to Gabe, "Don't take it personally. You don't have cleavage and you're not wearing a dress. They'll get over it."

She opened the door to see Mark sitting with the *Silvio f*older opened in front of him. Ted wasn't there. Mark waved Gabe to a chair. "Thanks, Teresa."

Teresa looked around. Mark noticed. "I sent Officer Hanson on an errand."

He looked at Gabe and then back to Teresa. "He's at Harbor Florists. You know that place, don't you, Gabe?"

"I do. That's where I sent Mrs. Woodward a dozen red roses after my unfortunate hand gesture."

Teresa turned to Mark. "Is there anything else, Detective?"

"No, please close the door."

He continued to look at Teresa as she walked down the center aisle, speaking to Gabe as he admired. "Such a lovely young woman. She'll probably break someone's heart one day. They say Helen of Troy launched 1,000 ships. I wonder what havoc Officer McGill will unleash."

He turned to Gabe. "Ted and I just entertained Jan Gillek. Such a lovely woman and quite a looker *herself.* Maybe you saw her on the way in?"

Gabe unconsciously started to drum his fingers, which Mark noticed. "Yes, I did. She's really dolled up today. Looks like she had the whole department lusting after her. Including yourself, I assume."

Mark blushed. He wasn't supposed to be the one on the hot seat. "Be that as it may, let's get down to business."

He leafed through the folder. "So, you're still maintaining that you were out driving on Wednesday night. Are you sure you weren't on the docks confronting Silvio?"

Gabe grabbed his chair lightly to stop from drumming his fingers. "And Mrs. Woodward attests to that. I am sure you've spoken with her."

"Mrs. Woodward stated that she can't tell the difference between you and your brother. She couldn't swear it was you."

"Have you spoken to Jim? Did he say he flipped Mrs. Woodward off?"

Mark pulled out Jim's sheet just as Ted walked in. He waved him to a chair, looked at Gabe and continued. "I have eyewitness testimony stating that you killed Silvio in a fight. You ran at him and head butted him into the water. Silvio fell back and hit his head going in. I imagine that caused the fatal injury."

Gabe turned angry and tried to look over to Mark's notes. Mark calmly closed the folder.

"Who is this witness? Maybe he killed Silvio and is framing me?"

"So you deny killing Silvio."

Gabe stood up. "I do. I was on the other side of town."

"Sit down, Cooper."

Gabe caught his breath, realized he had lost his composure, and sat.

"Look," he paused, "Gabe…I understand how these things happen. You were both drunk and Silvio started the fight from what our eyewitness said. Just come clean. This sounds like self-defense. There's no reason to drag this out."

Gabe sat there trying to regain his composure. He looked over at Ted, who had placed his hand on his leg near his weapon. Mark swung around and looked out of his office window. The squeak of the office chair caught the attention of both men.

Mark seemed to be thinking things over, and saw Lucy's in the distance. He turned back. "Ah, Mario. You think Mario will have you killed. Don't worry, we can place you into protective custody while this gets sorted out. We'll have people watching Mario. He won't come near you."

Gabe looked defeated. "He doesn't have to kill me himself. He brought someone into town who looks like he could do it."

Mark didn't know this. "Can you describe the man?"

"Yep. Your typical goon. Maybe six-two, dark hair, mean look."

Gabe paused for a few seconds and then smiled. "But that's not my problem. I didn't kill Silvio. Ask Mrs. Woodward."

The detective sighed and placed the folder into a desk drawer. "You've denied killing Silvio three times. I guess a cock will be crowing soon if I remember my New Testament."

Gabe stood up. "Silvio was no Jesus. Can I go now?"

He waved his hands and nodded. "You're free to go Gabe, for now. I'd steer clear of Mario Gallante if I were you. He's probably itching to avenge Silvio's death."

Smiling, he continued. "And he probably couldn't tell Jesus from Barabbas."

- - -

Jan sat in her car after the interview. She wondered about Gabe's alibi and if Jim wasn't the actual birder of Mrs. Woodward. She was also running on adrenaline from having turned on most of the Long Harbor male police staff that day. Dialing Jim's cell, she reached him in his rectory office as he was finishing Silvio's sermon.

"Hi, Jim. Meet me in the lounge of the Days Inn in an hour. Prepare to be there for a while. I need to unwind."

There was silence. Finally, Jim coughed and said, "I'll see you then." Jim hung up and sat back. So much for his return to the straight and narrow.

Folding his written sermon, he placed it in his top drawer. He stood to get ready to meet Jan, and realized he had an erection. Father Ray walked by at that moment. "Jim, can I speak with you in my office about Silvio's funeral?"

He leaned on his desk casually and said, "Actually, I was going out for a while. But, sure Ray. Give me a minute."

Ray looked at Jim's odd posture. "Are you okay?"

"I'm okay. I just stood up too fast. I'll be right over."

He brushed an imaginary piece of lint from his sweater and studied himself in the dresser mirror. Just stay professional, Jim, at least for now. He walked over to Ray's office and pulled out a chair as Ray waved him in.

"I want to go over the arrangements. Jessie already sent over the music she wants and I faxed it to Gloria. Are you ready with your sermon?"

"I just finished it up. It's not a puff piece, but I managed to make Silvio sound human. I speak a bit about him being in a better place. I didn't mention that we're all in a better place without him."

Ray laughed. Jim continued. "I don't think it will be a tear jerker. Silvio wasn't Mother Teresa and everyone knew it. I'll just talk of God's mercy and infinite capacity to forgive us all."

The pastor rocked in his chair for a second. "Well, Jim, not a bad approach to a difficult task. I was expecting something along the lines of *I came to bury Silvio, not to praise him.*"

Jim's jaw dropped. "That's amazing, Ray. I had thought of saying that." Ray smiled. "You don't minister for thirty years without developing the ability to read people or situations."

He sat up and looked Jim in the eye. "Now, take a few minutes to think about what direction you want for your life. You're a good priest, Jim, but you're conflicted. Decide what you want to do, and whom you want to do it with. You owe it to yourself, and to those who care for you, to be honest."

- - -

Mario sat in Lucy's having lunch and discussing business—football betting—with Vincent. "This season is too crazy. And there are too many injuries. It's a crap shoot."

He toyed with his tossed salad. He wasn't dieting by any stretch, but three squares a day at Lucy's had taxed even his capacity to chow down. He was playing with a reluctant cherry tomato when his cell rang; his favorite niece.

"What's new?" he asked. After about a minute, he looked around and lowered his tone. "So, Gabe Cooper. Is Porfino going to arrest him?" Sheila walked over and started to speak to Mario.

Vincent grabbed Sheila's arm. She turned towards Vincent, looked at his hand on her arm, and then looked back at Vincent with a stare that unnerved the gunman. He released her arm.

"Mr. Gallante is busy at the moment. Can you come back in a few minutes?" He reached into his shirt pocket, pulled out a twenty-dollar bill and handed it to Sheila. "And I'll have another Diet Coke."

She looked at the twenty, put it in her apron, shrugged and walked away. Mario ended his conversation with "Keep me posted," and hung up. He smiled. "Vincent, there are some people, like Sheila there, that you just don't mess with."

Mario filled him in on Gabe's interview. "Gabe Cooper looks guiltier by the minute. He just has this damned good alibi. Tony Wagner claims he actually saw Gabe kill Silvio. The problem is that no one trusts Tony. He could just as well have killed Silvio and framed Gabe."

He leaned towards Vincent. "We need to finish this up by tomorrow morning."

Vincent nodded, as he understood vengeance. "So, what should I do?"

"Get ready to take care of this tomorrow. Do it at the funeral. That'll send a message."

Vincent nodded. "Who am I delivering the message to, Cooper or Wagner?" Mario thought for a moment. "I'm not sure. Maybe both. I'll let you know."

- - -

Jim walked into the Days Inn avoiding eye contact as much as he could. He walked into the lounge, which was mostly empty on this early Tuesday afternoon. Jan was sitting at a corner table, drinking an Appletini and appeared to be flirting with a middle-aged man in a crumpled suit.

The man was about to speak to Jan when Jim arrived. He tapped him on the shoulder and spoke a firm "Get lost, pal. This is my girlfriend."

The man looked at Jim and wondered where he'd seen him before. He stood and nodded to Jan. "Sorry, Ma'am." He turned to Jim. "You have quite a beauty here, my man. Don't let her get away."

Jan was beaming at this as the man left.

"He's right about that," Jim said as he sat. The waitress walked over and scanned Jim. "Don't I know you?"

"I live in town." He looked at Jan's drink and then at the new Jan. "I'll have what she's having."

- - -

Mark closed the Silvio case folder and locked it in his desk drawer. It was six o'clock. He had let Ted leave at five. Mark turned off his desk lamp and swiveled his chair to look over downtown Long Harbor. There wasn't much happening outside on this Tuesday evening. There was enough street light so that he wasn't completely in the dark. He glanced over at his calendar. It was December 18, one week until Christmas. Maybe I'll have this mess wrapped up by Christmas Eve, he thought. "Time for some peace on Earth" he whispered to himself.

He was startled by a "What's that, Sir?" He spun around to see a woman from the office maintenance service smiling. "You were saying something about peace on earth?"

"I didn't realize I was talking out loud. That must mean it's time to go for the night."

Putting on his police jacket, he adjusted his collar and walked towards the door. "Have a good evening." He could now make out her nametag. "And have a happy holiday, Rosita, if I don't see you before."

Rosita smiled. "And you too, Detective. May you have the peace on earth that you speak of."

After saying his goodnights to the few officers and staff still on duty, he walked over to his BMW, pressed the Unlock button on his key chain and slid into the front seat. His good old Beemer, his refuge from this crazy world. He started the engine, turned on his radio, looked around for oncoming traffic, and drove away from the station. He stopped at the next red light. He was opposite Lucy's.

The brightly lit diner was mostly empty. Sheila was carrying a tray with an entrée piled high on a plate. She stopped and placed it before Mario.

The light turned green and Mark pulled into the entrance, parked near Mario's booth and turned off the engine. The sudden headlights startled Mario and Sheila, who shielded their eyes and looked out. Mark gave an embarrassed wave. Mario smiled and beckoned Mark in. Sheila walked a few steps, picked up a menu and placed it across from Mario.

Mark and Lucy exchanged greetings as he indicated he was joining Mario. "Ah, Mr. Gallante. This has become his home away from home. I don't usually care for the gangster type, but he's always pleasant and one heck of a tipper. He says he'll be leaving after Silvio's funeral tomorrow. We'll all miss him, especially Sheila."

She walked Mark over to Mario's table. Sheila was still there chatting him up. "Detective, I'll leave you in Sheila's capable hands. Try the chicken soup tonight."

Mark sat down, unzipped his jacket and looked at Mario's empty bottle. "What are you drinkin', Mario?"

Mario turned the bottle to show the demented hound on the label. Mark looked up at Sheila who was standing at the ready. "I'll have a Flying Dog, Sheila. And bring another to my thirsty host."

Mark looked at the menu. "So, what's good?"

Mario examined his plate. "I'm having the stuffed pork chop. Not bad."

Mark looked over Mario's plate, thought a second, and then looked at the menu. "The Chicken Parm sounds good."

The mobster shrugged. "My heritage prevents me from ordering Italian in a diner. It's sacrilegious to have Italian cooked by Greeks."

"Well, I'm half Italian myself, although lapsed, I guess. I'll eat whatever they put in front of me."

Sheila returned with the round of beers and a basket of warm bread. She stood at attention with pad out, awaiting Mark's order. "I'll have the Chicken soup and the Chicken Parm with mashed potatoes.

"Make that spaghetti," Mark corrected himself as he saw Mario cringe. I wonder if detente works like this, he wondered.

She left and Mark picked up a slice of bread and lightly coated it with butter. Mario looked into the basket, spotted the end piece, pulled it out and slathered enough butter on it to cover the surface area an eighth of an inch thick. He bit half of the thick slice, then loudly chewed the bread into submission so that the only proof that the half had existed was butter coated fingers and a bite mark that could have been taken into evidence.

Mark watched in awe. He took a swig of beer, put the bottle down, let out his own gasp of satisfaction and looked at Mario, who was stuffing the second half into his mouth.

"So, Mario. I heard you brought in a henchman. Is that to do away with whoever you think killed Silvio?"

After signaling that he never spoke with his mouth full, Mario cleaned off his fingers, took a swig of beer and thought this over. "You must mean Vincent. He's in town to help Gallante Plumbing and Fortunato Brothers get over the manpower shortage caused by

Silvio's death. Henchman? He's a master plumber. A wrenchman—maybe you didn't hear it right."

Mark smiled at the play on words. For a goon, Mario was pretty sharp.

"Look, Mario. We'll solve Silvio's death pretty soon. Let the law do its job. Silvio's killer will be brought to justice. We don't need outsiders coming in and shooting up Long Harbor."

Mario looked towards the kitchen. "Your soup is coming." Sheila placed the cup of thick soup in front of Mark and dropped two packs of saltines next to it. She asked if there was anything the men needed.

"My friend and I need to talk, Sheila," Mario said and reached into his pocket for a twenty. "Can you get me a newspaper? You can keep the change."

Sheila smiled. "I'll be back in a few minutes with your paper."

Mario smiled as Sheila walked away grinning. "She's a real card," he said, then turned serious. "Detective, I run a business. When a problem occurs, I solve the problem. My visit to Long Harbor will be over tomorrow. I am burying my friend and making sure my company is running again."

He picked up one of Mark's saltine packs. He smiled and then crushed the pack with his hand, opened it, and emptied the crumbs into Mark's soup. "It's better with the added flavor. Now, let's enjoy our dinner. We both have long days ahead of us tomorrow."

- - -

Jim lay on his side, spent and confused. "Where did that come from?"

"You didn't like?"

"That was amazing. It was just so unexpected. What came over you?"

"I believe it was you who came over me."

He looked at Jan in silence and wondered. Who is this woman and why am I just meeting her now?

She turned on her side to face Jim. "Look at me, Jim. I'm the same Jan. I just decided that I'm going to lead my life openly. No more rendezvous in a Starbucks twenty miles outside of town, no more shy smiles at my boyfriend, the priest. I want an open relationship where we can both be free," she said. "And I want honesty."

She sat up, losing the sheets. "So tell me. Did you flip off Mrs. Woodward on Wednesday night on the way to see me?" Jim stopped staring at Jan's breasts and rolled onto his back. He thought for a second. "Where did you hear that?" Jan folded her arms. "Detective Porfino, if you must know. You're not answering my question."

"Detective Porfino said that I flipped off Mrs. Woodward?"

"He indicated he thought it was you. Apparently, he likes you for the act and not your brother."

Realizing he had to choose between preserving Gabe's alibi and lying to Jan, he took a breath and made a decision. "No. It must have been Gabe." He sat up. "You believe me, don't you?"

"I guess I have to." She looked Jim in the eye. "Maybe the honesty issue needs to evolve. In the meantime, I'll settle for you committing to be open about us. I want an honest relationship, Jim. I want you to marry me."

She pretended to brush a speck from her left breast causing the nipple to harden, as Jim took note.

"Oh, and if it turns out you lied, I couldn't testify against you if I was your wife. Think about it, Jim. It's a win/win. You get me and my lady friends, and Gabe gets to pretend that he didn't kill Silvio."

"Are you asking me to leave the priesthood? It's my life."

"I'm your new life, Jim."

\- - -

Chapter 12

Let He who is Without Sin

Wednesday, December 19. Editorial page, Long Harbor Press. *Good Bye, Silvio* by John Gibson.

Silvio Fortunato, business owner and suspected bookmaker, will be buried today at St. Augustine's Church. His mass and funeral is expected to be attended by family, business associates, law enforcement, and friends. Fortunato disappeared a week ago on Wednesday, and his body was discovered on Friday morning floating in the bay near the harbor inlet.

His business, Fortunato Brothers Plumbing, was highly successful. But the real revenues for his enterprise are believed to be derived from the more lucrative betting empire that Silvio allegedly carved out here in Long Harbor.

Somewhere out there, Fortunato's killer awaits the funeral and hopes that his life can return to normal afterwards. I say killer because, although the cause of death is still listed as undetermined, many residents believe he met his fate in the same way he undoubtedly dealt with others.

This may sound harsh and even cruel to his family and friends. I do sympathize with his lovely wife Jessie and fine son Rico. I hope they find whatever solace they can in friends and the community. But Silvio, you lived by the sword and you died by the sword. Good bye and may God have mercy on your soul.

Mario put down the paper, took a sip of coffee and signaled Sheila for the bill. Boy, Gibson didn't pull any punches, he thought. I'll be glad to get out of this town. Well, one more day, Long Harbor. Let me take care of some loose ends and then, sayonara.

He considered the events of the last few days and the results of the interviews as communicated by Teresa through an unwitting Ted Hanson. It boiled down to Tony Wagner and Gabe Cooper. He hated Tony, but couldn't believe he would be stupid enough to dispose of

Silvio exactly as he had done to Enrico. After taking one final bite of toast, he took out his cell and dialed Vincent.

He looked around to make sure he wasn't being overheard. "Vincent. Please extend my personal regards to Gabe Cooper."

- - -

Jim awoke in his own bed the next morning after returning late from his time with Jan. He sat at his desk in his pajamas and read his Divine Office. He heard Ray moving around in the kitchen and smelled coffee. He craved a cup but couldn't face Ray at the moment; there would be time to talk later. For now, he needed to get ready for Silvio's funeral mass and burial. This might be one of his last official acts as a priest. Better to go out in style, he thought.

He closed his prayer guide, sighed, and walked over to his closet. He pulled out his clerical black pants and shirt, walked to his dresser and pulled out a collar. He attached it to his shirt and looked at himself in the mirror. "I guess some things weren't meant to last forever," he said aloud to himself.

"What would that be, Jim?" came Ray's voice from the doorway. He saw Ray in the mirror, holding two cups of coffee. Jim looked away and was silent for a few seconds. He then turned and walked towards the doorway.

"Ray, we need to talk. I've made a decision."

Ray grimaced and walked in. He made a gesture with his head towards two chairs. "Let's talk."

- - -

Lou walked into the trailer of Cooper Renovations at 7 a.m. and noticed an incoming voice message on the phone. Gabe usually got in around eight. Lou sat himself in Gabe's chair and dialed the voice service number. "Lou, this is Gabe. I'm going to Silvio's funeral today. I won't be in at all. Let the guys go home early today if you can."

He erased the message and sat down. Good old Gabe, he thought. What's good for the boss is good for the troops. I'll miss him if he doesn't come back.

Walking over to the file cabinet, he opened the bottom drawer, the one containing Gabe and Lou's secret stash of Jim Beam. Lou removed the files in the drawer revealing the whiskey, and took out the bottle. "Almost empty. Gabe's been busy. Enough left for two shots. I'll take one if you don't mind, Gabe. I'll leave you the other."

Emptying a shot into a paper cup, he sat back in Gabe's chair, sipped the Bourbon, and looked at the label on the bottle. *Bold Choice.* Lou laughed. "What bold choice is it to get plastered?" He held the cup up to an imaginary drinking buddy. "Here's to you, Gabe. I'm not sure how you're tied up in this mess, but I hope you get out okay."

– – –

Long Harbor Florists brought in fresh arrangements for the funeral. Gloria sat at the organ and leafed through the music chosen for the service. *Come Back to Me;* nice song. *On Eagles' Wings;* always a good choice. *Ave Maria;* the number one hit at funerals. That should get them crying, she thought, but I need to jazz this up. This is too somber for such a joyous occasion. It's not every day we bury the most hated man in town.

She mulled over catchy tunes that might speak "Silvio." She laughed to herself. How about *Sit Down, You're Rockin' the Boat?* She stood and looked over at the pews and the altar to make sure she was alone. She started to play the song from *Guys and Dolls.*

She heard the front door close, stopped, and opened the book of Catholic sheet music. Locating *On Eagles' Wings,* she started to play through it, hoping the visitor didn't hear her prior effort. She quietly sung the show tune to herself. The devil dragged you under, Silvio. He did us all a favor.

As Father Ray walked in, he heard a hymn that seemed vaguely familiar. The music stopped and then picked up. He recognized *On Eagles' Wings,* looked up to the choir loft and saw Gloria playing and quietly singing along. The odd thing was that the tempo of the words didn't match the slower cadence of the Catholic hymn. Gloria noticed him and stopped. "Good morning, Father Ray. I was just practicing for the funeral mass."

Ray waved and continued down the aisle. Gloria's a real pip, he thought. She was probably singing a show tune while rehearsing. He smiled. That probably wouldn't be a bad idea to lighten the mood of today's service. He looked at the flowers surrounding the altar. Boy, Jessie and Rico really did it up. Silvio's going to have quite a fancy sendoff.

The front door of the church opened again, letting in the sunlight on this crisp December morning. In walked a shapely younger woman in a black dress. "Our first mourner," Ray thought.

Walking to the last pew, she genuflected, made the sign of the cross, and shuffled towards the middle. She didn't kneel to pray but rather sat back, removed a tissue from her purse and let loose with a honk that could have woken the dead. She looked at the tissue, realized it had given it's all, and placed it back into her purse. Taking out another, she dabbed her eyes.

Ray decided to leave her in peace before the funeral procession arrived and walked past. He glanced over to satisfy his curiosity. It was Carla Ciccone, the waitress from The Wharf and Silvio's suspected paramour.

Carla saw Father Ray looking over. "Good morning, Father. I decided to come early and pray for Silvio. I won't be staying."

He was touched by the sadness Carla was feeling. "Please stay, Ms. Ciccone. God hears all of our prayers."

Smiling, she said. "Thank you, Father, but I don't want to cause a scene with Mrs. Fortunato. I will be at the burial though. Somewhere in the crowd."

Ray nodded and left the church, thinking over what was about to take place. Well, this is going to be some burial, he thought. A mobster mourned by people who either hated him or loved him, and probably feared him. All conducted by a priest who will soon be released from his vows so that he can continue to romance a parishioner. Long Harbor, you've come a long way from your humble beginnings.

- - -

The funeral procession arrived at 10:50. Father Jim walked in and headed towards the sacristy. He closed the door so that he could put on his vestments. After a few minutes, there was a knock on the side door. It was James and John McNally, identical twins and the altar boys for the mass. They had already dressed and awaited instructions from Jim.

"Light the candles, and make sure the wine and cruets are ready."

"Yes, Father," they said in tandem.

"Wait. I almost forgot something." Jim reached into his pocket and pulled out some cash. He rolled off two fifties.

"Here's fifty dollars for each of you for serving today. It's a consideration from Mr. Gallante, Mr. Fortunato's employer. Let's give the man his money's worth today."

Their eyes lit up as they uttered a simultaneous "Thank you, Father," then walked away to do their preparations.

Jim looked at the remaining cash in his hand. "And $200 for the preacher man. Mario, you're going to remember this day."

- - -

Angelo Danzetti, baptized Michelangelo, had been in the funeral business all his life. He ran errands for his father, Michael Sr., founder of Danzetti's, during his school years. He worked summers transporting flowers and dead clients, and served a three-year apprenticeship after graduating community college and mortuary school.

Now, after his father's retirement, Angelo managed Danzetti's. For him, funerals tended to run the same course: transporting the body, meeting the family, and making the arrangements. Then there was preparing the deceased for the viewing, overseeing the wake, and finally, on the funeral morning, transportation to the church and gravesite. It wasn't that Angelo wasn't compassionate; it was just that there was nothing out of the ordinary to make one funeral different from the next.

But, this was Silvio Fortunato; he'd been a big man in town if only because he was the biggest criminal. Angelo left his black Lincoln Town Car and walked briskly to the hearse as Lloyd, his assistant, prepared to remove the coffin. The pallbearers were in place: Rico, Mario, Sal, and three of Silvio's plumbers/runners.

Angelo jumped in and instructed the bearers on how to lift the coffin and place it onto the transport dolly. This was heavy lifting, but the distance was only a few feet. Mario grunted on the initial lift and appeared to strain during the transfer. When the coffin was in place, Angelo directed the rolling of the coffin into the church. Mario mopped his brow with a handkerchief.

"Are you okay, Uncle Mario?" asked Rico.

"I'm fine, just out of shape."

The coffin was rolled into the vestibule where it was met by Jim and the altar boys, who held candles. They both looked at Mario and smiled. Jim cleared his throat to reclaim the attention of the boys, led those present in a prayer for Silvio, and then preceded the coffin into the church. The mourners, led by Jessie, her sister, and Rico, followed as Gloria played *Be Not Afraid* on the organ. Jessie stopped beside the casket, touched the metal and wept. Rico walked over and led his mother into the first pew.

Jim saw this and was moved. This was never easy, he thought. Silvio was a cheating creep who neglected his wife and son, but here there is forgiveness and sympathy.

He blessed the coffin and shook holy water from a golden sprinkler, turned with James and John and climbed the altar steps. The funeral mass began with a greeting to those present and an invitation to pray for the salvation of Silvio and the comfort of his survivors. Jim took a second to look at the congregation. Mostly a full house, he thought. I wonder how many are cops?

It was a full mass at the request of Jessie. Rico and Mario did the readings. Mario struggled, not so much from sadness, but more because he was painfully shy in front of the assembled, and wanted to get the words out right.

Jim was surprised. Here was a man who controlled the lives of so many, yet he seemed ill at ease in front of a crowd.

He stood for the Gospel, signaled those assembled to rise, and walked to the pulpit. He then opened his hands and exclaimed "The Lord be with you."

Those in the assembly aware of the response said "And with your spirit." The others mumbled or grunted to feign a response. Jim opened the bible to Rico's selected reading. It was the Sermon on the Mount, with Jesus instructing on the Eight Beatitudes.

Jim thought a recitation of the Ten Commandments, especially *thou salt not kill* and *thou salt not commit adultery* might be more appropriate, but took a breath and read the gospel. When he finished, he said, "This is the Word of the Lord." The assembly answered, "Thanks be to God" or mumbled in sync.

Signaling everyone to sit, he closed the bible and cleared his throat.

"Jessie, Rico, Silvio's friends and associates, my brothers and sisters in Christ. This wonderful gospel was selected for this occasion by Rico, Silvio's fine son. Before receiving this selection, I had considered a different Gospel. I see now that he couldn't have made a better choice.

The Eight Beatitudes were given to us by Jesus to continue his message of love and forgiveness. In the Sermon on the Mount, Jesus chose not to rehash the Ten Commandments and their 'shalt not' theme, but rather to teach us all about humility, charity, and service to others.

Jesus gave us the beatitudes as a map, a path through life. He wanted us to look upon ourselves and our fellow man as co-heirs to God's kingdom rather than obstacles to self-gratification and success.

I'd like to review some guidelines given to us by the Lord to help us achieve the greatness of which we are capable. 'How blest are the poor in spirit; the reign of God is theirs.' What better way to become truly rich than to help and respect others.

'Blessed too are the sorrowing; they shall be consoled.' Jessie and Rico must continue on and we have the opportunity to help ease their way.

'Blessed are they who hunger and thirst for holiness, they shall have their fill.' This is sometimes worded as 'thirst for justice.' I like holiness better. Justice can be easily purchased and dispensed."

Jim looked at Mario.

"Even the frontier kind. Vengeance and hatred are empty tools of the devil. They don't solve problems, they just create new ones."

Mario looked down and pretended to straighten his tie.

"'Blest are they who show mercy; mercy shall be theirs.' This town has shown their dislike of Silvio's actions. That's understandable. But we must recognize that this man was one of us, trying to live his life, but full of the

same human limitations that we all possess. Let's understand that the next time we fall short.

Finally, 'Blest too are the peacemakers; they shall be called sons of God.' Let's get back to our Christian roots and dedicate ourselves to living as if each day we live and each human we encounter was made by God and deserves the tranquility that God gives.

My brothers and sisters, Silvio was flawed. No one doubts that. But aren't we all?"

He paused to scan the assembly.

"There's maybe a killer among us, maybe more than one."

Gabe scanned the mourners to see if he was being stared at. He noticed Tony Wagner and Mark Porfino looking directly at him, and looked away. Tony Wagner saw that everyone else was staring at him, including Miriam. He grimaced and looked straight ahead.

"I'd bet there's an adulterer or two also."

Many of those listening looked down wondering when their sin was coming up.

"Some of us take worldly possessions that belong to others. Some of us are gluttonous."

Most of the assembly looked at Mario, who gave an embarrassed shrug.

"And you don't have to look any further than this pulpit to see someone who has been unfaithful to his God and to his mission. So before we judge others, let's remember our own shortcomings and also the Lord's admonishment, 'Let he who is without sin cast the first stone.'"

Jim closed the bible and seemed lost in thought for a moment. He looked up.

"My brothers and sisters, God understands human frailty. He understood why Silvio did the things he did. Yet in all of Silvio's actions, God never loved him any less. God couldn't love less if he tried.

Let's not leave this service today convinced that we are any better than when we came in, or that we are any better than our neighbor. Leave today committed to loving God, loving yourself and loving your neighbor by living the beatitudes as well as we mortals can."

Waiting a few seconds to let this sync in, he continued. "Now let us pray."

- - -

At the completion of the mass, he motioned the assembly to stand and signaled James and John to accompany him to the coffin. There, Jim gave a final blessing to Silvio and sprinkled holy water on the metal casing. He then signaled Angelo Danzetti who, in turn, motioned the pallbearers to come forward. Angelo whispered instructions to the men and led them forward down the aisle, rolling the coffin. James and John followed with Jim walking slowly behind. He stopped for a moment to console Jessie and Rico, who then left their pew after him.

He snuck a glance at Gabe, who appeared to be distressed. Across the aisle, Mark Porfino saw this and elbowed Ted Hanson, who nodded. Jim continued to take in the mourners as he continued down the aisle. Tony Wagner appeared to be having an emotional, whispered conversation with Miriam.

Maybe she now thinks Tony killed Silvio, he thought. What a mess. How will this straighten out without Gabe getting arrested—or killed?

Passing Jan, he saw she was beaming. Her star pupil had knocked it out of the park. Maybe this is all just a dream, he thought. He reached the last pew. Father Ray sat there by himself. They made eye contact and nodded.

No, I guess this is real, he thought. He turned and walked towards the sacristy, allowing the coffin and the mourners to leave the church and assemble for the ride to the graveyard. He removed his vestments and put on his cleric's suit coat.

As he was hanging up his vestments, he heard "The end of the road, I guess." Jim turned to see Ray.

Jim smiled. "And I didn't even leave them laughing."

- - -

Holy Innocents Cemetery was the main burial site for the Cambria diocese. The holy and unholy alike rested in peace on a hilly overlook facing Long Harbor. Silvio had bought a four-grave plot years ago when the prices were cheap. Enrico, his older brother, was the only current occupant. The adjacent plot was unassigned. The other two were for Silvio and Jessie. Silvio had insisted that their names and birth years be placed on the stones. Jessie was uncomfortable with that and felt it was bad karma. Silvio prevailed.

The hearse and the funeral procession turned into the gated entrance. Mario was in the third car, after Jessie, Rico, and Jessie's sister Jeannette with her brood of sullen kids.

Mario was angry at being third car. After all, he was like a favorite uncle to Silvio, and his mentor. He was more important to Silvio than Jeannette from Cambria, but decided not to make a scene. After all, she had stopped hugging trees long enough to attend. He saw the ornate sculpture of the Holy Innocents at the cemetery gate. Not many innocents here today, he thought. Gabe, two cars behind, thought the same as he turned in.

At the end of the twenty-car funeral procession, Jim pulled in, stopped near the gravesite, shut off his car, and adjusted the rear view to check his appearance. He saw a small orange Kia pull in and park away from the crowd.

Carla. He hoped she'd stay in the background. A scene between wife and girlfriend was the last thing they needed here.

He picked up his bible, left his car and walked to the burial site where the mourners assembled.

Leaving her car, Carla adjusted her black dress and veil, and walked to the edge of the mourners. She scanned the crowd and saw Jessie and Rico seated, Mario standing directly behind, and various co-workers and friends of Silvio. In the next row stood Gabe, Tony Wagner, Mark Porfino, and Ted Hanson. She edged closer to Gabe.

Mark and Ted were more intent on watching the assembled crowd than following the proceedings. On the perimeter of the site, Long Harbor officers—dressed as workers—looked out for suspicious activity. Another worker on the site was Vincent Ferrante. He raked leaves, feigning ignorance of the gravesite activities.

Walking to the front of the crowd, Jim cleared his throat, and opened his bible to the Committal Service. He recited the prayers for the salvation of Silvio's soul and prayed for the comfort of those he left behind. In the back of the crowd, muffled tears from the lady in black. Not so muffled though, to escape the notice of Gabe, Tony Wagner, Miriam, Mark and Ted.

On the hill overlooking the rite, Vincent continued his raking until he was behind a large oak. He looked around, determined that he could not be seen, and pulled a canvas case from his leaf bag. He assembled his TRG 42, placed the rifle on a branch of the Oak and looked through the gun sight. He swung the sight slowly until he spotted Gabe next to Tony Wagner.

Jim was throwing dirt onto Silvio's coffin and uttering a final prayer for Silvio, when Carla, facing Gabe and Tony, pulled a .25 caliber semi-automatic from her purse. She shot Tony point blank and got off three more before she was tackled by Ted Hanson.

The mourners turned at the sound of the gunfire. Screams erupted and people ducked or ran. Vincent pulled back his rifle and started to disassemble it. He saw the plain-clothes officers running from near-by down to the sight of the shooting. He placed the rifle into the canvas case, carted his leaf bag away to his car, removed his rifle and placed it into his trunk. He sat in his car and waited a few minutes as police cars arrived. He then drove out of the cemetery.

Carla was handcuffed by Ted and placed into a police sedan. Mark was consoling Miriam and asked a female police officer to see to her needs. He walked over to Jessie to see if she was okay. Rico and Jim were calming her.

Tony lay on the ground, a bloodstain soaking his suit coat. Ted was kneeling next to him, waiting for the paramedics. Gabe stood glued to his spot. Ted looked up, asked him if he was okay, and suggested that he accompany him to the police station later on to give a statement.

The cemetery custodian had come over after hearing the police sirens. He instructed his men to complete Silvio's burial after Jim indicated that he had finished. The remaining mourners withdrew.

- - -

Chapter 13

Let There Be Peace on Earth

Interrogation Room A, Long Harbor Police Department, was a stark room with three scuffed white walls and a fourth with one-way glass. Carla sat in a small uncomfortable chair at a bare metal table topped with cheap Formica. She was bound at the waist with a sturdy metal chain attached to the chair. Her hands and feet were cuffed, and the cuffs attached to the waist chain. Teresa McGill stood guard.

Mark walked in and observed Carla, shackled and somber. Carla nodded, causing her metallic jewelry to jingle. He removed her handcuffs. She rubbed her wrists and folded her hands together, elementary-school style, and stared forward. Mark realized she had been crying, but wanted to remain stoic.

He looked at the padded chair next to him. It was larger than Carla's and designed to accommodate the donut-eating habits of the Long Harbor police. Pulling out the chair, he flopped down. The contact of gluteus to pleather caused a muffled fart sound. Mark and Carla both involuntarily smiled at the unexpected sound at such a serious time.

Walking into the room holding a recorder, Ted searched for a place on the table to position the device. He carefully placed the microphone between Mark and Carla and pulled out his padded chair as he met Carla's eyes. His semi-glare was intended to show Carla she was in for a tough interview. As he settled into the chair, it emitted fart sound number two. Mark and Carla both let out a short laugh and looked down. Teresa also smiled, covering her mouth to hide the reaction. Ted looked at the three of them. "What?"

Turning on the recorder, Mark started the interview. "This is Detective Mark Porfino. It is Wednesday, December 19, two p.m.

Present are officer Ted Hanson, assistant detective for the Long Harbor Police Department; Officer Teresa McGill; and suspect Carla Ciccone who has just been arrested for the attempted murder of Tony Wagner, retired detective of the Long Harbor Police Department. Note that Tony Wagner is currently undergoing emergency surgery to remove the bullets fired by Miss Ciccone. If Tony Wagner dies, the charge will be upgraded to murder."

He turned to Carla. "Miss Ciccone, do you understand that we are taping this interview and that anything you say can and will be used against you?"

"I do."

Ted positioned the microphone microscopically closer to Carla. Carla returned an annoyed stare.

"Let the record state that Miss Ciccone has agreed to confess to this matter. This statement is being taped to verify that Miss Ciccone is testifying of her own free will. Detective Hanson, can you please supply your badge number and your association to the case?"

The officer leaned over, face almost in the microphone. "Patrolman Ted Hanson, Long Harbor Police department, Badge 1857. I have been assisting Detective Porfino in the investigation of the death of Silvio Fortunato. I was present at the Fortunato funeral when the shooting of Tony Wagner occurred."

Mark turned towards Teresa. "And Officer McGill?"

Surprised at being asked to speak, she took a step forward and called out, "I am Officer Teresa McGill, Badge 1855. I am assigned to guard the suspect. I was not present at the funeral."

Mark turned back to Carla and smiled, hoping to relieve her tension. "Carla, let's get down to matters. Why did you shoot Tony Wagner?"

"That bastard killed Silvio just like he killed Enrico three years ago."

Mark pushed back Ted's hand as Ted attempted to move the recorder an additional millimeter towards Carla. "What led you to believe that Tony Wagner killed Silvio Fortunato?"

The woman started to cry, but took a breath to collect herself. "Silvio told me that he knew who killed his brother. He had evidence that it was Tony Wagner. He had arranged to meet him later and was going to confront him. I told Silvio to be careful; Tony could kill him, too, and probably get away with it. Silvio wasn't concerned. He told me he could take care of himself."

"Why didn't you tell me this when I interviewed you?"

Returning an angry stare that caused Mark to sit back , she said, "The Long Harbor Police Department takes care of its own."

She looked up at the one-way glass and raised both hands in a simultaneous one-fingered salute.

"That includes you, Chief Benson, protector of the town. The only person you protected was Tony."

Looking back at Mark, she continued. "On Wednesday night around ten-thirty, I was taking my break out back. I had talked with Silvio earlier. He was drunk, but was gonna meet Tony later that night, anyway. I saw Silvio walk over to his Explorer and then look at his front tire and a puddle underneath. He shouted 'That bastard,' got in and drove away. Boy was he pissed."

She wrung her hands. "Just then I heard a truck door open about twenty yards away. It was Tony Wagner. He climbed into his truck, pulled out his cell, and called somebody. He put his cell away, and floored it out of the lot in the same direction as Silvio. I tried to call Silvio, but he didn't answer his new cell. He was proud of his "Sopranos" ring tone, but said the phone crackled and just dropped off at times. He was gonna return it the next day."

Mark looked at Ted for a reaction. Ted nodded. That explained the fractured 911 call. Mark looked back at Carla. "There was a call to 911 from Silvio's phone near the time of his death. We never found the phone."

"How convenient for Tony."

Mark turned towards Teresa. "Officer McGill, please take Carla back to her cell."

As Teresa led Carla back to her cell, Mark saw her smile at Ted and wink.

- - -

The men walked towards Mark's office.

Ted sighed. "Maybe she got the right guy after all."

"It would appear that way," Mark said, nodding. "You got Tony's cell records. See if Carla's story is correct. Find out who he called that night. Let me know what you come up with."

Pulling out his cell to check the call records, Ted tapped in 'Tony Wagner,' and started to scroll. He reached Wednesday the 12th, ten p.m.

"He called Miriam Walker and spoke for about fifteen seconds."

Looking at the next message, he continued. "11:15, Miriam again, thirty seconds this time. What can you say in thirty seconds?"

"Maybe that the job was done."

"Should I bring in Miriam?"

"Not yet. Let her worry about her brother."

- - -

Tuesday, December 24. Father Ray Lowery, now the sole priest of the parish, was preparing for Christmas Eve mass. The church was full with poinsettias and the altar lit with candles. The congregation filed in. What would normally be a modest crowd for a regular Sunday mass became an overflow assembly of finely dressed regulars and CAPE Catholics—Christmas, Ash Wednesday, Palm Sunday, and Easter. Where are these people the rest of the year, he asked himself. He spotted the crucifix on the opposite wall. I know, be nice.

James and John McNally, alter servers for the mass, entered the sacristy as Father Ray was straightening his robes and checking himself out in the mirror. They stood at quiet attention in their cassocks until Ray saw their reflection.

Ray turned and smiled. "We have a full crowd tonight, Boys. Let's do St. Augustine's proud."

The boys smiled and said 'Yes, Father."

He took a second to look at the brothers. If only they could stay this innocent, he thought.

Opening his drawer, he pulled out two envelopes. "Merry Christmas, Boys."

They eagerly grabbed the envelopes and pulled out a twenty-dollar bill. Their smiles faded as they held the small denomination. After a second, the twins simultaneously realized that gratitude was due. "Thank you, Father."

"What's the matter, you expected more?"

James, the more vocal of the two, said "Sorry, Father. It's just that Mr. Gallante gave us fifty dollars each for Mr. Fortunato's funeral. We figured we would get at least the same for Christmas Mass."

"Look, this is a blue collar parish. No one's getting rich here. Mr. Gallante has a lot of money at his disposal."

"Yes, Father."

"You'll learn in life that money can be a blessing and a curse. Be careful where and how you make your money. An honest couple of bucks beat a dishonest wad of cash any day."

He looked them over and smiled, "Now, let's go out there and honor the birth of a man who forsook wealth for greater rewards."

"Yes, Father." The three then left the sacristy and headed towards the middle aisle. As Ray followed the boys, he silently prayed "Lord Jesus, save the McNally brothers."

- - -

Gabe entered St. Augustine's alone. He dipped his finger into the Holy Water and blessed himself as he walked in, although he didn't feel particularly holy or solemn this Christmas season. After all, he had killed someone and another man was killed in retribution. His brother covered for him and lied to the police. Now his brother had asked to be removed from his sacred obligations so that he could marry his girlfriend.

He knelt in the back pew and blessed himself, then slid down towards the middle. He said a prayer for Silvio, for Tony Wagner, for Jim, Jessie, and Rico, and anyone else he could think of whose life he had altered with that one drunken act.

A thirty-something woman, a man who had to be her husband, and six kids between what appeared to be maybe twelve at the oldest and two at the youngest, piled into Gabe's pew as he slid over to make more room.

Two males immediately started to poke each other. One of them landed a slight punch onto the arm of the other. "Hey," he cried out. The mother seemed oblivious.

The father shook a finger at the boys. "Stop it. It's once a year. Be nice."

Gabe smiled to himself. Brothers. They've been fighting since Cain and Abel. They eventually bond to each other. Sometimes they even throw their lives away protecting each other.

He looked towards the altar and made a silent prayer. "Lord Jesus, protect this family and these brothers. Let them grow up and live normal, happy lives. We have too many Silvio and Enricos, and Gabe and Jims. Let these guys grow to respect themselves and each other and remain faithful to you and their community."

The ringing of hand-held bells announced the beginning of mass, and everyone stood as Gloria started into *Oh Come All Ye Faithful*. The McNally twins walked up the aisle holding tall candles. Behind them was Father Ray, done up in his finest robes for the solemn occasion. He was singing and encouraging others to join him. He made eye contact with Gabe, grimaced, and nodded as he continued singing. Gabe nodded back. God help the brothers Cooper, they both thought.

Jessie and Rico sat on the main aisle, towards the front. They both turned facing the entering altar boys and Ray. Jessie saw Ray and Gabe exchange nods. She put her arm on Rico's shoulder to steady herself. He turned to his mother and smiled. "We'll get through this," he whispered, then opened the songbook, pointed to the hymn. They joined in the song.

Mark Porfino sat opposite Jessie and Rico. He wasn't even Catholic and rarely attended any religious service, but he loved the solemnity of this occasion. As Ray passed, Mark held up the songbook and joined. Ray smiled and started to sing even louder. Maybe there is a chance after all for peace on earth, he thought.

\- - -

Father Ray finished the gospel and signaled everyone to sit. He walked out from behind the pulpit and stood in the front of the altar. This was unusual for Ray and got the attention of those who might have been tempted to doze off.

"Welcome everyone on this most holy night. I see many of our traditional faithful decked out in their finery. You look very nice indeed. I also see a few friends who choose to save the expression of their faith for occasions such as this."

There was embarrassed laughter with some coughing.

"Welcome all. May God keep you in his grace for the coming year. We are here on this happy and solemn occasion to commemorate God's gift of his Son to his people. God passed on the pomp that might be expected for the birth of a king. Rather, our Father chose a humble beginning for a Man destined to change history.

My friends, Our Father was telling us to judge a man based on his actions and not on external expressions of importance and power.

As we finish a long and eventful year in Long Harbor, we are right to reflect on those we lost during the year. Be it a husband, father, brother, or other loved one lost to senseless violence, a revered parish priest who chose to return to secular life, or some other friend or loved one no longer among us.

It is right and just for us to grieve for our losses, my brothers and sisters. We just need to remember that God is always present among us, showing us the path to salvation just like the star on that holy night led those seeking Him.

When life seems too difficult to handle, when the pressures of daily living tear away at your inner strength, remember that God gave us His Son."

Ray turned towards the manger.

"This simple, yet holy, child was born to lead us back to The Father and away from the worries and distractions of this world.

My brothers and sisters in Christ. Let us resolve in the coming year to follow the star leading us to God's son. We can do this by forgetting past injustices and focusing on being a better people. It won't be easy. It's simpler to dwell on the past. Just know that God gives us the strength to handle whatever comes our way. We just have to accept God's grace and pay it forward. For it is in giving that we receive."

Ray turned back to the pulpit and took a few steps, but stopped and turned again.

"Now let's finish this celebration of God's gift to man so that we can put on our civvies, enjoy our families, and tear into those presents."

This brought a laugh from the assembled.

Ray decided to speed through the remaining portion of the mass. The church was hot from the lights, candles, and the sheer number of people present. Many had opened their coats and were fanning themselves. He decided to skip some of the more formal singing during the consecration. Just the meat and potatoes so that we can get out of here without someone passing out, he thought to himself.

After communion, the final blessing, and announcement that the mass had ended, he signaled Gloria for the closing hymn. Gloria spoke into her microphone. "*Let there be Peace on Earth*, number 126."

He walked to the front of the altar, preceded by James and John. They genuflected together, turned and started to walk down the aisle as Gloria worked the keyboard like a Swedish masseuse and belted out the lyrics. The congregation smiled at Gloria's enthusiasm and joined in the singing.

Ray nodded to Jessie and Rico as he walked by. So brave to bear up through this all, he thought.

Looking over at Mark on the opposite side, the detective gave a thumbs-up. Ray smiled.

As he passed, Gabe returned a grim nod. The poor soul, Ray thought. To be in the line of fire of a mad woman, and then to see his brother turn away from his vocation in one week. What must be on his mind?

Standing outside the front entrance, he received the congregants, many happy souls glad to get out of the hot church and ready for a quick shot of Christmas spirits. I could go for a Flying Dog myself, he thought.

Mark stepped forward. "Wonderful service, Father Ray. You Catholics really do it up right. I liked the part about moving on. That's sound advice."

"I'm glad you liked it."

"I'm not sure if the police can follow that advice. There's too many loose ends about Silvio's death." Ray was confused by this.

Gabe followed a minute later, unaware that Mark was standing off to the side. He offered his hand to Ray.

"Bless you, Gabe. Say hello to Jim when you see him. He'll always be a friend."

Gabe smiled, showing cheer for the first time in weeks.

As he left Ray, Gabe spotted Jessie and Rico standing a few feet away. Jessie was shivering from the cold but gamely smiling and talking with those wishing her well and offering, again, their condolences. Gabe walked over and shook hands with Rico. "Merry Christmas. If there's anything you need, just let me know."

Jessie turned to Gabe, who turned to face her. "Jessie. Merry Christmas. There will be better days ahead."

Gabe extended his arms and Jessie took a step forward to embrace Gabe. "Thanks Gabe," she said. "You've always been there for us."

The hug then lasted an awkward amount of time. Rico was somewhat embarrassed as people stopped, observed Jessie's death grip on Gabe, and spoke to each other with hushed words.

Mark saw this, too. Rico tapped Gabe on the shoulder. "Gabe, we have to be getting home now. Maybe you can stop by during the holidays." Gabe let Jessie go; she was crying. Rico put his arm around her. "Let go home, Mom. It's cold out here."

- - -

Part 2: Lent

Chapter 1

The Wedding Feast

It was fifteen months later and Lent had begun. Jan and Jim were about to be married. Their relationship had been public since Christmas a year ago. Jim kept his Catholic faith and was now using his masters in Religious Philosophy to teach at Cambria College, a small, non-sectarian school. Jan continued to work at the real estate office. They shared Jan's small home in the Willows.

Jan's family had known Jim for several years, both as assistant pastor of St. Augustine's and as a community leader in helping the less fortunate find housing and jobs. Ralph and Sue Gillek held Jim in high regard. Sue once joked to her quiet and shy daughter, "Why don't you find a nice young man like Father Jim?"

Ralph and Sue's northeastern liberalism had been put to the test when Jan and Jim stopped by just before that Christmas and announced they were dating, Jim was leaving the priesthood, and—to top things off—they were moving in together. Sue forced a smile and said, "I'll make coffee." Ralph: "I'll get the Flying Dog."

Over beer, coffee, pepperoni and mushroom pizza and garlic knots, they subjected Jan and Jim to an impromptu third degree. "Are you sure about this? Have you really left the priesthood? Are you prepared for what people will think and say?"

Jan and Jim were ready for the intensity of the grilling. They held fast, expressed their love for one another, and convinced Ralph and Sue that they could face what may come. The parents looked at each other and shrugged. Ralph stood up, walked over, and shook Jim's hand. Sue embraced Jan.

Now Jan was visiting the bridal salon for a fitting with her mother. Sue was relishing being Mother of the Bride. After the fitting, they walked to a Starbucks down the street and ordered coffee and biscotti.

Jan had kept a second secret from her mother. After a sip of the strong Latte and a bite of the biscotti, Jan put down her drink, took a breath, and said "Mom, I'm pregnant."

Sue spit foam and sweet hot fluid from her Caramel Macchiato onto the table and even caught the sleeve of a male patron at the next table. He looked up, saw a drop of brown fluid on his sleeve, started to utter, "What the f…" but thought better of it.

Picking up a napkin, Sue dabbed it in water, and wiped the young man's sleeve. "Sorry. Too hot."

"That's okay. It's the most exciting thing that happened to me today."

Sue looked at Jan. "I wish I could say the same."

- - -

Six months earlier, Lucy Morgan had sold Lucy's to Sheila and run off with her friend, the TV chef. They planned to open a small restaurant in New York City: bean soup and cheesy bread served on the Great White Way. Sheila had kept the décor unchanged. She did have the electricians replace the neon *Lucy's Eat and Go* marquee with a brighter and more animated *Sheila's Diner*. She also tinkered with the menu, adding Polish recipes. Besides that, it was the same old reliable hometown diner. Gabe walked in with Jessie and Rico. After a nine-month mourning period for Silvio, Jessie and Gabe had resumed the relationship that had started in high school. First, there were impromptu meetings for coffee or lunch, and then a slow, progressive advance into a simmering romance.

Upset at first by this, Rico saw how his mother lit up at the sight of Gabe and thought about how much Gabe had helped both of them over the years. He still wasn't comfortable with the intensity of the relationship, and then with Gabe moving in, but was happy for his mother's newly found happiness.

As for him, after graduation from the community college, Rico was hired by Mario as an assistant to Nicky, his bookkeeper. Mario instructed Nicky to focus Rico on actual plumbing transactions until

Mario could groom him for bigger things. Rico liked his job even though Gabe and Jessie had warned him about Mario's connections.

The young graduate appreciated the opportunity offered by his father's mentor and assured Gabe and Jessie that he would steer clear of anything unseemly. In the six months he had been there, nothing aroused concern.

Sheila had given up waitressing, devoting her time to running the register and browbeating the cooks. A new waitress, Donna by nametag, walked over to their table and smiled. Her white teeth and trim figure got Gabe and Rico's attention. She gave a special "Hi" to Rico who returned a shy but cheerful "Hi, Donna."

Noticing Gabe and Jessie staring, he said, "Donna is a student at the college. We spent study time together before I graduated."

"He was such a smart student. I learned a lot from him. And so handsome."

Gabe saw the need to end Rico's discomfort and turned towards Donna. "I'll have a Flying Dog...Jessie?"

"An iced tea for me, please."

They were now both smiling at Rico, who shook off his fog and ordered a Diet Coke.

"You got it, and I'll be right back with cheesy bread."

The waitress swayed away to the appreciation of both men. Jessie elbowed Gabe in the ribs; realizing he'd been caught in the act, he looked down at his menu to avoid further reproach.

Jessie turned to Rico. "That's a nice young lady, and pretty, too. Now that you're employed and have some money, you should ask girls like that out. You're quite a catch, in my book."

"Thanks, Mom." Rico looked at his menu, following Gabe's approach to confrontation avoidance. "Oh, look. It's bean soup night."

Gabe and Jessie both laughed.

Donna returned with the drinks and cheesy bread. The three ordered their meals: Bean soup all around, meatloaf for Gabe, a chef salad for Jessie, and a turkey burger for Rico. Donna returned another white-toothed, killer smile and left to place the order. Gabe pretended to check his cell for messages to avoid any temptation to watch her walk into the sunset.

Turning to Rico, Jessie said, "So have you bought a suit for Jim's wedding next week?"

Rico lightly slathered a piece of cheesy bread. "I did. It will be ready by Thursday."

"Maybe you can invite that nice young lady to join you."

Seeing Jessie eyeing him and tilting her head towards Rico, Gabe took the hint and spoke up. "Of course. That's a great idea. Go for it."

"I just might. I'm not going to do it here though, in front of my mother and her boyfriend."

The front door cowbell announced the entrance of new patrons. It was Mark Porfino accompanied by Mrs. James and her daughter, Linda. If Jim's leaving the priesthood and moving in with Jan was town gossip number one, and Gabe and Jessie's romance number two, the unlikely pairing of Mark and Linda was a close third.

This confirmed bachelor had given up his monk-like devotion to his job to date this quiet, pretty offspring of the outgoing Mrs. James.

Not only that, Mark was converting to Catholicism, with Mrs. James as his sponsor. Father Ray was also taking a personal interest in Mark's spiritual journey. Maybe adding Mark to the fold would allay the loss of Jim, he thought. And who knows? Maybe Mark could also become a Sunday afternoon football and Flying Dog buddy.

Sheila was walking Mark and the James women past Gabe's table. The detective stopped to greet them. After saying hello, Gabe returned to checking his cell to avoid further conversation.

But Mark was looking straight at him. "What a difference a year or so makes to all of our lives. Gabe and I have found companionship amidst all the turmoil of the past and this young man has blossomed into his own. How are things going at Gallante Plumbing? I'm sure there are enough bookkeeping transactions to keep you occupied."

Annoyed at the reference, Rico managed a smile. "It's going great, Detective. You have no idea how many leaks need fixing. It's a challenge to keep up with the paperwork."

Mark wanted to pursue this, but thought the better of it. "Why am

I discussing business this evening when there's cheesy bread to be consumed?" Mark looked over to the approaching Donna, carefully balancing the entrees. "And here's your meal."

Leaning over to Rico, he said, "I think your waitress is giving you the eye. Go for it, young man. No time like the present."

Seeing Sheila standing at their table, he said, "I must be off. Mustn't keep Sheila waiting."

- - -

Ted Hanson interviewed Miriam Wagner shortly after her brother's death. Miriam confirmed that there was enmity between Tony and Silvio, and that they indeed had planned to meet that night, but she denied the allegation that Tony intended to kill Silvio, and no evidence was found to support it.

There had been calls between Miriam and Tony around the time of the death, and a few calls between Tony and Silvio prior to the killing, but nothing that could point with any certainty to Tony planning to kill Silvio.

The Silvio case file was left in the open state. Carla's confession laid the killing on Tony, but Mark and Ted both felt that Gabe was still a suspect. However, there was no point in pursuing Gabe while his alibi stuck.

Both men had testified at Carla's trial. The judge and jury were sympathetic to Carla, the distraught lover, but she was found guilty and sentenced to ten years in Cambria Adult Correctional, known as CAC, considered a country club in law enforcement circles. The sentence and assignment weren't bad, considering she had shot someone in cold blood in front of dozens of witnesses.

The romance between Ted and Teresa McGill had heated up and then, nine months ago, abruptly ended. Mark and Ted had both suspected a leak within the department during the Silvio investigation. They subpoenaed Mario's cell records and unearthed a series of calls from a disposable cell.

One night at Teresa's, Ted noticed a cell different from her normal phone. When she was in the kitchen, Ted opened the cell and checked the last calls. They were to Mario's cell. Ted looked into Teresa's background and discovered she was Mario's niece.

On confronting Teresa, she admitted to being Mario's informant. Asked how he knew, Ted admitted looking through her phone; end of romance. Still, Ted had strong feelings for Teresa and offered to allow her to resign. If she left, he would not turn her in. Teresa moved to Cambria and was reportedly working for Mario and dating Rico. Small world.

Three months later, Ted Hanson was promoted to Police Investigator and now reported to Mark. He headed up certain investigations with Mark mentoring. They met almost daily to go over the status of cases they were working, and would occasionally kick around the Silvio case.

Ted was in the station this Saturday even though it was Mark's weekend for coverage. Mark, through his relationship with Linda James, a friend of Jan's, had been invited to Jim and Jan's wedding. Ted reviewed his cases and then picked up some files his boss was working on. Mark permitted Ted to review his files and encouraged openness between them on all cases. He found the *Silvio* folder and opened it. So tell me, Gabe, he thought. Where was your mistake? What's going to lead to your demise?

- - -

The Knights of Columbus Hall in Cambria had a thriving wedding business. It could seat two hundred plus and had a fully equipped kitchen. More importantly, there was a large finished bar to support such a crowd, and a Whiskey Sour fountain.

Ralph Gillek, father of the bride and financier of the wedding feast, had gone top shelf on the liquor and local brews, but lower budget on the whiskey for the fountain. He assumed that those dipping in would not notice any quality difference from the top shelf.

After the entrance of the bridal party, the bandleader asked Gabe to say a few words toasting the bride and groom. The crowd came silent as Gabe stood. He cleared his throat and turned towards Jan and Jim.

"Jan, Jim, this is a very happy and blessed day for all of us. We here are privileged to share in your happiness and wish you the best of luck as you begin your new lives. Jim, you've married a beautiful bride from a wonderful family." Ralph and Sue smiled at this as the crowd applauded.

"Jan, you married a caring, giving man, who above all is a faithful friend through thick and thin." Gabe then paused and appeared to be tearing up. "Treasure each other."

He turned to the crowd. "Everyone, please join me in toasting Jan and Jim."

Voices responded "To Jan and Jim" and everyone drank. Gabe went over to Jan and hugged her. He then shook Jim's hand and they embraced. Not a dry eye in the house except possibly for Mark Porfino. Through thick and thin, he thought. Maybe thick as thieves.

After the toast, Gabe walked around to mingle and spotted Ray. He sat and they talked. Ralph, grinning and almost giddy from the moment, joined them. He was relieved that the reception was going so well.

When the catering manager walked over and whispered to Ralph that the Whiskey Sour fountain was a big hit but was running low, Gabe, Mark, and Ray heard him. Best Man Gabe stood and said, "I got this."

Walking to a quiet corner, he called Lou and asked him to bring over a case of Crown Royal. Fifteen minutes later, the whiskey arrived, and the caterer directed the bar staff to mix in the new batch.

Shortly after, the manager walked over to the table where Gabe, Ralph and Mark were sitting.

"Ralph, that new batch of sours is great. People usually serve the lesser brands after a few hours. This stuff is premium."

Ralph turned to Gabe, "Gabe, you saved the day."

Ray, who had earlier switched to the whisky sours and was feeling no pain, looked at Gabe and held up his glass. "It's a miracle," Ray proclaimed, as he stood to get a refill.

The detective shook his head and thought, the man is unbelievable. He's going to be difficult to trip up with all of these guardian angels.

- - -

Chapter 2
Revelations

Carla Ciccone walked through Cambria Park. It was a sunny afternoon, warm for late March. The park was a favorite of the locals. Ducks and turtles swam in Cambria Creek. Children ran about flying inexpensive plastic kites after their fathers untangled enough string to allow flightworthiness. Parents chatted with each other as they kept an eye on their kids from a distance.

She stopped walking and took a deep breath. It felt good to breathe clean air and be warmed by the bright sun. A pair of screaming, laughing children ran by and brought her out of her solitude. One of them dropped a Frisbee. Carla bent down, picked up the green disk, brushed off some dirt, and handed it back to the young girl. She appeared to be wary of Carla, but muttered a "thank you" and ran off to join her friends. The friends were eyeing Carla, but went back to playing when the girl joined them.

She spotted a bench facing the creek and walked over. A man in a dark suit sat, watching the small stream flow by. Starting to ask if she could sit, she noticed that the man seemed almost trancelike. Deciding not to destroy his peaceful state, she sat, looked around, and took time again to take in the pleasant surroundings and the people enjoying the spring day.

The man emitted a gurgling cough and seemed to labor in his breathing. Carla looked over. "Are you okay, Sir?" The man turned to her. He had a large red stain on his suit coat and the shirt underneath. Tony Wagner. "Hello, Carla. Sorry, I've had trouble breathing ever since you shot me."

She went pale, speechless for a moment. Gathering the courage to respond, she replied, "Well, you shouldn't have shot Silvio. He was all I had to live for. You deserved to die." Tony coughed and again took a moment to catch his breath. "Well, it's too late now, but you shot the wrong man."

He smiled. "All the same, I did kill Enrico Fortunato, so I guess you saved someone else the effort."

She faced Tony and looked him in the eyes, which was quite a trick since they had decayed in the last fifteen months. "You're denying still that you killed Silvio? Why? You're dead and must have had to confront your maker." Tony smiled. "That I have. All things considered, I'd rather be in Cambria," Tony said and laughed at this, channeling W.C. Fields.

"I saw you follow Silvio that night. He knew you killed Enrico. He told me that he was meeting you and that you both were going to have it out. You killed him to keep him quiet."

Tony coughed again and needed a minute to catch his breath. "A hearse is going down the street when the back door opens and the casket falls out. It's a steep hill and the casket starts to slide down. The undertaker and his assistant try to slow the heavy box but they're losing the battle. It continues to slide downhill. The undertaker sees a drug store and directs his assistant to keep pushing back while he gets help. He runs into the pharmacy and goes up to the counter. The pharmacist puts down a prescription he's filling and asks is he can help the excited man. The undertaker says "Quick, give me something to stop this coffin."

The dead man laughed so hard that he had to hold his side. New blood oozed from his wound. "That joke is funnier when you're dead." Tony turned serious. "Sorry, Carla. I didn't kill Silvio. You shot the wrong guy. I did see who killed him though. I'm not sure why he didn't just call it in. It was self-defense."

"Who was it?"

"It's always the quiet ones you need to be wary of. Think about it. Who else did Silvio have major issues with?"

Carla thought for a moment. "Gabe Cooper. But he had an alibi."

Tony looked up at a kite that had broken loose and was flying away from a crying child. "Alibis are like kites. They hold up for a while, but the flimsy ones come apart. Ask Detective Porfino to stay on the trail. Gabe's flimsy plastic cover will come loose eventually."

He smiled. "Oh, by the way, I wasn't the only witness to the killing. Mr. Richardson's four-legged-ball-of-energy was there that night. That's why Reggie goes crazy when he sees Gabe. Reggie loved Silvio. If he could finger Gabe for the killing, he would. Maybe man's best friend can help our Detective Porfino. Maybe he can undo Gabe's alibi and show how it flies away."

Carla woke up gasping. Looking around, she realized she was in her cell, ten by six feet of grey walls and a cold cement floor. She walked over to her one amenity, a thinly lit opening with an obstructed view of Cambria Park. Taking a minute to collect herself, she located the creek and the wooden bench. The bench was empty. Nearby was a broken plastic kite.

– – –

Mark walked into his office on Monday morning whistling *YMCA*. The wedding band may not have been great musicians, but they could get a crowd going. Mark had even participated in the Chicken Dance. On top of that, after dropping Mrs. James off at her house, he and Linda went back to Mark's apartment and did it like crazed rabbits. He now understood why marriage was such a valued institution. Getting laid afterwards was just a matter of letting the emotion of the day take its natural course.

Ted walked to Mark's doorway and was about to knock as a matter of form when he noticed that Mark was staring out the window and humming what appeared to be *Macho Man* from the Village People. Ted hadn't seen Mark so tuneful before. He decided to knock lightly to give him a chance to return to terra firma.

The detective stopped whistling between the macho and the man and spun around. Seeing Ted, he smiled. "Just remembering Saturday. Come in."

Ted walked in, pulled back the padded chair and sat. A muffled noise. "This is from Interrogation Room A, isn't it?"

Mark shrugged. "Nicer than mine. I swapped one out. Why should the accused have all of the fun?" Mark took a breath and turned serious. "So what's going on, Ted?"

The young detective straightened, avoiding another pleather incident.

"I was looking over the Silvio file again. What did we miss? We both know that Tony was too smart to kill Silvio the same way as Enrico." He sighed. "I'm coming around to your thinking. It probably was Gabe Cooper. Maybe we should focus on undoing his alibi."

Mark drummed his fingers on his desk. "I'm convinced it was self-defense. I don't like open cases, though. Gabe will unravel somewhere along the line. I'm walking a fine line on this. Since he moved in with Jessie, I just can't accuse him outright of killing her husband. I need solid proof before I disrupt her and young Rico's life. But don't worry, I'm not giving up."

"I'll keep looking too, Mark. There has to be an opening somewhere."

"Ted. For now, this conversation does not go beyond this office. Mario may have a mole here."

He looked at Mark for some indication that he might have known about Teresa. "Okay Mark, mum's the word."

Ted left the office and Mark watched as his young charge walked away. Now let's see if that gets to Mario, he thought.

Mark turned on his laptop and waited for it to boot. His phone rang and he considered having it go to voice mail, until he noticed the number was from Cambria Adult Correctional. The operator identified the call as collect. Mark accepted the charges and awaited a voice on the line.

"Detective Porfino, this is Carla Ciccone. I think I made a big mistake about Tony Wagner." There was a pause as Mark absorbed this. "Are you there, Detective?"

He squeezed his eyes shut and reluctantly answered. "Yes, Miss Ciccone. What makes you change your mind about Tony after almost a year and a half?"

This time, the pause was on Carla's end. "I spoke to Tony last night. He cleared it up for me."

- - -

Mark arranged to visit Carla in the afternoon. He considered telling Ted but decided to see how the visit went. May be just the ranting of a mad woman, he thought. He cleared his afternoon calendar but left space for a 4 p.m. meeting with Stanley Richardson. Mr. Richardson and Mark had become friends in the last fifteen months. Stanley asked for the meeting but didn't explain the purpose.

Leaving his office at noon, he stopped at Popeye's on the way to the prison. Feeling hungry after his morning '80's revival, he ordered the 3-piece combo meal with mashed potatoes, topped off with a large Coke. Minutes later, he wiped off his fingers and slurped the last of the drink. He slid into his car and started the engine, then spotted the spearmint gum and unrolled a piece. Have to hide the chicken, he thought. Linda will kill me later on if she knows I went off my diet.

Mark arrived at CAC thirty minutes later. By that time, the effects of the grease and large soda had kicked in and he was squirming as he signed the visitor's log and asked to see Warden Cummings. He sat in the Warden's outer office, as Ed Cummings was late returning from rounds. Mark stood up and walked to Sherry the receptionist. "Sherry, can I use the men's room before I see Ed?"

Noticing the anxiety in Mark, she took pity. "You can use the warden's bathroom. I'll let you in."

He closed the door and landed on the porcelain just seconds before Armageddon. Reaching for the paper to conclude his business, he flushed his sins away. As Mark washed his hands, he noticed there was no exhaust fan and no window either. He waved his arms as if this would dispel any evidence of the foul deed and returned to the waiting room.

The warden appeared a few minutes later, walked over to Mark, shook his hand and invited him into the office. As he approached his desk, he stopped cold. "What the hell?" he said, looking towards his bathroom.

"Sorry, Ed. I think it was something I ate."

Ed opened a drawer, pulled out a strawberry scented candle, held his breath, walked into the bathroom, lit the candle, and closed the door.

He looked at Mark, who was having trouble making eye contact. "Popeye's," Mark mumbled.

"I understand. I love the stuff but have the same consequences. We're not twenty anymore, Mark."

The warden turned away from the bathroom as the candle only accomplished so much. "So how can I help you?"

"I've arranged to talk to Carla Ciccone today. She called me and said that she thinks she killed the wrong man. She said that Tony Wagner told her who the real killer was."

Ed sat up straight. "Tony died the night she shot him. You know that. Do you think she's going for some insanity deal? Maybe to lessen her sentence?"

Mark shrugged. "She *sounded* clear-headed to me. What do you think?"

"She's one of the sanest inmates in here. Hers was a crime of passion, but she's no nut job."

"I agree. This is probably a wild goose chase, but I want to hear what she has to say."

Ed picked up the phone and called the guard station. "Tell Monica I have Detective Porfino from the Long Harbor Police here. He needs to question Carla Ciccone. Please tell her to escort him to the Visitor's Center and stay with him throughout his questioning."

He put the phone down and looked at Mark. "Monica Stevens will escort you back. She's pretty close to Carla. Let her observe. She might have some insight into what's going on."

Picking up the Strawberry Lysol, he took the long walk to his bathroom. Mark could hear him blowing out the candle. He opened the door, spun around, and sprayed for ten seconds in a sweeping motion. He then walked back to his desk. "Oh, and keep your guard up. These inmates can be manipulative. Don't believe everything she says."

- - -

Stanley Richardson and Claire Woodward met for lunch at Sheila's diner. Mark Porfino had introduced Stanley to Claire shortly after the events surrounding Silvio's killing and the later shooting of Tony Wagner. He had spoken to both individually about the events and noticed a common spark of vitality. Mark wasn't normally a matchmaker, but saw no harm in introducing the pair. Stanley and Claire hit it off right away. The clincher was Reggie's affinity for Claire. Reggie was not easy to win over, but Claire treated Reggie with such affection that the terrier never had a chance.

Now, fifteen months later, Stanley and Claire had become a regular topic of the town gossip mill. Today, they were having lunch in their favorite meeting place. Sheila herself waited on them and the entire crowd greeted the couple as local royalty. After the clam chowder, grilled cheese, and tapioca pudding, Stanley ordered coffee for them both.

As Sheila went to fetch the brew, Stanley reached into his coat pocket and pulled out a small velvet box, stood while balancing a hand on the table, walked over to Claire's side of the booth, and went down on one knee. He opened the small box and revealed a simple diamond ring. He cleared his throat. "Claire Woodward, will you do me the honor of marrying me?"

At first, Claire thought Stanley was joking, but soon realized he was serious. She also noticed that the surrounding patrons and gradually the entire diner had quieted and was watching the event. Claire looked at Stanley, who seemed nervous yet happy. He also appeared to be tentatively keeping his balance in this position. Claire took a breath and said, "Of course I will, you old fool." She leaned over and hugged Stanley, who struggled to stand up in mid-hug. The diner erupted in applause.

He placed the ring on Claire's finger to a second round of approval. Sheila came over, put down the coffee, and hugged them both. Claire held out her hand to show the ring. "It's beautiful," Sheila said. She took a step back to look at the happy couple. "Let me know when you set a date."

Stanley smiled and looked at Claire, who laughed. "It will have to be soon. We're not getting any younger." The crowd cheered.

– – –

Monica arrived at Ed's office and, after a quick introduction, led Mark to the visiting area. She called the guard station and instructed an officer to bring Carla down to the Visitor's Room. Mark was led into the empty room and shown to an uncomfortable chair with a counter containing a black phone.

Across from him was a glass partition. Monica left Mark saying she would return with Carla. In a minute, she walked through the door on the inmate side holding her by the arm.

The officer led Carla to the chair across from Mark. She picked up the phone and instructed Mark to do the same. Monica then pressed the Speaker button on Carla's phone. "I'm putting this on speaker Carla, so know in advance that there should be no expectation of privacy."

"I understand."

Mark spoke into the mouthpiece. "What do you have, Carla?"

She took a breath. "I know this will sound crazy, Detective, but I met Tony Wagner last night. In a dream. He told me he didn't kill Silvio. He said that Gabe Cooper killed Silvio during a fight. He said it was self-defense."

"Carla, what's going on? It's too late for an insanity defense."

"I know it sounds crazy, but it got me thinking. If Tony killed Enrico, he would be too smart to kill a second time under similar circumstances."

Mark shrugged. "We realize that. This case isn't closed, Carla. It's just that we can't undo any other alibis yet."

"Tony says that alibis are like kites; the flimsy ones break apart in a steady wind." She paused for a second, thinking. "Besides, there was another witness."

Mark sat up. "Someone who saw the killing? Who?"

Carla looked around as if divulging a state secret. "Mr. Richardson's dog. He saw the whole thing."

He covered his face with his hand, thought for a second, then looked up at Carla. "And how do you suggest we get Reggie to testify?"

Carla looked towards the ceiling and thought a second. "Tony told me Reggie goes crazy when he sees Gabe. Maybe you can arrange some meeting between them. Maybe this will get Gabe to drop his guard."

Carla sat forward and fixed Mark with a stare that unnerved him.

"Look, Detective, I know this sounds crazy. Maybe it was just a sleep-deprived fantasy, but I just can't lie here at night wondering if I shot the wrong man."

"I'll see what I can do, Carla. In the meantime, try to dream of more pleasant things. You shot a bad guy, just for the wrong reason."

He put down the phone and waved to Monica. As Monica was leading her from the room, Carla turned and smiled, "Like a kite," she said. She seemed oddly at peace with herself and chatted with her jailer as they went out the door.

Mark waited until Monica returned. She smiled. "What do you think?"

"I'll see what the dog says," he replied.

Returning to his car after saying goodbye to Ed Cummings, he switched on some jazz and drove off. He looked at the console clock. Now for my appointment with Stanley Richardson, he thought. What other revelations are left for today?

After returning to her station, Monica clocked out for her break, which had been delayed by Mark's visit. She went to the staff dining room and chose a quiet corner away from the other staff on break. She pulled out an unregistered cell and dialed the only number stored.

After a few seconds, a man answered. Monica looked around one last time. "Detective Porfino was just here talking with Carla Ciccone."

There was a pause as the man responded. "Yes, the woman who shot Tony Wagner. She's having second thoughts. She thinks Gabe Cooper shot Silvio."

She took a breath as she responded to the next question. "Apparently Mr. Richardson's dog saw the whole thing." She winced at the third degree. "No, I'm not drunk. Just telling you what happened."

"Okay. I'll see what else she has," she said as she heard a click.

- - -

Returning to his office just before four, Mark motioned Ted in. "Carla tells me that she shot the wrong man. It was Gabe who killed Silvio."

Ted shrugged. "We pretty much believe that, too. What made Carla decide this now, after fifteen months?"

"She met Tony in a dream. He explained it all to her."

Ted didn't know how to answer. Was Mark pulling his leg? "What else did she say?"

"There was another witness to the killing.

"Who?

Mark drummed his fingers, slumped in his chair and sighed. "Mr. Richardson's dog, Reggie."

Ted's second moment of stunned silence. He collected himself enough to smile. "Well, that explains why Reggie goes crazy when he sees Gabe. Here I thought it was because he was a hyperactive mutt."

Mark sat up. "Mr. Richardson will be here soon. Maybe keep that opinion to yourself." Mark laughed. "We don't want to aggravate the star witness or his master."

- - -

At four, Officer Manning from the front desk called to say that Mr. Richardson was here for his meeting.

Mark looked at Ted, "We play this straight, Ted. We're at a dead end on the Silvio case. Let's see where this leads."

A few moments later, John Manning knocked on Mark's door. He stood next to a beaming Stanley Richardson. Mark stood, as did Ted, following Mark's cue. "Come in, Stanley." He looked at the officer. "That will be all, Officer. I'll see Mr. Richardson out when we've finished." Manning nodded and turned to Mr. Richardson. "It was a pleasure meeting you, Sir."

Stanley walked in. "Such a pleasant young man. He saw my picture of Reggie when I opened my wallet to show ID. Turns out he has an adorable pooch also— Maxwell, I believe." He turned to Ted. "Man's best friend, although some folks may not think so."

The young man gave an embarrassed smile and pulled out a chair for the elderly visitor. Mark smiled at Ted, who was realizing that there was more to Mr. Richardson than met the eye.

"Now how can I help you, Stanley? What brings you in this afternoon?"

"Might as well share this with everyone. Mark, today I proposed to Claire Woodward. We're getting married in two weeks."

Mark sat back, open-mouthed yet silent. After a moment, he said "That's wonderful, Stanley. I knew you two were dating, but this comes as a real surprise."

"Congratulations, Sir," chimed in Ted.

Mr. Richardson nodded his thanks to Ted. "Now Mark, I've come to know you as a friend and a straight shooter over this last year. I can't think of anyone else I'd like to stand beside me on my wedding day. Will you be my best man?"

Mark laughed. "Of course, Stanley. I'd be honored."

"Great. It will be a small wedding party, just you and me, Claire and whoever she chooses." Stanley smiled. "Oh, and Reggie, of course. He's going to be ring bearer."

- - -

Claire Woodward drove directly from Sheila's to the Willows section of town, giddy after leaving Stanley to his appointment with Mark. She decided to line up her Maid of Honor without delay. In the last fifteen months or so, she had developed a close friendship with Jan. Initially, it was the maiden aunt advising her young charge on the ways of the world. Later, the women attained an equal footing as Jan's assertiveness blossomed.

Now they were close friends, confiding in each other, and complaining about the men in their lives: Jim, the loving, but sometimes secretive, ex-priest; Stanley, the observer of all things, who didn't shy away from expressing himself. Claire had been delighted when Jan and Jim announced their engagement; Stanley had been more subdued. He didn't seem to trust Jim.

Now Claire was going to ask Jan to be Maid of Honor. She drove to 118 Longshore, and parked, noticing that Jim's car was there but not Jan's. Truth be told, she didn't quite care for Jim, either.

Something gnawed at her about him. She initially considered waiting for Jan to arrive home, but decided to greet Jim and wait inside.

Claire left her Nissan and walked up the gravel driveway. Noticing a curtain open, then close, she smiled. "There's no hiding, Jim. I will soon be at your door."

She rang the bell and heard the typical "company's here" ding-dong. After a minute, the sound of footsteps and then a squeak as the door opened. Jim smiled, though it seemed somewhat forced to Claire. "Claire. Please come in. Jan's on her way home."

Claire smiled and walked in. Jim took her coat and led her into the living room. "Please sit, Claire. Is there anything I can get you?"

Declining, she sat on the couch. Jim sat in an easy chair across from her. Next to the chair was a bible with a piece of paper slicking out, presumably marking Jim's place. The paper looked like a sports betting slip. Next to the bible was a pencil. Jim noticed that Claire had spotted the paperwork.

Jim nodded to the scripture. "Catching up on my New Testament for my Religious Philosophy course. I haven't picked up the bible as often as I should after I left the priesthood. Still, it comes back quickly."

Claire smiled. "I guess old habits die hard."

He wondered if she meant the bible reading or the betting. He now knew what Claire and Stanley saw in each other. They enjoyed being inscrutable. A squeak preceded the door opening and a skirted leg appeared. After a few seconds of key jangling, Jan walked in juggling a bag of groceries. Jim jumped up and relieved Jan of the load.

Jan spotted Claire, smiled, and offered a warm hello as Jim took the groceries to the kitchen.

"What a surprise! What brings you here today?"

Jan sat next to Claire on the couch, while Jim returned and sat in the easy chair. He picked up the bible, tucked in the betting slip and put the bible in a drawer.

Claire held out her hand. Jan spotted the ring and gasped. "Did Stanley propose?"

Jim sat forward. He hadn't noticed the ring.

"Just this afternoon. Right in the middle of Sheila's, in front of the lunch crowd."

Jan laughed. "That's wonderful, Claire. You two were meant for each other."

"Absolutely. I was just thinking that," Jim agreed.

Claire smiled and stared at the diamond. "The old coot got down on one knee and asked me to marry him. I felt like I was 20, not 78."

Jan took Claire's hand to look closer. "Very nice, and very sweet. So have you picked a date?"

"Yes, two weeks from Saturday. We're not getting any younger. Plus, we wanted to get it done before Holy Week. And Jan, we have been such good friends for this last year or so. I trust you more than anyone. I would like you to be my Maid of Honor."

Jan looked at Jim, who nodded. "Of course, Claire. I'd be honored."

Claire stood. "Well, no time to delay. I'm going to contact St. Agnes's and also start writing the invitations. Let's meet Saturday morning at Long Harbor Bridal. I hope they have something in my size. I wonder if I can still wear white."

"You'll be beautiful," Jan said.

Jim stood up and reached for Claire's coat. "So, who's going to be Stanley's best man?"

"Detective Porfino. Stanley and Mark are close friends."

She looked skyward in thought. "It's almost like they share some secret that they will someday spring on the world."

Jim paled, but collected himself and helped Claire with her coat. She thanked him and said, "Oh, and I'm inviting your brother and family, too. Stanley speaks of Gabe often. He remembers the days at Jackson Place. How he'd take walks with Reggie and talk to Gabe. I think he and Reggie both miss Gabe."

- - -

Chapter 3

Suffer the Little Ones

Christy's Salon was popular with the men in Long Harbor despite the presence of large hair dryers, women's magazines, and other trappings of female cosmetology. This was because a small back section had been transformed into a man cave with a large screen HDTV, Predator cheerleader posters, sports memorabilia, and stylists in low-cut white blouses who charmed even the crustiest holder of both an X and Y chromosome.

Gabe and Rico walked into the salon and were greeted by Antonio, co-owner with his sister Christy. Antonio was as flaming as you could get, but loved his Predators and the man cave he had developed himself. He welcomed the men, regular customers, and led them back to the inner sanctum.

He called out "Yoo hoo, Gina. Two more regulars." Gina Vivaldi appeared from behind a curtain. She was chewing gum and sniffling from a slight cold, but her firm, shapely figure made her look like Helen of Troy to the handful of tonsorial clients present. She was also wearing a gold necklace that must have set some admirer back.

"Okay, who should I do first?"

Gabe and Rico looked at each other and laughed. "I guess I need it more," said Gabe.

She waved him to a chair and put a cloth drape around him as he settled in. Rico found a chair facing the TV. On the 55" screen, a March Madness tournament game was in progress. Duke was throttling an Ivy League team as the announcers were already discussing their next opponent. He decided to reach for a *Guns and Ammo* magazine that looked like it had been well leafed through.

"So Gabe, what can I do to you?" Gabe looked up to see Rico

smiling as he looked over the latest Glocks.

"Just a trim, Gina. I'm going to a wedding next week."

"Oh, whose?"

He caught Gina's eye in the mirror. "Stanley Richardson and Claire Woodward."

The young woman laughed. "I heard about that. I think that's wonderful. I hope old man Richardson can still hold up his side of the bargain. No use for the bim and the bang if he can't deliver the boom." The assembled males laughed along with their stylists.

Gabe thought a second. "I hadn't really thought of that. I think it's great that they found each other this late in life. Once someone finds their soul mate, everything else falls in place and nothing that came before really matters."

The ladies and Antonio let out a collective "Aaaah," but the male patrons stared at Gabe uncertain how to react. Sounded a little too gay for them. Rico looked up to see Gabe smiling at him. He nodded. Gabe had been good for his mother, and she for him.

Gina clipped away with the scissors and started to babble. She had attained styling nirvana years ago and was capable of chatting on all subjects that crossed her mind regardless of her captive client. In the spirit of the upcoming nuptials, she was discussing her love life and her recent breakup with off-and-on again boyfriend, Guido.

Gabe had lowered his listening switch as had most of the assembled males. The stylists and Antonio, though, were listening and nodding. Gabe's autopilot was interrupted by the ring tone of Gina's cell. It was the theme to the Sopranos.

Gina stopped cutting. "Do you mind if I answer this, Gabe?"

"Go ahead.

She examined the incoming number. "Speak of the devil," Gina chirped as she raised her hands in exasperation just missing Gabe's ear with the scissors. "Yeah, what's up Guido?"

Silence as the whole man cave listened in. "What? Tell you what, you can have it back when you take back that *Guido* tattoo that I have on my ass."

Hanging up, she shoved the cell into her pocket. "That creep wants me to return this necklace he gave me on Valentine's Day."

Antonio and the stylists stopped cutting and groaned.

The men were quiet. They knew they were just visiting Planet Estrogen and had better watch their step. They were also collectively thinking of the tattoo.

After a few seconds, a brave male called out "Hey Gina, where'd you get the ring tone?"

She stopped cutting again, just missing Gabe's ear. "Actually, the creep got that for me, too. He wanted me to remember him whenever I got a call. What a controlling bastard."

The man slumped in his chair and remained quiet. Gabe frowned and said aloud, "Where have I heard that ring tone before? I remember that it surprised me when I first heard it. It was a while back, I think."

He thought for a second and caught Rico staring at him in the mirror. Gabe realized the tone had been on Silvio's phone that night. "Oh, well, not important I guess," he mumbled.

After a second, he looked back to the young man, who appeared to be sullen and lost in thought.

Gina continued cutting. "So Gabe, what were you talking about before? Oh, yeah, the wedding between Richardson and Claire Woodward." She thought for a second. "I think you're right Gabe. Once you find a soul mate, it doesn't matter what else happened before."

- - -

Rico rolled off Teresa McGill, looked up at the ceiling and sighed. Teresa looked at him, thought a moment, covered herself in the sheet, and asked, "Is everything okay? You seemed distracted."

He looked over at his sex buddy and smiled. "I'm all right, Teresa. I was just thinking about something that happened this weekend."

She propped herself on the pillow, exposing her left breast. "So tell me. Anything happen with you and your girlfriend?"

He shifted and turned towards Teresa. He tried to answer as he examined her perfect areola.

"Donna? No, it's all good."

Touching most of his body as she slid over, she also ran her hand down his back. "Does she know about us?"

There wasn't enough blood rushing to Rico's brain to answer right away. "No. This is just a late night at the office."

She was upset by this and paused for a few seconds. "Maybe we can make this more than just passing time."

"Teresa, I dated Donna more on a dare from my mother than because of anything wrong between us. Remember, we were just casual friends who dated once in a while at the time I asked Donna to Uncle Jim's wedding."

"Would you break up with Donna if I asked you?" Teresa removed her hand from Rico's back, slid it to the front and fondled him. "What if I said pretty please?"

At that point, he would have promised to walk barefoot through coals.

"I will. I'll tell her tomorrow."

He thought for a second as he lay losing control of his thought faculties. "What are you doing a week from Saturday? How would you like to go to Mr. Richardson's wedding with me?"

– – –

St. Agnes church in Cambria was filled with colorful spring flowers that evoked life emerging anew. Stanley was insistent on this. "Nothing that looks like a funeral arrangement," he told the florist. For a man of modest tastes and presumed similar means, Stanley had wowed Claire and the various wedding merchants with his willingness to spare no expense. "I'm only getting married once. Let's do this right."

Monsignor William George himself was going to preside. Stanley and the monsignor had become friends while sharing too many whiskey sours at Jim's wedding.

Today, Bill was going to join Stanley and Claire Woodward in holy matrimony. Another Lenten marriage. He hoped that the bishop would understand. Stanley, like Ralph Gillek, made a tidy contribution to the building fund.

Bill still couldn't get over Stanley's decision to tie the knot at his age, but gladly agreed to preside. This was out of affection for Stanley and the promise of a rip- roaring reception. He walked through the church and made sure that all was in order. He looked up at the choir loft. He had convinced Gloria from St. Augustine's to play the organ. His parish organist Susie was competent, but not flashy. Gloria was the rock star among organists in the diocese. She could get Mormons singing at a Starbucks opening (her little joke).

Gloria was practicing as Bill waved at her. What was that song? he asked himself. It sounded like *Sit Down You're Rockin' the Boat* from Guys and Dolls. Oh well, as long as she sticks to traditional wedding songs during the ceremony.

Walking into the sacristy, he opened the closet, looked at his vestments, studied his color combo, and thought. Violet for Lent. It blends with the flowers anyway. He put on his white robe followed by the violet stole and chasuble. Examining himself in the mirror, he thought himself quite the dashing vicar.

In the mirror, he saw Mark and Mathew Clark walk in. These were the altar boys for the wedding as they were also top-of-the-line among his altar servers: tall, handsome boys who would someday break ladies' hearts. Mark and Matthew could also sing well, a rarity for servers. Their father was choir lead and quite the crooner.

He turned to the boys. "Mark, Matthew, we have a big day today. It's not often that people in their seventies get married. Let's do it up right."

Reaching into his pocket, he removed some cash. "Oh, and Mr. Richardson, the groom, wants you to have this." He handed the boys a fifty each. The twins let out a "Whoa" that signaled their approval. "Let's make this a day they'll talk about for years."

\- - -

Stanley looked in the mirror. His black tuxedo fit his gaunt frame like he was born to wear it. "Not bad, if I do say so myself."

Mark stood back and looked at the self-admiring groom as Reggie, wearing a mini tux of his own, circled Stanley for a closer inspection. "Stanley, you look great. If I wasn't straight, I'd marry you myself."

Both men laughed and Reggie emitted his shrill terrier bark of approval.

Stanley looked out the window to take in the arriving guests. Jim

Cooper was by himself since Jan was Maid of Honor and attending to Claire. He was talking to his brother Gabe, Jessie, Rico, and a woman who appeared to be Rico's date.

"The Coopers are here," Stanley called out.

Mark stood behind Stanley and looked at the five guests chatting. Rico appeared to be introducing his date.

"Well, I'll be." Mark uttered. "It's Teresa McGill. She must be Rico's date. It's a good thing Ted's not here."

The elderly man shrugged as he watched the intros, which appeared to be somewhat awkward. "Life goes on, Mark. I never did understand why she left so abruptly."

Mark shook his head. "Me neither. She just said 'personal matters.'"

Stanley walked back to the mirror and seemed to be speaking to the mirror as he checked for any sartorial flaws.

"I always found it funny, though, that Mario Gallante's niece would be working for the police department."

Mark's jaw dropped. "I didn't know she was his niece."

He turned back to watch the fivesome walk towards the church. Of course, Mark thought. I wonder if Ted knew about that.

– – –

Claire and Jan sat in the back of a white stretch limo rented by Stanley for the occasion. Sammy, the chauffer, had greeted the ladies in his slight but charming African accent, helped them into the Lincoln, and explained the amenities. He opened a small fridge, brought out a bottle of Champagne and two flute glasses. He poured the liquid and handed a glass to each.

"Ladies, enjoy. I'll get you to the church on time."

The women laughed and clicked their glasses. Sammy circled the car for a last inspection and slid into the front seat. He looked through the glass separating himself from them. "If there's anything you need, just let me know."

Claire looked at the handsome graying man, emptied her flute, seemed to think a moment, and sighed. "Are you married, Sammy?"

The driver looked into the rear view mirror. "No, Ma'am. I guess I haven't found the right woman."

Claire laughed. "I'll keep you in mind if this doesn't work out."

Sammy tipped his cap and started to drive.

Jan took Claire's glass. "Maybe you should go easy on this stuff; mustn't be seducing the chauffeur on your wedding day."

The both laughed. Sammy smiled and started to whistle *Get Me to the Church on Time.*

- - -

Monsignor George walked into the room where Stanley and Mark were waiting. Also in the room was Eddie Smalley, Stanley's nephew. Eddie was holding Reggie and petting him gently. Stanley handed Eddie the ring box.

"Ready, Eddie? This is Reggie's big moment."

The young man smiled, "Ready, Uncle Stan." He looked at the terrier. "Ready, Reggie? Let's give them something to remember."

Mark and Matthew walked into the room, grinning. Stanley seemed to understand why they were so happy. Monsignor George took this in but didn't comment.

"Okay. So just like we practiced. Mark, you walk out first, followed by Stanley. Both of you stand to the side of the altar. Mark and Mathew will follow and I'll follow them and stand at the top of the altar, waiting. I'll cue Gloria to start the processional music. Then the Maid of Honor will head down the aisle followed by our ring bearer."

He turned to Stanley. "I hope you know what you're doing."

Stanley smiled. "Don't worry, we practiced."

After the men and boys aligned, Bill looked up to the choir loft and signaled Gloria. The organist began *Canon in D* by Pachabel. Those assembled stopped their chatting and turned towards the back. Jan walked through the entranceway and stepped down the aisle. Jim smiled at her and she returned a happy glance. She completed her walk and stood opposite Mark.

Next, the sound of a bark followed by Eddie Smalley whispering, "Reggie, chill." The assembled laughed and whispered to each other. Gloria raised the volume on her organ to whip the crowd into silence.

After a few seconds, Eddie whispered in Reggie's ear and placed the terrier on the runner. Reggie had a black sock-like sleeve on his tail with two gold rings attached. He trotted down the aisle, wagging away, as cameras flashed.

When he approached the midpoint, Gabe Cooper stepped into the aisle to take a photo. The terrier spotted his nemesis and stopped. He barked loudly and ran for Gabe's feet. He grabbed onto Gabe's pants and tugged while growling and backing up as Gabe attempted to steady himself on the arm of the pew.

A few seconds passed as everyone sat, frozen. Finally, Eddie Smalley ran up the aisle and pulled Reggie from Gabe's pant leg. The boy looked up. "I'm sorry, Mister. I don't know what got into him."

Eddie walked a little further up the aisle, whispered soothing encouragement to Reggie and pointed him towards the altar. Reggie turned again to Gabe, barked once, then turned facing the altar and continued his walk towards his master.

Gabe looked around, shrugged to the assembly, smiled and slid back into the pew. Jessie's lips could be read asking, "What was that about?" Rico stared at Gabe. He weighed what had happened this week. First, Gabe's comment on the ring tone which his father had loaded the day he died. Now Reggie, believed by townsfolk to have been present at the killing, was literally tearing into Gabe.

Up on the altar, Mark watched Reggie complete his walk, stood in front of Reggie and retrieved the rings. Reggie wagged his tail in appreciation.

He bent to Reggie's ear. "Good boy. Don't worry, my friend. I'll take care of the bad man." He then looked at Gabe. On making eye contact, Mark nodded. He knew Reggie's secret.

The remainder of the wedding was uneventful; mostly. Claire staggered—just a little—as she walked down the aisle, accompanied by another nephew who was giving her away. Most attributed this to nerves, but Jan knew it was the Champagne. When Claire reached the front of the church, she kissed her nephew and turned towards Stanley, who smiled. "You look beautiful."

She smiled back. "You too, Big Guy. I can't wait to jump your bones."

Monsignor George smiled and looked down. The remainder of the wedding party—including Mark and Matthew—laughed. Bill nudged his servers and they restored their game faces.

Once outside the church, Gabe examined his pants. They were ripped, and damp from Reggie's drool. Jessie handed him a tissue and tried to avoid the glances of the attendees walking by. Rico was a few steps away, staring at Gabe. "Could it be true?" he asked himself.

Teresa had excused herself for a moment and was speaking on a cell about thirty feet away. She nodded, hung up, and walked back to Rico.

"How's your mother?" he asked. Teresa seemed puzzled for a second. "Oh, she's fine. I was just checking in on her."

- - -

The wedding reception was held at the Knights of Columbus hall in Cambria, the same venue Jim and Jan had used. The liquor flowed freely, as Stanley saw to it that the bar was well stocked; there was no need for Gabe to produce a miracle this time. Just as well, since Gabe wasn't feeling very savior-like. Guests stopped by, expressed their sympathy for his embarrassment, and speculated that Reggie must have been over-excited. Gabe smiled and said, "It must've been my cologne."

Jessie laughed. "Never a dull moment with this guy, I guess."

Jim and Gabe exchanged glances, then both looked over to the head table where Mark was chatting with Jan. The detective glanced over at the brothers. He held up his Whiskey Sour, saluted, and said something to Jan as he tilted his head towards Gabe's table. Mark and Jan started to walk over, smiling. The reason for each smile was different though.

Mark stopped at the table, nodded to Jessie, Rico, and Teresa. "Teresa, we have a lot of catching up to do. Maybe we can chat later."

He turned towards Gabe and Jim. "And the brothers Cooper. Another family reunion." He held up his glass and eyed the guests. "To family. Through thick and thin, they stay together."

Jan looked at Jim starting to understand what Mark was getting at. Everyone raised a glass. "To family," they responded.

- - -

The reception went smoothly, with most everyone dancing and chatting. Jim was especially outgoing this day and drank well beyond his normal limit. He kissed Jan and nuzzled her to the discomfort of Gabe and the rest of the table. Gabe took Jim aside in the Men's room.

"Jim, maybe you should slow down on the scotch, or maybe switch to beer. Those are strong drinks you're putting down."

Jim patted Gabe on the shoulder. "Gabe, don't you realize. Porfino is onto us."

Gabe looked around, walked towards the stalls, and carefully looked under each. "Jim. One crazy dog isn't going to get me arrested. Just relax and enjoy the reception. And switch to something lighter."

Monsignor George walked in. Gabe and Jim smiled. "Boys, quite a reception, huh?" The brothers nodded. "Well, if you'll excuse me, as Archie Bunker once said 'you only rent beer.'"

He looked around, spotted a urinal, walked over and unzipped. As fluid hit porcelain, the muffled, prolonged sound of gastric discharge was also heard. Bill half-turned towards the brothers. "Well, as Newton said, 'every action has an equal and opposite reaction.'"

Gabe smiled and guided Jim to the door. "See you back at the table, Monsignor."

Bill went on urinating and discharging. As Gabe and Jim were exiting, Mark was walking in. He nodded. "Gentlemen. Quite a reception, huh? This will be a day to remember."

Gabe smiled and continued pushing Jim, who was raising his hand and appeared to be ready to say something. "Sure is, Mark," Gabe responded. Jim dropped his hand, more due to the squeezing on his other arm by Gabe than discretion.

"Well. We need to get back to our table."

Mark nodded. "Mustn't disappoint the ladies now, must we?"

He walked into the Men's room as the brothers nodded back and walked towards their table. From the Men's room could be heard, "Whoa, Monsignor."

- - -

Following the cake cutting and the oddly sensual removal of Claire's garter by Stanley to the strains of Ravel's *Bolero,* the reception wound down. Some guests lingered and chatted, others stood and walked over to Claire and Stanley to express their thanks and wish the couple many long years of happiness. Gabe looked at Jessie, Rico, and Teresa. They were ready to leave also. He studied Jim, who continued putting away the scotch. Jan seemed angry at this but smiled at Gabe. Maybe Jim was due a bender occasionally.

The group walked over to the bride, and Claire hugged her Maid of Honor. Not a dry eye. Jim, inspired by this, stepped forward, reached for Stanley's hand and gave it a firm shake. "May you two have many years of happiness. I'd give you a blessing, but I lost my license." He chuckled and hiccupped.

Jan shrugged at Claire. The men smiled bravely and navigated Jim to the door. Jessie, Teresa, and Jan issued a collective and embarrassed, "Good Bye" and followed the three men out of the reception hall. Stanley and Claire joined to make sure Jim was all right.

Deciding she needed to drive, Jan jumped into the driver's side before Jim could object. Gabe opened the front passenger door, gingerly deposited Jim onto the seat, and attached the seatbelt around his sibling.

Jim grinned at Gabe. "Brothers, through thick and thin. Right Gabe?"

Wincing as he took in the smell of scotch, Gabe took a breath and responded. "Right, Jim. Through thick and thin."

Gabe started to walk towards his car. Jan, distracted by Jim's behavior, and slightly angry at the position she was in, pulled out without looking. Another guest honked and swerved to avoid them. Jan looked at the driver and mouthed an embarrassed, "sorry."

Turning angry, Jim raised a hand and turned towards the other car. He issued a one-fingered salute to the driver. "Fuck you, pal."

Jan shouted, "Jim, stop." The ex-priest, realizing that he had embarrassed them both, sank low and mumbled a "sorry." The other driver waved Jan on. She smiled politely and drove out.

Claire and Stanley saw the near crash and then Jim's flip. "Oh My God," said Claire. "I was wrong all along."

– – –

Chapter 4

The Passion and Judgment

Rico settled himself into his small cube after lunch. Anxious about the events of the weekend, he distracted himself—at least temporarily—with a high-cal-low-nutrition Popeye's meal. His fingers were still greasy, and he licked them to get a last taste and avoid smearing his screen or keyboard. He restored his Outlook screen; an email from Mario summoned him in bold contrast to his previously opened mail.

He sighed, hoping for a low-key day. Craning his neck and peering over to Mario's office, he spotted Mario's secretary Irene—a slight, blue-haired ball of fury if you crossed her. She sensed being observed, and looked up to meet his gaze.

Embarrassed at being caught, he stood, brushed some biscuit crumbs from his shirt, and walked towards Irene's lair. She had resumed her typing and appeared oblivious to the approach. He stood before her desk as she continued typing. Rico knew this dance. Clearing his throat, he said, "Good afternoon, Miss Wallace. Mario asked me to stop by and see him."

After a few seconds, she looked up and peered over her bifocals. "I'll see if he has the time."

Standing, she walked to Mario's door, knocked once, and entered. After a minute, she returned and, not looking at Rico, sat at her desk and looked at her screen.

He was about to say something when he heard "Come in" from Mario's office. He smiled at Irene, who grunted and returned to her typing.

He was just in time to see Mario crumpling a McDonald's wrapper. He held it in both hands, eyed a wastebasket near Rico, and simulated a crowd noise. "He dribbles, three seconds left, he shoots."

He flung the paper towards the basket. Rico saw that it was going to fly past the basket and deflected the crumpled sphere, causing it to land in the basket.

His boss stood again and made a crowd noise. "And Fortunato lays it in after a great assist from Gallante." Mario sat quiet for a second, somehow admiring his athletic feat. "Rico, my man, close the door and have a seat."

Rico had to laugh. Mario was quite a character, but he paid well. He walked over to the visitor chair and sat. A muffled noise emanated from the pleather.

The mobster laughed. "Man, I love that chair. So, Rico, how was your weekend?"

Sitting forward to suppress the sound that would set Mario off again, he replied.

"It was a good weekend, Mario. I went to Mr. Richardson's and Miss Woodward's wedding. I took Teresa, we had a good time."

"Yes, I spoke to Teresa," he responded, smiling. "I understand the Cooper brothers livened up the action. First Gabe dueling Reggie in the aisle, and then Jim saluting another guest and wishing him intercourse."

Mario loved his own wit. Rico thought a second. He wasn't comfortable dating Mario's niece. Anything he said or did might get back to Mario. Still, Teresa's death- defying agility in bed caused Rico's northern reasoning to be overruled by the southern caucus. Rico nodded. "Yes, they did liven things up. Jim surprised me. I didn't expect that."

"I wonder how many times Jim has flipped people off. Maybe this wasn't a one-shot deal," Mario said, sitting forward.

"You know, someone flipped off Mrs. Woodward the night your father died. She thought it was Gabe but maybe it was Father Jim."

After silence from Rico, Mario continued "Yet, that was Gabe's alibi for the night of your father's killing. Without that, he would be suspect number one."

Rico shifted. Another muffle but no one noticed. "What can I do Mario? Go to Detective Porfino and demand that he reopen the case?"

"Porfino already knows," Mario returned.

Rico was surprised by this. "Rico, in one rash move, Carla Ciccone did away with Tony Wagner and created an out for Mark Porfino to drop your father's investigation."

He leaned back and started to swivel. "Porfino isn't your friend, Rico. He's just a cop trying to close cases."

Rico sat there, uncertain what to do next.

Walking over and sitting on the edge of the desk, Mario pointed a finger at Rico. "Rico. Think over what your father would have done in a case like this. He would have taken matters into his own hands. He was prepared to avenge Enrico's death just before he died."

He let these words settle and watched the young man. Rico thought a few seconds and then looked up. "Do you mean, kill Gabe myself? I understand obligation, Mario, but I'm not a killer. Besides, how would I do it? Shoot him? Where would I get a gun?"

Mario leaned forward and patted Rico on the shoulder. Returning to his chair, he opened a drawer and pulled out a Glock. "I can give this to you for your personal protection. You never know who you're going to meet out there."

He set the safety and checked the chamber. "And, who knows, maybe one day this may come in handy."

"I have to think about this, Mario."

"I understand, Rico." He leaned forward and forced eye contact "Remember how we talked about a man needing to honor his father and respect his heritage? This is your chance."

The confused young man slumped and didn't respond.

Mario sat back and smiled. "Think it over, Rico. This is a big decision. Just don't worry about being traced to the gun. We can make it vanish."

Rico stood and walked out of the office. Mario put the gun away, picked up his 32- oz. Pepsi and started to slurp. He noticed the empty packet of fries. He crumpled it, walked about five feet from the wastebasket and arched a toss towards his goal. The packet hit the back wall and bounced in. "Still counts as two points," he cheered while looking around. "Now, where's that Snickers bar?"

- - -

Claire Richardson (nee Woodward) entered the Long Harbor police station at ten Monday morning. She wanted to talk about the Silvio Fortunato case.

The officers milling around the front desk greeted her. The females examined her ring and asked about her married life. Claire beamed and whispered something that made the women giggle. The male officers looked at each other. Maybe Stanley still had it in him to satisfy a woman.

Ted took this in and cleared his throat, signaling the assembled to return to their duties. Walking up to Claire, he offered his hand. "Mrs. Woodward, sorry, Richardson. I'm not sure if you remember me. I'm Officer Hanson. You were kind enough to speak with us at your home during the Silvio Fortunato investigation. If you don't mind, I'll be sitting in on your talk with Mark."

The new bride smiled. "I remember. And Stanley speaks highly of you. We wondered why Teresa McGill dumped you. She was at our wedding with Rico Fortunato."

Ted seemed embarrassed and looked around. The few officers in earshot were smiling but pretending not to have heard. "Yes, Mark told me."

She patted his shoulder. "Don't worry, young man. Life goes on." She looked around. "Maybe you should hook up with one of these nice young ladies."

Now everyone was laughing, making no pretense of not having heard. "Good advice, Mrs. Richardson. Shall we go see Mark now?"

The pair walked down the aisle of cubicles towards Mark's office. Administrative staff, detectives, janitors, all stopped for a moment to smile and nod, some wishing her congratulations.

Ted smiled at Claire. "How's it feel to be a rock star?"

Shrugging, she replied, "I guess I do look somewhat like Mick Jagger."

"Stanley's a lucky man, Mrs. Richardson," said Ted, laughing.

He started to knock on Mark's door, but stopped when the detective appeared. Beaming, he said, "Claire, you look lovely. Marriage agrees with you."

She smiled. "Thank you, Mark." Leaning in, she continued, "When are you going to make an honest woman of Linda James?"

Everyone laughed. "Back to work, folks," he called out.

"Claire, please come in. I see that you've met Ted on the way in." Picking up his phone, he asked his admin to bring some tea.

After settling in a chair, Claire turned somber. "Mark. I think it was Jim Cooper who gave me the finger the night of Silvio's death. I don't think it was Gabe Cooper, like I first thought."

"What makes you think so?"

Claire explained about the incident Saturday as Jan and Jim were leaving the reception.

Ted turned towards Claire. "Mrs. Richardson, can you say with certainty that it was Jim who—" Ted paused.

"Flipped me off? Gave me the one-fingered salute?"

Ted laughed. "Yes, in so many words."

She paused. "I probably couldn't testify to it, if that's what you mean. But I am certain."

"Does that mean Gabe killed Silvio?" she said as she turned towards Mark.

Mark looked at Ted and then back at Claire. "We were never able to shake his alibi."

"I feel so bad about that. Maybe if I hadn't been so certain before, Tony Wagner would be alive now. Oh dear."

Sue Becker walked in with Claire's tea. There was a lemon wedge, sugar, and Girl Scout Savannah Smiles, Thanks a Lots, and Samoas on the tray. Claire thanked Sue and looked at the tray. "I think I need something stronger than this."

Mark opened his drawer and pulled out a bottle of Scotch. Walking over to his credenza, he picked up three glasses, turned and saw Sue looking at the three. He turned and picked up a fourth glass.

"Sue, close the door and have a seat."

He looked at Claire. "It wouldn't do to have people say that Claire Richardson was drinking with two strange men at ten o'clock on a Monday morning."

Sue smiled and pulled up a chair after closing the door. Mark walked over and poured a shot glass for each of them. He then examined the cookie tray and selected one of each. The others did likewise.

Sue looked at Mark. "What are we drinking to?"

Mark grimaced. "Murder most foul."

- - -

Rico opened the front door Monday night in time to see Gabe setting the table and Jessie bringing out a pot roast. Gabe grabbed Jessie by the waist as she passed, and Jessie turned and kissed Gabe. They embraced and prolonged their kiss. This became more passionate and would surely have lead to a delay in the evening meal had Rico not cleared his throat. It was clear that Gabe and Jessie loved one another, but intercourse alongside the red meat was more than Rico could have stood.

Gabe released Jessie, who smoothed her hair and straightened her skirt after Gabe removed his hand. "Hi, Rico. Just getting ready for dinner."

"Sorry I'm late. Things going on at work."

He looked at Gabe. "How was your day, Gabe? Still working the wood?"

"SSDD as they say, Rico. Same shit, different day," Gabe replied with an embarrassed smile.

Studying Gabe and Jessie, Rico realized that in just a few days they had gone from loving couple to murderer and unsuspecting girlfriend. "Give me a minute to wash up," he said as he went upstairs.

Gabe looked at Jessie. "Should we tell him now that you're pregnant?"

Dinner proceeded as most weekday dinners. There was small talk, passing of serving dishes, discussion of the day's activities, what's on TV tonight, and what was planned for tomorrow. Rico and Gabe had a glass of Chianti, but Jessie begged off, which was unusual; she never passed on wine. Occasionally, Gabe would look at Jessie and they would both smile. To Rico it appeared they were sharing some personal thought or secret. He considered a 'Hey, what gives?" but thought the better of it.

After dinner, Jessie took the dishes back to the kitchen as Gabe beamed at her. Rico took a breath, then said "So Gabe, why do you think Reggie barks so loudly when he sees you?"

Surprised by the question, Gabe appeared to be formulating an answer. He looked towards the kitchen. Sounds of plate scraping indicated a few moments of privacy. "Who knows what's in the mind of a terrier?" Gabe smiled. "He sure ruined a good pair of pants."

Rico leaned forward. "I was talking to Mario today about the wedding on Saturday. He heard about the attack from Teresa,"

Appearing to lose his composure, Gabe frowned, then took a breath. "Imagine Teresa being Mario's niece. Small World."

Rico looked towards the kitchen door; the sound of a coffee brewer belching out caffeine. "Mario thinks you and Reggie shared some unpleasant experience that Reggie won't let you forget about." Rico strummed his fingers. "Any thoughts, Gabe?"

"Mario has had more unpleasant experiences than I'll ever have. Why don't you ask him about his unpleasant experiences? I'm sure there aren't many creatures, human or otherwise, willing to remind him of them."

"No, I guess not," Rico agreed. "Mario seems to take care of business when he thinks it's necessary. You have to give him that."

Jessie returned from the kitchen with a plate of Girl Scout cookies. There were Trefoils, Thin Mints, and Samoas. "Girl Scout cookie time. Dig in."

Observing Gabe and Rico, she was struck by how quiet and somber they appeared. She smiled. "Well, what's up with *you two*?"

\- - -

Mark sat in his office that evening and thought over the meeting with Claire. He and Ted were convinced that Gabe had killed Silvio now. They also knew that they had no real grounds to arrest him. The changed testimony of an elderly woman who had only briefly seen her assailant through a car windshield at night wouldn't cause the District Attorney to reopen a 15 month-old case. On top of that, Claire could only testify that she *thought* her flipper had been Jim, based on a later action.

What a mess, he thought. Silvio's dead, Tony's dead, Gabe is now living with Jessie. They seem to be very happy. Maybe I should just let sleeping dogs lie.

He opened his drawer and pulled out a box of Trefoils and the nearly drained bottle of J&B. He poured a shot and opened a sleeve of the cookies. Picking up the shot glass, he poured a few drops onto the shortbread masterpiece, bit off a chuck and sucked the alcohol out of the soggy but delightful treat. He drained the remainder of the scotch and put the glass down with a dramatic clunk.

Swiveling in his chair and spinning a half-turn to see the night lights of Long Harbor outside of his window, he thought to himself: well, sleepy town, I am sworn to do my duty. Even if it involves persuasion more than evidence.

Spinning back around, he whacked his knee on the side of his desk. "Fuck." Opening the Silvio folder to Gabe's information, he found Gabe's cell number and dialed.

A few rings later, a tired and somewhat angry voice responded "Hello?" He wondered what Gabe was doing that would evoke this response. "Gabe. This is Mark Porfino."

After a tense silence, the sound of a chair pushing back and footsteps indicated Gabe was finding somewhere more private to talk.

"Hi Mark, what's up?"

Mark took a breath, poured the remaining scotch into his glass and picked up another Trefoil. He drained the scotch and tapped the cookie on the desk. "Gabe, we need to talk, but I don't want to drag you into the police station one more time. We need some privacy."

Silence for a few seconds. "What's this about, Mark?"

He selected a cookie, put half of it into his mouth, and then sucked the life out of it, enjoying the sugar rush but not enjoying what he would say next.

"I think we both know, Gabe. Let's meet and see what we can come up with." Mark bit off the soggy portion and chewed. "It's time, Gabe. It's time we cleared up this mess."

More silence, then a sigh. "Okay, Mark. Where and when?"

Mark looked at the photos of the dock with Silvio's bloated body being examined like a prize shark. "The waterfront at Greys Street, right where we pulled in Silvio. Eight tomorrow night."

Silence again. Mark drained the scotch. Finally, "Alright, Mark. But just you and me, okay?"

"You got it. No SWAT team. Just the two of us." Mark picked up his glass and saw a perfect print of his thumb. "Gabe, this is your last chance to clear up this mess. Nobody wants Mario settling it."

Gabe sighed. "See you then, Mark,"

Putting the phone back into the base, Mark picked up the J&B bottle and examined it for any remaining sustenance. Another dead soldier, he thought as he dropped it into his wastebasket.

Gabe returned to the table. Jessie looked at Gabe and asked about the call. "It was Mark Porfino."

He looked at Rico, who was looking at his plate of uneaten cookies. "He wants to meet me tomorrow night, eight, at the waterfront at Greys Street."

The men exchanged glances. Jessie put down her napkin. "But why?"

Gabe looked at Jessie, then at Rico. "Unfinished business."

- - -

Rico went to work Tuesday morning more troubled than ever over his father's death and Gabe's likely involvement. He felt both betrayed and a compelling need to bring his father's killer to some level of justice. He considered calling Detective Porfino and forcing him to admit that Gabe was the killer and that he'd be arrested that night.

After a few hours of looking over invoices and answering email, Rico decided that he had to do something. He picked up the phone and dialed the Long Harbor police. When Officer Hanson answered, Rico thought a second, then hung up. "What can I say to *him?*" he thought. "Arrest my step-father...and oh, by the way, I'm sleeping with your ex-girlfriend?"

He sat at his desk and watched the clock. Mario walked into the office carrying a Burger King bag and a large Coke. Rico shook his head and thought, eleven o'clock. When they investigate Mario's death, the likely suspects will be Popeye, Ronald McDonald, the Burger King, and that Taco Bell Chihuahua.

He stood and walked to Mario's office. Irene was on break, so at least no centurion to overcome. Rico knocked on Mario's office door. Mario saw Rico, and, picking up a sleeve of fries, waved him in. "Come in Rico. Care for a few fries?"

He entered, closed the door, and shook his head. "Not hungry, Mario. I have something on my mind."

Mario held up one finger, picked up his super large drink, and took a long drag on the straw. His bliss confirmed that Mario was pleased with his dining choice.

"Have a seat, Rico. What's troubling you?"

"I'm more convinced than ever that Gabe killed my father. Detective Porfino is meeting him tonight at eight o'clock at the waterfront at Greys Street. It sounds like he might arrest Gabe.

"Gabe described it as unfinished business," said Rico sitting back.

Mario wiped his hand on one of the thirty or so napkins he had stuffed into his bag. "I know, Rico. I have my contacts within the Long Harbor police." He picked up a few fries and stuffed them into his mouth. Rico waited for the mastication to cease. Mario was thinking as he chewed.

"What makes you think Mark Porfino is going to arrest Gabe? Wouldn't he look like a fool for having been deceived for so long?"

Rico considered this. "Then, why else would he meet with Gabe?"

"To plan a way out of this. The pressure is mounting, with Carla convinced that she killed the wrong man, and Reggie attacking Gabe in church."

Sitting back, Mario peeked at his Whopper with Cheese, then closed the box and studied Rico. After a few moments, he continued. "Who knows, maybe he'll get Gabe to cop a plea, or maybe he'll convince him to skip town. Maybe they'll concoct a story on how he just disappeared."

Mario took a large bite of the Whopper causing mayo to spill from the corner of his mouth. Chewing, he took another sip, then grabbed six or so napkins and wiped his mouth.

"So. Let's say Gabe agrees to plead to self-defense. Mark chews it over and thinks 'why not?' Gabe maybe gets six months suspended for obstruction of justice, and before you know it, he's sitting at the dinner table passing the roast beef and thinking of the next time he'll sleep with your mother."

"He won't go to jail?"

Mario laughed. "No, he's too connected...and people didn't like your father. Sorry to say that Rico, but your dad had a lot of enemies."

He pushed his lunch to the side; a rare act of self-denial. Sitting forward, he looked Rico in the eye. "The only way to get justice for your father is to make sure Gabe pays the price right then and there."

Mario opened his side drawer, pulled out the Glock and, reaching further into the drawer, pulled out a bullet magazine. Putting both into his suit coat pocket, he opened Outlook and emailed Irene that he would be out on business this afternoon.

Picking up his Whopper, fries, and Coke, he signaled Rico to stand. "Let's go out to a place I know where we won't be disturbed. I'll show you how this works."

Rico hadn't stood yet. "Hey, if you decide to let the police resolve this, I'll understand." He patted his suit coat pocket "I'm just presenting you with more options."

The young man stood and staggered, unsteady on his feet. Was he seriously considering killing someone?

"That's the spirit." Mario pulled out the fries. "You sure you don't want some? They're extra tasty today."

- - -

The waterfront at Greys Street was a popular location for socializing during the day. Office workers would stroll the dock or sit at the few benches facing the water. They ate lunch and chatted about work or the coming weekend. At night, the waterfront was a lonely quiet spot, sparsely lit and empty.

Mark stood near the water and shivered from the late March chill. It had been a mild winter overall, but this last week, Holy Week, had turned colder. There were even forecasts of a possible snowy Easter this Sunday.

He looked at his watch—8 p.m.—and peered around. Dark and quiet, and no Gabe. I'll arrest him tonight at home if I have to, he thought angrily, as he rubbed his hands.

Then footsteps from behind. Mark turned and saw Gabe walking towards him and the dock. "Gabe. I didn't hear you. Glad you made it. Where's your car?"

Gabe reached into his pocket and pulled out keys. He turned around towards the parking lot and pressed the 'lock' button on his key chain. His car lights flashed. "It's a Prius," Gabe responded. "I sneak up on everyone."

He walked to within a few feet of Mark. He appeared solemn, maybe even angry. Rubbing his hands, he shivered, "Let's get on with it, Mark. It's freezing out here."

Mark turned towards the water and took a breath.

"Fifteen months ago, Silvio fell into the water from this dock. I think he was fighting someone. Maybe he was the instigator. Whomever he fought had enough strength and wherewithal to push Silvio into the water. Silvio hits his head on a pylon, goes cold, and drowns."

Mark turned again towards Gabe but didn't make eye contact.

"A few minutes later, the killer calls 911. On Silvio's cell of all things. Maybe he is remorseful. Maybe it was self-defense and he wants to be a standup guy and report what happened." Mark forces eye contact with Gabe. "But he panics. Silvio is connected. Mario will have him killed. He hangs up and, I'm guessing here, throws Silvio's cell into the water."

Gabe was no longer angry; pale, but in control. "Go on."

Mark rubbed his hands to warm them. "And then, of all things, after going home as if nothing happened and trying to resume his life, he is presented with an accidental alibi. He was clear across town when Silvio died. Thank God for old ladies who complain about being wronged."

Reaching into his jacket pocket, Gabe pulled out a stick of gum. "It's times like this that I wish I smoked."

Mark reached into his jacket, pulled out a Canadian Club flask, opened it and took a quick gulp. Stepping forward, he handed the flask to Gabe, who spit the gum into his other hand and tossed it into the nearby bush.

Gabe opened the flask and took a long sip. He coughed as he reacted to the strength of the whiskey.

Mark waited for Gabe to stop coughing. "It was you, Gabe. You killed Silvio."

"It was self-defense, Mark." Gabe closed the flask but didn't hand it back to Mark. "I was walking home from The Wharf. Silvio must have seen me as he drove by. He pulled up, got out of his Explorer, came over, and confronted me."

Taking another swig, he continued, "He had accused me in the past of hitting on Jessie. We had words in The Wharf that night." Gabe laughed. "Then, after I left, I pissed on his tire. I guess that was the last straw for Silvio. He loved that Explorer more than he loved Jessie. I had defiled both of them in his eyes."

Handing back the flask, he walked towards the dock. Mark followed and stood next to him, looking out. "He then beat the shit out of me." Gabe turned and pointed. "I landed in the bushes right there. Right on top of fucking Reggie, who had taken a crap just seconds before. Silvio thought that was hilarious. He said that he was going to do something he had planned to do for a long time. He reached into his jacket and pulled out something black. I thought it was a gun."

Shuttering from the cold and the memory, Gabe half spoke and half cried, "I stood up and ran towards him, head-butting him and knocking him down. He was mad. He reached for the black object again. I ran at him and pushed him into the water. Silvio hit his head falling in... it turns out it was his cell."

He was quiet, and then said "Oh, God. What a mess I've made."

Waiting a moment for Gabe to collect himself, Mark offered the flask, but Gabe shook his head. "So, what now?"

Mark put the flask into his coat, and then both men turned as they heard footsteps. The noise stopped. Mark turned to Gabe. "I have to arrest you. I think if you tell the District Attorney what you told me, he might be willing to be lenient."

He looked behind Gabe to see if anyone was there. "Lucky for you, Gabe, that everyone hated Silvio. You'll have a lot of sympathy."

The footsteps resumed from the shadows and Rico appeared. He was holding a gun at his side and appeared to be nervous and angry. "You killed my father, Gabe."

He turned to Mark. "And you knew it and didn't do anything." Rico raised the gun and held it in two hands to steady himself.

Mark raised his left hand to try to calm Rico. With the right, he released the safety on the Glock in his hip holster. "Rico, you don't want to do this. Let the law take care of this. I'm going to arrest Gabe."

Not responding, Rico continued shaking. "Rico, put the gun down. Put it on the ground. If you walk away now, we'll forget the whole thing. Think about it. Don't do anything you'll regret," Mark pleaded.

The young man was crying. "Detective Porfino. You hated my dad just like everyone else. Is a jury really going to convict Gabe?"

Stepping forward, Gabe called out, "Rico, this doesn't help anyone. Your mother doesn't need this. You can't go to jail, too. Listen to Mark. This is the best way."

"My mother doesn't need the man who killed my father sleeping with her and pretending nothing happened."

He raised the gun, causing Mark to reach for his Glock. Gabe stepped forward in front of Mark. "Rico. At least let Mark go."

Mark raised his gun. "Gabe. Move."

Rico closed his eyes and fired as two muffled sounds like a hammer hitting a nail rang out. Gabe gasped and stumbled.

Mark crouched as a reaction to the shots and then reached for Gabe to try to shield him. He looked up at Rico and raised his gun. Rico dropped the gun and stood trancelike. "Get face down on the ground, Rico. Hands out."

Rico was transfixed. "Rico. Do it now!" Rico seemed to come out of his trance and looked at Gabe.

"Oh, my God. What have I done?"

"Down on the ground, Rico."

Rico continued to look at Gabe, who was bleeding profusely. "Oh, my God."

The detective stepped over Gabe and walked towards Rico. Rico turned and started to run. "Stop, Rico."

Continuing to run, Rico crossed into Greys Street. There was the loud blare of a car horn causing Rico to stop and turn. The SUV driver applied his brakes, but not in time. Six thousand pounds of minivan hit Rico head on, hurling him to the ground thirty feet from the impact.

The driver shouted, "Oh, my God," threw his transmission into Park and ran out to Rico. Mark pulled out his police cell and dialed 911.

"This is Detective Porfino. I have a shooting and a car accident at the Long Harbor dock at Greys Street. Two men injured. Send police assistance and ambulances."

Ted Hanson arrived first. He saw a mangled body in the street with the driver bending over him. He looked over to Mark, who was kneeling next to Gabe. The ambulances arrived as did two police cruisers. Ted directed the first ambulance crew and two patrol officers over to the auto victim. He waved the other crew and set of officers to follow him towards the man who must have been the shooting victim.

When Ted reached Mark he was about to say, "Who is it?" when he realized it was Gabe, who was breathing, but had lost a lot of blood. Mark waved to the ambulance crew and stood as they reached Gabe. "Two shots, both to the chest. He's pretty bad." He looked at Ted. "Now, let's see how Rico is doing."

\- - -

Mark called Jessie after checking on Rico. Silence, then a sob. She cried out and collapsed.

"Jessie?" No response. Mark called 911 again and told the operator to send a cruiser to the Fortunato home to check on Jessie and bring her to the hospital.

Now thirty minutes later, she was sitting in the Emergency Room. The two men in her life had critical injuries. Mark walked in and saw Jessie before she saw him. He realized that Gabe's blood was on his shirt, so he zipped his jacket up. He walked over and sat down. "Jessie, I'm so sorry."

Jessie dabbed her nose with a tissue and looked up at Mark. "How could this have happened? Rico never owned a gun, and he loved Gabe. What led him to do this?"

Not sure how to answer without further hurting Jessie, he looked ahead, averting her gaze.

"Who knows what drives a young man over the brink? Rico loves you very much. So does Gabe. Sometimes that love causes people to do things that they can't take back."

He looked towards the doors to the Emergency room. "How are they?"

Jessie looked towards the doors, then turned angry. "How do you think?"

She started to cry again. Mark put his arms around her, letting her cry into his jacket.

Jim and Jan arrived a few minutes later. Jan and Jessie hugged and sobbed as Mark and Jim looked at each other. "This is really fucked," Jim sobbed.

Mark looked over at Jim. "We'll talk later."

"Oh, my God," said Jim, burying his face into his hands.

Ten minutes later, two ER doctors came through the automatic doors and stood before Jessie. The doctors looked at each other as if to say, "Who first?" The more senior of the men sat next to Jessie. "I'm Doctor Stevens. This is Doctor Roberts. I'm afraid that neither man made it."

– – –

Chapter 5

The Resurrection

Easter Sunday morning. Early April. St. Agnes Church in Cambria. Monsignor Bill George looked out at the congregants filling the pews. The CAPE Catholics were streaming in, chatting away, and renewing friendships with those they don't see except on special holy days. Oh well, he thought, better once in a while than never. He put on his cassock and then his Easter white vestments. "They better dump some money into the basket."

Mark and Matthew were standing at the doorway of the sacristy. They looked puzzled. "Did I say that out loud?" The boys smiled. Bill looked at his watch. "Showtime boys."

Bill and the boys walked out of the sacristy and assembled with the lector at the back of the church. "Hold your horses," came a voice from the front door. Bill turned, annoyed. It was Stanley Richardson with Claire.

"Whoops, sorry Monsignor. I didn't mean any disrespect. We were just running late."

Bill smiled. John Simpson, the lector, seemed angry and about to say something, but Bill winked at him then turned towards the newlyweds. "Welcome. You're just in time. We'll wait."

Claire gave an embarrassed smile as she walked by. An "oof" from Stanley indicated a deserving jab in the ribs. The couple found a pew after Claire called out "shoo in" to a couple who was clinging to the aisle seats like they might fall into a black hole if they slid towards the middle.

When the pair settled, Bill signaled John, Mathew, and Mark to start up the aisle. Susie, the organist, announced the beginning of Mass and ordered, er, asked, the congregation to rise. She then started on *Morning Has Broken*.

Bill proceeded up the aisle and looked at the assembly. Easter was like the Super Bowl for Catholics; he enjoyed the crowd. He passed Claire, who smiled back. Stanley was wincing and rubbing his side, no doubt wondering if Adam made the right move giving up his rib in exchange for what became of it.

Farther down, Bill passed Mario Gallante and Sheila. They were sharing a hymnal and singing. Well, well, he thought. It wasn't beauty that tamed the beast. It was bean soup and cheesy bread.

Helen James, Linda, and Mark Porfino appeared next. Mark and Linda were sharing a hymnal also, although Mark seemed distracted, looking at someone in a pew towards the front.

Approaching the altar, Bill decided to stop his star gazing, but then noticed Jim and Jan standing in the second pew. Jan was singing but also looking over at Jim with concern. He was attempting to join in but seemed in a trance. He looked pale, almost on the verge of fainting

Bill realized Jim was the object of Mark's attention.

John Simpson walked to the lectern and positioned the Bible. Matthew and Mark walked to the candle stands and settled the procession candles in place. Bill ascended the steps in front of the altar, circled to the other side so that he was facing the assembly, bent and kissed the altar.

He then walked to the three altar chairs. Mathew was standing at the left, Mark at the right. Bill stood in front of the middle. Facing the assembly, he waited for Susie to finish. When the music ended, he smiled at the assembly.

"Welcome, everyone, on this joyous day. Put your troubles aside. Today we celebrate the resurrection of Our Lord. This is the day when Our Lord conquered sin and death and saved God's children from the clutches of the devil."

After the opening prayers and the Gloria, the readings proceeded followed by the gospel. The gospel recounted the Holy Mother and Mary Magdalene discovering the empty tomb and hurrying to report to the apostles, Peter and John running to the site, discovering the body missing and the burial garments wrapped. Jesus having risen just as he had foretold.

Bill closed the bible and signaled everyone to sit. He took a few moments to look at the assembly. He saw Jim sitting still motionless; sorrow at the loss of his brother.

"My brothers and sisters in Christ, today we celebrate the triumphant resurrection of our Lord. Today, Jesus conquered sin and death. He put the problems of the world in perspective and gave man a cause to rejoice in God's forgiveness and unbounded love.

I know that sometimes we may not feel loved by God. Sometimes we may even think that God has abandoned us. My brothers and sisters, God cannot abandon his children. God is the eternally loving and forgiving parent.

In the last week we have experienced the last stages in the life of Jesus; His triumphant entry into Jerusalem, followed by his last meal with his closest friends, and finally his betrayal and death. It was a pretty bleak time by all standards. Yes, what happened, the betrayal by Judas, the anger of those who worshiped him just a week before, and a brutal agonizing death were events that would break the best of us.

But Jesus loved his own, his sheep. He died for the sins of all of us. However, he died knowing that he would soon rise and triumphantly conquer death for all time."

Jim had been only half listening to the sermon, but some words roused him. Jesus has died for our sins, just like Gabe had died because Jim had put brotherly love above reason. If he had only convinced Gabe to come clean, Gabe would be alive today. But Rico had turned on Gabe and became both Judas the betrayer and Pilate the final judge and executioner.

Gabe also loved his own: Jessie and Rico, his adopted family; his brother; and probably even Reggie. He smiled at this thought. Gabe, the things brothers do. We did it all, even being idiots to the end.

"My brothers and sisters in Christ, enjoy this wonderful day. Enjoy the warm weather, the Easter dinners, and especially those chocolate bunnies."

The assembly laughed at this. They appreciated Bill's gift for preaching, but also knew his affection for sweets and liquor.

"But never forget that the true meaning of today is that our Lord has delivered us from the clutches of Satan. He has re-established our pure relationship with God the Father. Forever, from that point forward, we became redeemed children of God. Adam's failure in the garden, a failure which blemished all of his children, was wiped away.

We have been saved, brothers and sisters. Let us repay the Lord for his generosity by leaving the church today praising the Lord and carrying out the good works that please God so much. Forget your earthly worries, for one day we will stand before the Father knowing that his Son has already reserved a room for us in God's eternal kingdom."

Bill lifted his hands. "Please rise as we renew our baptismal vows." He led the congregation through the renewal of the vows of Christianity. Walking to the altar, he continued the Mass.

Jim was struck by Bill's words and even a bit jealous of his mastery at the pulpit. That used to be me, he thought. He looked over at Jan, who was singing the offertory hymn. Did I make a big mistake? Did I give up my calling to pursue earthly pleasures and to protect my brother? He studied Jan, resplendent with her belly bump. I love Jan and I love our child. Still…I wonder.

Bill completed the mass in a respectable fifty-five minutes. He followed Mathew, Mark, and John down the aisle as Susie whipped up the assembly with a rousing *Jesus Christ is Risen Today.*

As he passed Jim, the man nodded. Bill was relieved by this. Jim had suffered so much in the last few days, and tomorrow he was going to bury his brother. He said a silent prayer for Jim and continued down the aisle.

Mark, Helen James, and Linda smiled also. Mark looked calmer than when Bill had walked up the aisle before. Maybe Mark had found some inner peace himself after this terrible week, he mused. Sometimes, catching the bad guy isn't all it's cracked up to be.

When Bill approached the Richardsons, Stanley pulled a cellophane package from his pocket, unwrapped it and pulled out a yellow Peep. He saluted Bill, bit the head off, and chewed. He smiled through marshmallowed teeth.

Bill shook his head and smiled. How do you top that?

He stopped in the front foyer and turned to greet the worshippers as they left. He thought of the Peep. "One more mass and I can pop a few of them myself. Praise be to God."

– – –

Jessie returned to Cambria with Jeannette, her sister, after the joint funeral for Gabe and Rico. After two weeks of holding down a park bench and watching children fly their kites, she realized that, for better or worse, it was time to return to her hometown and resume her life.

Standing in the empty dining room, she pulled out a chair, sat and closed her eyes. How sweet to remember the happy times at the table: the joking with Gabe and Rico, downing a few glasses of wine. She gently massaged her stomach as she opened her eyes. Young man, or young lady, she thought, choose wisely in life. There are going to be people who break your heart.

What now, she wondered. In the full-length mirror opposite her, she noticed envelopes scattered on the floor near the door. Walking over, she scooped the mail into a pile, picked up the envelopes, and returned to the table.

The condolences were sincere, yet unhelpful. After a few minutes, she placed the remaining mail into a drawer and walked into the kitchen, where unsympathetic plates and glasses awaited washing and the return to their cabinet sanctuary.

Realizing there was nothing better to do, she filled the sink with hot dish water and submerged each soiled soul. She scrubbed away the impurities and put each in the rack to dry. Starting to feel her composure fall away, she picked up the dishcloth, staggered to the kitchen table and wept into it. Why me, God? What have I done to deserve this? How do I go on?

She felt a movement in her stomach. She smiled and massaged her future child. She whispered, "You are my new life, young child. You are my chance to make things whole again."

Her cell rang; Jeannette checking on her. Letting it go to voice mail, she dried her eyes and walked into the living room. She switched on the TV in time to catch the last few part of *Days of Our Lives.* Minutes later, she was asleep.

\- - -

Father Jim Cooper turned in the direction of the sunlight streaming through the stained class. It was a Saturday afternoon in late April, two weeks after Easter Sunday. The designer of St. Agnes Church had the foresight to include a small window in the confessional located at the rear of the church. The light streaming through gave a beatific air to the small room, which contained two padded yet uncomfortable chairs and a kneeler. Few people used the kneeler these days, choosing instead to face the priest chair-to-chair.

Jim took in the warmth of the sunlight as he lifted his face and closed his eyes. Heaven on Earth, he thought. Looking down at his bible and his March Madness selection sheet, he remembered the pep talk from Monsignor George. After welcoming him back to the priesthood, Bill had emphasized the importance of a good sermon to inspire the faithful.

Now he was expected to produce a thoughtful sermon each week, no regurgitation of the gospel just read. He opened his Missal to the Sunday readings, and decided to focus on the brotherly relationship of Christ to his apostles. The memory of Gabe was still fresh and he wanted the congregation to understand the special ties between brothers, good and bad.

Taking out his mechanical pencil, he dragged over the kneeler and placed the notebook and betting sheet on the padded ledge. He glanced at the sheet. Boy, how could Butler have lost to Valparaiso? A few more upsets and I'm out.

Clicking his pencil, he took a breath and started.

My brothers and sisters in Christ. During this Easter season, we've focused on our Lord revealing himself to the apostles and preparing them to lead the church after he left them. Christ and the apostles were a true Band of Brothers. They conducted a campaign of truth and promise to those needing to know that God had not forgotten them. They withstood hardship together and enjoyed the admiration of the community.

Brothers today follow the same principals. While they don't always understand each other, as I'm sure the apostles didn't understand Jesus, they stick together, through thick and thin.

During the night of the passion, Judas succumbed to earthly needs and betrayed our Lord. Brothers do that, too. Even worse, they remain too faithful and allow a brother to walk down the wrong path.

Jim heard footsteps and then the turning of the doorknob. Putting his notebook and selection sheet away, he turned to the side and allowed the penitent to enter. The visitor did not sit. Jim turned and said, "Welcome."

His brother stood before him, wearing a white shirt, white khakis, and loafers.

"Gabe. I thought you died."

Paraphrasing Mark Twain, the deceased replied. "Reports of my death are not greatly exaggerated.

"Not bad, Jim," Gabe continued, examining the room. "The light through the stained glass adds something."

Jim sat forward to make sure he was really looking at Gabe. "Then you *are* dead."

Gabe nodded at Jim, who smiled. "Well, it's still good to see you. It's awfully lonely without you."

"Jim, I miss you, too." He shrugged his shoulders. "Shit happens."

"So tell me, are you in Heaven or Hell?"

Gabe shook his head. "Confidentiality agreement. I can't tell you. Peter made that clear."

You don't converse with a dead man every day. Jim searched for questions.

"Are you at least comfortable? Have you met anyone you can talk to?"

Gabe laughed. "You'd be surprised who's there." He looked at the slip sticking out of the missal. "You'd lose money betting on who is and who isn't."

They both laughed as Gabe leaned forward. "Attila the Hun is a real hoot. Not a bad guy at all."

Jim clasped his hands together to help himself think. "So, why have you come today?"

"I came to tell you that I should never have involved you in the Silvio mess. I forced you to compromise your principals. I could tell you were uncomfortable with that." Gabe smiled. "But you were a true brother and put that bond above your personal happiness."

He stood and brushed the wrinkles on his pants. "Don't worry, Jim. They understand. There's a long history of brothers in the bible." Gabe laughed. "And besides, God grades on a curve." Gabe let out a sigh, "Lucky for me."

Jim heard footsteps approaching the confessional. Gabe patted him on the shoulder, but Jim did not feel the touch. "Be good, Jim. And most of all, forgive yourself."

"I'll try, Gabe. Say hello to anyone I might know."

Gabe raised his hand to his forehead and saluted. "Soldier on, Brother Jim. Soldier on."

The deceased started to fade as the doorknob turned. Realizing that this short visit may be his last time to talk to Gabe, Jim shouted towards the door. "One moment please. I'll be ready in a minute."

Gabe continued to fade. "Gabe, don't go. Gabe I need to talk to you. Gabe…Gabe."

Jim's shouting woke Jan. She looked over and saw Jim swinging his hands as if trying to grab hold of something. Jan gently tapped him on the arm. "Jim, you're having a nightmare."

Jim did not awaken. Jan shook his shoulder "Jim…Jim!"

He awoke with a gasp and looked around. After a few seconds, he sighed and relaxed, catching his breath.

"Jim, you were calling to Gabe."

He looked around. There was no kneeler, no chairs, no Gabe. He looked at Jan, who looked at him with sadness and love.

"I said goodbye."

CPSIA information can be obtained
at www.ICGtesting.com
Printed in the USA
BVOW03s1819110717
489089BV00001B/19/P